A WOMAN AND A LAKE

A NOVEL

DORIT AMIKAM

A woman and A Lake.

ISBN: 0615847137
ISBN-13: 9780615847139
Library of Congress Control Number: 2013912549
CreateSpace Independent Publishing Platform
North Charleston, South Carolina

Published in the United States of America by Dr. Dorit Amikam

First edition published 2014

Front and back Design by Dorit Amikam ©

Cover art work and interior art work by Artist and Scientist Dr. Dorit Amikam ©
www.doritamikam.com

Edited by Dorit Amikam

1. Inner strength in women-Fiction 2. Romances and love-Fiction 3. Success , challenges and empowering -Fiction 4. Title

A woman and A Lake: A Novel of Love, Inner Beauty and Strength, Sprinkled with a Light Touch of Science and Much Art/ Dorit Amikam

DEDICATION

To my father Arie Achizeev Amikam, who was my best friend, my Gibraltar rock, my ever and always there for me.

My role model who was admired by everyone who had the privilege of his acquaintance, and by me.

I will try to live to his legacy and always be with hope and inner strength, as he said "I am so very proud of you Dorit, you are so talented, everything you touch turns out to be gold.

And I love you very dearly, you are very precious to me…we are so very close, and always will be. Where ever we are on this globe and this world"

Thank you father for being my Dad, Abale`.

It was, is and always will be a tremendous priceless privilege.

ACKNOWLEDGMENTS

To my string of friends who are my most precious jewels, they adorn my soul and provide me with the safe haven I needed to write. Each in their own way. Each for many years, before writing this book, during the years of writing this book, and I am so blessed to know that they will surround me with their love and devotion for many years to come.

They are a *constant* in my life, in a dynamic world and century when nothing is!

To my readers: should my book bring a smile to the lips of any, and touch the soul of a single person, then I am fulfilled.

For I have been so blessed all my life to receive and thus am so blessed to be able give…in my way, my own way, through my science, my art, my book and my soul.

Because, in the end, this is what life is all about, when enjoying the giving… a smile will shine, light and lead our path in life. ….

I have been so fortunate to have the love, care and kindness of my family surrounding me at all times. I have been privileged to share the good times in my life, my success and accomplishments and also my challenges and my hardships with my engulfing and forever protecting family.

Thus they are and forever will be with me, in life and embedded in my heart and entity. Always!

CONTENTS

Determination...Femininity,
Fragility and Strength...Her...

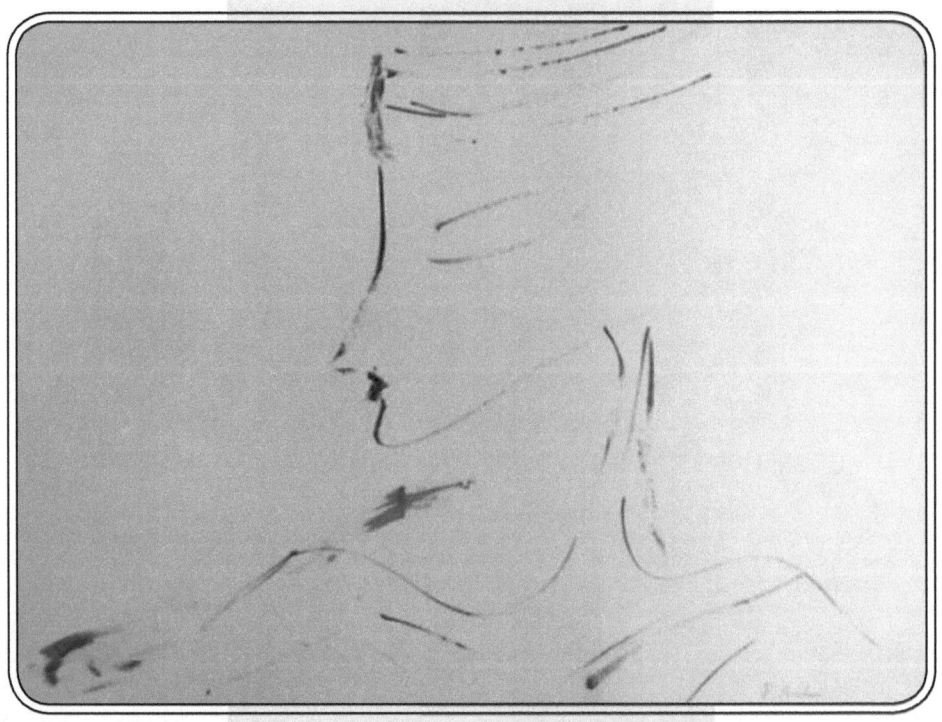

CHAPTER ONE

THE HIBISCUS, THE BOUGAINVILLEA AND THE WEEPING WILLOW, MAJESTICALLY BOWING

The morning was a beautiful sunny winter morning, with the air as fresh as can be. When I looked at the garden, I was amazed, as always these last days, how beautiful it is, with the Hibiscus still flourishing, the bougainvillea still standing there with her colorful leaves challenging the winter. The weeping willow majestically bowing, with its still green slightly dew-wet, long branches. All these calming views were entering my tranquil bedroom, emerging through my see-through, cream-colored, slightly moving with the wind-draperies, while I was listening to Bach. The discordant noise of the phone, somewhat startled me but I went over, bending to pick up the receiver, with a fully confident, but questioning, gesture, who could be calling now, at this midmorning hour, and invading, my so sweet privacy.

"Hi" she said, and I immediately recognized her voice; my friend Marian. My thoughts raced in my mind. What could she possibly want? What does she need? Is my father OK? I have not heard from my childhood best friend, for almost a year, and before that, the last time I saw her was at the Shiva of my husband, about four years ago, to which she made me feel as she is sacrificing a lot to be with me at my home, while grieving for my beloved husband who died and left me all alone in this world.

Yes, before that she would phone from time to time, and always with a request, a need, a want.

We were so close when we grew up. I spent days at her house and she practically lived at our home. We would go to the beach together, ride our horses together and come home, content and tired, as one, happy and devouring dinner that either her Swedish mother has prepared, or my mother had cooked.

But, we drifted apart.

I wondered what is it this time.

"Danielle" she said "how are you?" She asked, and I felt there was nothing behind that question, but a mere entrance to the conversation ahead. I opened my business-like, voice-drawer, and answered semi cold semi familiar-like "I am fine, what is up with you?"

"Well, I have done a DNA test, and it seems that I have inherited from my mother, a gene that is causing cancer, it's called BRCA"

I was speechless. I knew all too well what the BRCA gene is. I am a molecular oncologist by profession. How many times have I taught about this Gene? How many times have I lectured about this Gene? What is she telling me now? She has inherited the BRCA Gene? She is a carrier of the BRCA Gene? She has harbored this Gene, for all her life, The Gene that now I am beginning to understand has also killed my so beloved mother?

"How do you know? Why have you done the test now??" I bombarded her, semi accusing, semi curious, because, as a genetic counselor and a cancer researcher, my subconscious, knew better. It knew that as she has it, as she has inherited this gene from her mother, there is a 50% chance that I might have inherited this gene from my mother.

My God, all those genetic counseling sessions, where I told other families, other people, of them being carriers of a cancer causing gene, trying to be detached as to not be vacuumed to their reality, to their impossible, so frightening reality, and now, I my self, might be included in this club, of brave, of miserable, of frightened and strong people.

"Well" she answered "I have had some aches, and since my Mom died 18 years ago I have been following the values of CA125, and they have risen a bit and so I decided to take a DNA test, it took a whole month, and they have just phoned and informed me, and so I wanted to tell you"

I was shocked, how brave she is to do the follow up with this ovarian cancer marker, through the years. How brave she is to take the DNA test to this ovarian cancer causing Gene. I, never wanted to give it a second thought, as long as I was just teaching about it, researching it, diagnosing it in my lab at the Medical center, and giving genetic counseling to families harboring cancer causing genes, I was safe-I felt. I was protected.

Yes, my mother died of ovarian cancer too. But I was protected.

I always stood there on the podium, in my lectures, whether it be before my students, or in international conferences, detached, strong, informing and revealing of my published papers and my research, from a point of distance and safety, thus semi personal due to the hard and sad findings of cancer stricken individuals, cautiously self assured and in control- It will not happen to me, I am protected.

"What are you going to do?" I asked, still, with my mind focusing on HER, still unable to transfer the possible potential this news might have for me. For Me Personally. Maybe it will be just about her. If it is just about her, I can afford emotionally to be and to sound a bit more concerned, although, during the last years, I have closed my heart to my friend, Marian. I trained myself not to open, not to be tempted to respond, to her sometimes so warm, so defenseless, so reminding me of our wonder-land world of childhood, voice.

But this was different.

My primal instincts were awakening slowly and my entity wanted, needed to protect my friend. My sleeping for years, emotions, rebelled, and all of me was screaming and craving to love her. But my brain told me to slow down, receive the information and go from there. Be calm, do it step by step, and not put myself again in a vulnerable position for I have learned so many times, Marian hurts me.

"How come she never shared with me, this follow up, she was pursuing all those years, checking her CA125 values" I thought, questioning myself in my mind, but I quickly brushed it off.

"Go, and make yourself an appointment" she said.

I, still like a stork bearing its head in the sand, answered "yes, maybe next week"

"No, I will give you the phone number, phone now and make an appointment" she insisted, but using a tone of persuasion, since she knew all too well, that with us, neither me nor her is telling the other what to do. Suggestion is ok, telling, no. But this is an important matter, nothing to take lightly, so she repeated her persuasion, in a rather tempting tone, and so I took down one wall of my Marian-defending-walls, and reconsidered the rightness of her suggestion, after all the sooner the better, I have to know, where am I standing. Am I to face this new traumatic knowledge, regarding myself as well, when I have not yet totally recuperated from my previous traumas, the loss of my beloved husband, and the separation from my new- so attracting to me, lover, Jan-Paul.

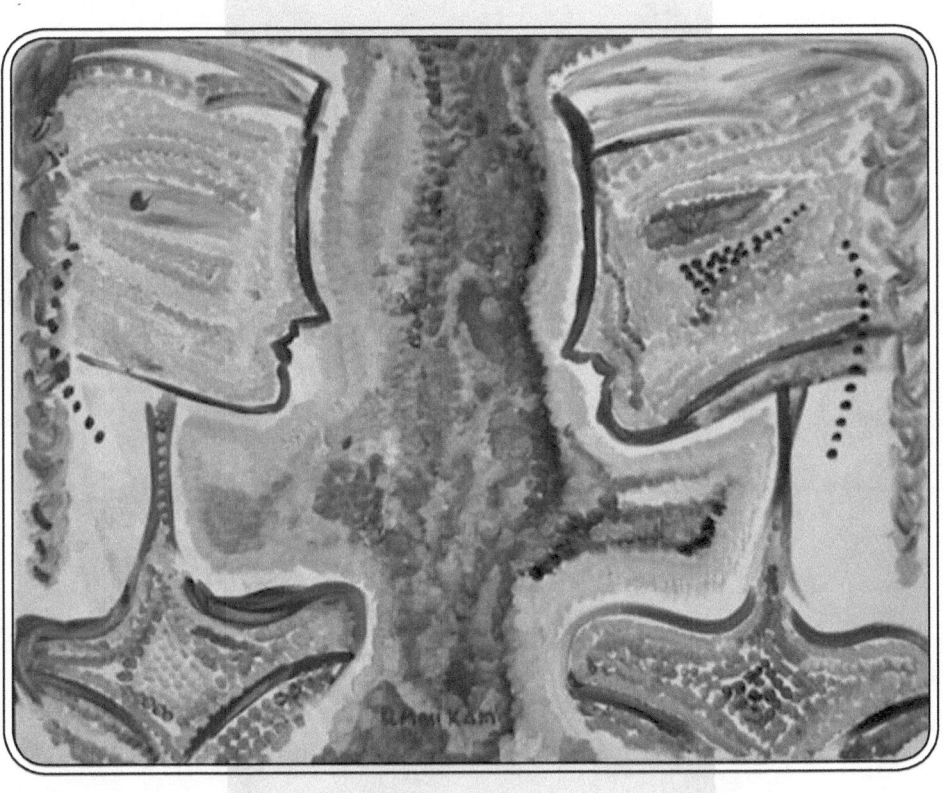

CHAPTER TWO

A WOMAN, A SCIENTIST, A WIFE AND A LOVER

I looked at the beautiful Persian carpet, laying there near the dark burgundy and blue-colored Afghani carpet, both always gave me a sense of home and security, with their elegant, classy yet warm and cozy feeling, puzzled at the threatening news. My emotional world was closed intuitively, and my mind was set to the analytical, practical mode, and thus, coldly and detached, I dialed the number, and began my journey getting to know my possible to be new mate in life, The BRCA gene, the gene that puts a woman at up to 54% risk of having ovarian cancer and her risk of having breast cancer approaches to 85% and there is also a risk of having uterus cancer. Also some other forms of cancers but at a very low risk, though higher than what is observed in the general population.

My new Gene, possibly. A gene that I have inherited from my mother, whom I loved so much. A gene, that I, if indeed inherited, would love and embrace as my own.

I phoned, Mayan, the women in charge of these DNA tests, partially uncomfortable.

I, Dr. Danielle Goldbear, the scientist, the genetic counselor, who was sitting in sessions with her, informing patients that were found to harbor a mutated gene that is thus causing cancer, was in need of her help. I was in need of a DNA test for myself. It was always others, now it is for me.

The phone rang, and Mayan finally answered and I could hardly begin the conversation. My voice harbored a mixture of vulnerable, yet in charge-professional tones, distant, yet friendly tones.

"Hello Mayan, it's Danielle Goldbear, my friend Marian has just received the results of the DNA test from you, and as you remember, my mother died of ovarian cancer as well"

"Oh, Danieeelllle" she was holding to my name as long as possible.

"Hello" she said, immediately recognizing me, with a warm, worried, engulfing tone, projecting she is all there for me, she will do anything for me, if she could, she would take all this situation away from me and erase it.

"Don't forget Danielle, it is just a 50% chance that you have inherited the Gene yourself" she told me, and some of me has transferred somewhat to a regular person, with her being the professional, although it is I who is the doctor, the scientist, and HER the technician.

It was I, the lecturer, who have explained to my students numerous times that one, has only a 50% chance of inheriting a gene from one's parents according to Mendel's genetic laws of Inheritance. I knew this all too well. And here she is, informing me, of the scientific data.

She is informing me.

It was a new experience.

A puzzling one.

But part of me was welcoming the remark.

I leaned heavily on her remark.

This was the first time that I was a bit striped from my achievements, from my credentials, from my authority, all of which represented for me an integral part of my personality. An important part of my personality. I was, as I perceived myself, a woman, a very strong woman, a scientist, a goal oriented very successful professional, a wife and a lover. All in a mixture, but the career oriented woman in me, definitely took a great part, even a dominant part in my personality. I was feeling belittled. It took away some of my confidence.

On the other hand it was nice to let yourself be cared for by someone else, to be comforted and draw some positive thinking from someone else, for a change.

I subconsciously realized that I am to step into a new reality. From now on, I will have to keep a balance between letting myself receive emotional support from other people, and between drawing power and strength, from me, from myself, from my inner being, by remaining detached and strong and also by keeping my world from feeling belittled or lessened by whatever event or reality that I would have to face.

That I might harbor a cancer causing gene, does not make me less of a talented, smart, warm and loving person.

That, I might be in a position of need, does not make me less strong.

I am me. No one can take away my achievements, my characteristics, my talents and what I have become through the years, along my life.

"Why don't you come tomorrow after hours and I will take a blood sample from you" she offered.

Tomorrow? I thought in my mind, why so soon, can't we make it like, late next week? What is the hurry?

"Well I am busy tomorrow" I said, although my calendar did not show anything too important.

"Danielle, come tomorrow and I will have them do the test within a week" she urged. Usually it takes a month for an outsider; she will push it so I will have the results within a week. Do I want this? Can I handle this pace? How nice of her. She must really like me and respect my work, being so cooperative.

"OK, I will see you tomorrow, and thanks a lot Mayan, you are great," I muttered trying to inject some pep to my answer.

I marked in my calendar, the appointment for tomorrow, writing only her name and not the purpose of the appointment, knowing fully that I refuse yet to face all possibilities that could result from the test, and thus, nothing indicated as to the reason for my appointment.

Brian was supposed to start communicating via a chat within a few minutes. I must not let him feel even the smallest clue as to what I have experienced just now. He is usually starting our chat my noon time, in Zichron, Israel, his very early morning, Washington DC. He would want to sense, feel, and interact with a warm, loving, secure yet somewhat dependent woman. He was charmed and fascinated with my professional achievements, and was looking to find a feminine, soft and welcoming woman along with it. Our daily conversations were, a cocktail of delight mixed with a draining effort to find as much as possible about each other and a yearn for closeness, dipped in a fear from openness. Brian's mails had always harbored a metallic texture, falling off guard very rarely to a more humane less cold tone, never really warm. I attributed it to him being in the exploring phase. I knew he was attracted to me, very much so, and I wanted to strengthen those feelings of his for me, and thus recruited all my energies, all my knowledge and tools, to tighten his appeal for me.

It was already 4 years since I have lost Michael, 3 of which were quite hard years, requiring an immense effort, just to exist. My mind sometimes escapes to these years but as soon as I would realize that, I would force my entity to focus and concentrate on the now and the future. Since I knew that I possess a very warm and family oriented personality, I was seeking a mate, a partner, a lover, a new friend for life. I have realized last summer, that I can fall in love again, since I fell deeply in love with Jan-Paul. We separated since then. I was deeply disappointed with what I have learned about Jan-Paul when being with him, and was deeply hurt by him.

Thus, getting to know Brian symbolized for me, a new future, a new possibility, and a sweet, silly, small emotional revenge to Jan-Paul; I am a very worthy woman, and men do want my presence, my closeness and a serious committed relationship with me.

I needed to re-build my confidence as a woman.

I knew all too well that I am a very feminine and attractive woman. I was always sought after, by men, in the Medical Center, where I was heading my research lab, in international conferences to where I was invited to lecture about my work, in the University where I was a staff member and taught my courses and where ever I met them, there would always be a man or two that needed to impress me, to be with me, to have me. There would always be a man or two that were fascinated by me and were seeking my presence.

Come with me to Berlin? I remembered the German scientist, in the international conference in Niece, France, asking me, pleading with me to return with him from Niece to Berlin, instead of back to Israel. That was the first conference that I attended after Michael died. I accepted their offer to lecture about my work, more as a tool for me to learn how to live again, without my husband, then to present my scientific data to the world. I succeeded, with flying colors.

But, it was so very difficult for me.

Yes, the world known scientist, Finch, came especially to hear me, and was there listening to me very seriously, with his eyes following every gesture of my body, trying to capture every bit of my presentation.

Yes, this same day, and the next day, where ever I met them, scientists congratulated me for my presentation. I was very deeply touched by a woman scientist, who crossed the road, when I was walking from the lecture hall to the hotel, especially to tell me how much she enjoyed my lecture.

I assume, they all, have also read the dedication to my beloved husband, a world known scientist, whom the whole scientific world mourned and was devastated for the loss.

So was I.

Devastated.

No one, but no one, knew, how hard it was for me to stand there, on the podium and present my data.

To travel alone to Niece, to the conference, the first time in over 20 years.

To sleep alone in my bed, in the hotel in a foreign country, for the first time in over 20 years.

I was, for them, the very attractive, blonde, talented scientist.

They did not know, that when I came back to my room, I cried so desperately. So, sorrowfully.

They did not know, that every evening, during my stay, when at the days I was so active and smiling in discussion groups, making conversation with my colleagues I phoned, so grief stricken, to my father in Israel to find some comfort, some condolence for my-so eternally-seeming grief and sorrow.

When I lost my so beloved husband, I lost some of my confidence as a woman.

The turnout of my encounter with Jan-Paul, damaged it as well.

I knew, deep down in my mind, due to my very capable analytical mind, that Brian is actually not the man for me. I was a very choosy woman, not only because I felt I deserve a highly capable loving friend, being myself very unique, but I was built in a way that this was what I needed, and should I make too many compromises, I would be unhappy and my entity would rebel and I would leave an unsuitable man, as I left Jan-Paul, although I loved him so much. I was not equipped, like many other women, to overlook undesired characteristics, to settle for what I thought I could not.

Sometimes, I wished I was more simple, and more like other sensible women, and able to settle for much less, as what I wanted, what I needed, was hardly there to find. Thus, Brian is definitely not for me. But on the other hand, Brian was an intelligent man, and I felt I should give it a chance. Who knows, maybe he IS the man? He did have some very appealing qualities. He was well educated, being a trauma, emergency room doctor, physically a kind of a man I could be attracted to; tall, blue eyes, and he was looking for real quality in a woman.

The sound of the starting chat coming from my PC startled me. I was caught deeply in my thoughts. I breathed deeply as I was sitting on the Marie Antoinette period, antique-pink-colored sofa chair, and got up towards my computer, in my den. I tried to draw out my business-like writing- mood tone, dipped gently with a little bit of warmth.

"Hello?!" I wrote.

"Shalom" Brian replied, with one of his numerous attempts of trying to get closer to me, thus using the Hebrew word for hello.

"Hi, how are you?" I answered, always finding it difficult to talk with him. He was not a fluent talker.

"I am fine, would you lie in a relationship?" He questioned.

I was startled. He had his way of bombarding me, out of the blue, with a question, or some questions, that he had prepared and thought of, in order to get to know me, whether I am the right person for him. Sometimes, it felt like he has a check list, and every now and then he would demandingly ask, not explore, not delicately feel around, but rather very childishly, as six year old do, just ask very undiplomatically.

"No, Brian, I would not lie. Would you lie? Have you been lied to?"

"Well, he said, I would not lie, but my wife, that is my ex-wife had an affair twice in our marriage"

Twice, my gosh, Brian was married for 33 years, and one of the reasons that I did want to give our relationship a chance was that I perceived him as a loyal man and friend. How come a woman betrays her husband twice?

Either she is not my cup of tea, and looks for and needs constant excitements, or maybe Brian has become a very boring partner in a relationship. An unsatisfying partner. Maybe they just stopped being compatible. I was for over 20 years with my husband, and every year was, like a good wine, better than the previous one.

"And how did you separate?" I asked, giving him enough lee-way to answer as he wished and just bypass the question with a merely, "fine," as an answer.

"She left" he said with his very metallic-matter of fact-chatting tone, of which I thought, must either be his protective way or reflects a rather cold personality.

"I would like to hear more about your life, Danielle" He said.

"Well, ask away Brian and you shall be answered" I promised, chatting back. "What are your plans for the coming weekend?"

"This coming Sunday I'm visiting New Orleans to celebrate my daughter's 25th birthday. She wants me to go with her to some museums. From there we'll probably go to some art galleries. Do you know New Orleans at all?" He inquired.

"Some, I confessed, not as well as you" I replied.

"What will you be doing?" He asked.

Well, I thought, besides figuring out the new information I have received an hour ago? What shall I tell him?

"I will be receiving some guests Brian, for lunch. Since it is a very nice season now, we will probably be eating lunch in the garden. It is already several weekends, that the hot summer is over, and there is spring-like cool pleasant temperature, thus very enjoyable for spending time in the garden." I playfully filled him in with my plans.

"That's nice" he sighed, "can I join? Please?" He chatted pleadingly, forgetting for a minute his metallic chatting tone.

I laughed with all my heart, and said "yes, sure, get on your private jet, and hop over for lunch" I tempted warmly, yet making it still sound as the pleasant joke it is.

"The following Friday I am flying to southwest Arizona to spend a long weekend with my two other daughters" Brian continued.

That's nice, I thought. I liked a man who spends time with his kids. "We're staying at an upscale Resort/Spa--I plan at least two massages (along with a lot of hiking). Do you give back rubs?" He asked and I could feel his semi smile. I was not sure Brian could really smile. Maybe laugh, but to smile warmly?

"The truth, Brian, no, as we said no lying, and I do not lie as a rule. I have a very bad memory, and lying is good for people who remember what they have said. Additionally, Brian, I find the truth always better, even when unpleasant. So, no, I don't, but surely I can leaaaarn???" My message held so many possibilities, for him, for us, alluring and appealing.

He either did not catch on or did not want to relate to my insinuations.

"During the first weekend of September I am running in a marathon at Naples, Florida and may spend some time looking around for a house to buy (a weekend getaway). Where exactly in South Carolina is your place? Literally in Hilton Head?" He asked.

"No" my chatting tone returned to the regular- nice tone "it is in Myrtle Beach" The conversation started to be somewhat of an effort, which could be natural due to the limited short time of our encounter.

"Well I have to get ready for work, and you must need to be back with your activities, so it was nice talking to you" He ended dryly and I, patiently, taking it down with a hope that this will change, finished the conversation politely biding him goodbye, and closed the chat.

Brian was for some times, pressing for us to talk on the phone. I was glad, today that this has not yet happened, and that I held up to his pressures and did not give him my phone number, yet. I felt, I still wanted and needed my privacy, and would like to control the times of our interactions.

Today especially, it was nice to be again, in my reality, my own protected so safe and engulfing bedroom, home, village and country.

I went about my daily plans and activities, part of me so intuitively well deciding to "go business as usual" and the other part, so dominantly belonging to my personality, craving to think about what has happened this morning, to analyze all the possibilities, to process my morning and built a controlled, solution-accompanied scenario and possibilities to all that has happened.

I had several goals in my life now. Quite heavy goals. Two of the most important ones were changing my career, and finding a new friend for life. These were under no circumstances easy goals. In fact they account for the most important aspects in one's life; work and home, career and spouse, the outside world and the inside world. And here I am, I was thinking to myself, still trying to emotionally recuperate from my separation from Jan-Paul, making an effort with Brian, and let's not forget Pierre, from whom I was expecting a burning love email, really trying my best to make for myself a new and enjoyable life, and there, out of the blue, another, so unplanned factor came into the so thoughtfully calculated formula, A GENE, The BCRA Gene.

Well, I thought, why don't I get on the treadmill, for now and see how things go. Running my 5.5Km on my treadmill always gave me comfort, cleared my head and presented new solutions for everyday reality presented tribulations.

CHAPTER THREE

MAYAN

I felt great driving my Honda CRV. I specifically chose this jeep, a small little dream that I had for years, possessing a jeep, 4 wheels, with the spare tire attached to the back door, thus having this appealing contradiction that I liked, a very feminine lady, woman, driving this supposedly rough vehicle. By the time I have purchased it, it was already quite common in Israel, but never the less, I enjoyed it tremendously, driving it, and also appreciated the looks, of mainly men trying to capture the image of this passing picture of the blonde in the Jeep. As my nice neighbor Karen said smilingly to me after admiring the new car, Danielle, it is "a babe magnet." She was right, it really was.

The lovely streets of Zichron were passing by me as I drove, but this time, my mind was not fully aware of the beautiful calming surroundings. I loved Zichron, being a small village of only 10,000 people, green and tranquil, and coming from the hectic city, with a very demanding life of a scientist, Zichron represented to me a place of sanctuary. A hiding place from my everyday work and life. But this time, my drive was somewhat different. I was on my way to Mayan, to let her take my blood sample, for a DNA analysis, to find out whether I am indeed a BCRA gene carrier, like Marian. I was very relaxed and calm, and planned to have my authority-wise personality, going through the procedures, being somewhat friendly, yet detached, not letting any of this enter my entity yet. What for, maybe it will all be just like a bad dream that passes when one is awaked.

"Wow, you look like a young girl Danielle" Mayan said when meeting. We haven't seen each other for several years, and she too, I said, looked very nice. We entered the meeting room, the big room where I used to sit as the molecular oncologist, presenting the results, with the staff members, the Gastroenterology clinician, if it would be a colon cancer analyzed family, or the onco-gynecology clinician if we were analyzing a BRCA family as to breast, ovary and uterus cancer, and such. The big room with its big brown table and numerous empty brown chairs felt familiar, but cold. I felt suddenly out of place. I felt very uncomfortable, now at the other side of the coin. I tried to disconnect myself from these thoughts and feelings and concentrate at how good Mayan looked and she walked me, very slowly and warmly through the paperwork, enquiring as to my family history, writing everything down on a paper sheet. It was strange seeing, there, black on white, my name, my age, and my own personal family data, detailed on Mayan's sheet.

"Well, come along and we will take some of your blood," she said cheerfully, but exactly the right quantity, not too much, we were not experiencing a happy occasion after all, but not too little, this is not finished yet, and it might very well be that I am not a carrier.

Also, for the first time, I started playing with idea, that if it will be positive, I will find a way to face it. I have to. There is no other option. But, I quickly returned to the reality at hand, unable to take this thread of thought further.

"When will you be able to give me some results, Mayan?"

"Usually as you well know, Danielle, it takes a month" Yes, indeed Marian told me it took a month for her to get her results back.

"But let me introduce you to our accomplished lab head, and we will ask him to do it as a rush job. I am flying for 4 days to Europe, I will come back for 3 days to Israel, and then I will be flying to the US for several weeks. So, I would like to be done with it as soon as possible, letting you take the necessary action."

What action? What necessary action? I will take my time understanding the results, and figuring out what to do.

It is rather peculiar, I thought, that Marian mentioned, I remembered, that they have referred her, very urgently, to an onco-gynecologist, for an oophorectomy. She was puzzled as to why is the rush. "Why is it so urgent?" She asked me. Marian did not like to be forced into a situation, to say the least. Marian needed to be in control, as much as reality allowed, of whatever situation she was confronted with. She was 55 years old. I was 52 years old. Her mother died of ovarian cancer at the young age of 56. Maybe they rushed her because of her approaching her mother's age? With me it will be different, should the results be positive, God forbid, they will not rush me. I will have all the time in the world thinking of my options. Processing the possible new reality.

We went through the corridor to the lab and as soon as we opened the door, I encountered the familiar smell which I like so much of the lab, the growing bacteria in the liquid bacteria agar-food, the smell of the different reagents, all so familiar after swimming like a fish in this world for over 30 years, and heading my own lab and research, supervising my own PhD and MSc students.

After exchanging some words with a colleague we ran into, we continued to the lab. I was beginning to be impatient, and wanted all this to be done with and over. I recruited my patience with my will power, but to an outsider, I probably looked like I have all the time in the world and am just going through with the procedure, as required, totally uninvolved emotionally.

"Anry" she cried out loud for the lab manager. He approached us. "Anry good morning, this is Danielle Goldbear, Dr. Danielle Goldbear, Danielle, this is Dr. Anry Bale" I smiled politely, and he looked at me with what I was thinking an admiring look? Do I know him? "Hi Danielle, don't you remember me? From Berkovitch's lab, I was the manager there?"

Berkovitch's lab was on the fifth floor, mine was on the seventh floor, in Rashi Medical center. He must know me. I don't remember him at all. "Yes, sure how are you? What are you doing here?"

"Danielle," he told Mayan, still admiring me, his eyes, shyly looking at me, standing at a respecting distance, "was heading her lab 2 floors above me." With his constant smile, projecting his respect and happiness that he, Anry, can be of help to the famous, Danielle Goldbear, the Danielle he admired and thought so much of, he answered, "well, I am running this lab now". His gaze could not leave my face.

"How quickly can you have the results for us Anry?" Mayan enquired very softly and delicately, implying that it will be nice to have it as soon as possible, but aware that he is the head of the lab and thus has the authority here. "Oh, anything for Danielle. Within a week for sure" He said.

"Well I am off within four days to Europe, can we have it by then?" She asked. "Yes, absolutely" He said, shifting his eyes, smilingly between her and me.

"I see you are doing a very good job here Anry" I said complimenting him and trying to sound professionally admiring him as much as possible. After all, he knows me and remembers me, so fondly and respectfully and is going to carry out my DNA analysis, I have to be as complementary as I can. The whole situation was beginning to be somewhat draining for me, and I was happy that Mayan called for me to enter the other room for blood withdrawal.

On the way back home, part of me was captured with the beauty of the road, and part of me was trying to understand, process and figure out what has happened today. How was I going to proceed with my life for the next 3-4 days, until I will get the results from Mayan? I loved the route I was driving. In the mornings, towards Haifa it had it's beauty, when the day was entering and the sun was coming up. A route I was taking almost every morning on my way to work. To my left was the Mediterranean Sea, majestically spread out, with all its beauty. Sometimes calm, sometimes in winter, very angry and stormy and gray. But always a breathtaking view. Also, in the late afternoon, like today, the view was breathtaking.

The twilight, calming-pastel-soft- color and the slow, repetitive, secure movements of the waves, were very soothing. One knew for certainty, that the next wave will come, with the same predictable slow movement, engulfed by the white foam. It was almost hypnotizing, but I had to concentrate as always on the road, driving, and, yes, today I was also somewhat bothered with the events that took place.

I am going to be strong, take this new issue out of my mind, and try and go on with business as usual, until Monday. Then phone Mayan and get the results. I have learned the hard way that one cannot crave for what one cannot have. One should not, because it is unobtainable. I learned that, when I wanted my husband back. I used to dream that all that has passed was a nightmare, and I will awake up and find my husband with me. Find that he did not die. It was part of the phases that I went through when mourning for him, and I learned that ***one can't crave for what one can't have.*** I can't have him back.

With my eyes still watching the yellow sand, the vast open horizon filled with the deep blue sea, I understood, that I have no control of the outcome, I will just have to face whatever next week holds for me, and do the best I can to deal with the reality imposed on me.

I felt, all of a sudden a huge feeling of peacefulness, of calmness, of strength. The understanding that I have no control over the outcome of my DNA test, actually gave me a feeling of control. My mind was clear, my heart was beating quietly and repetitively, feeling safe and secure.

I rolled to our driveway, with Ginger already barking his welcome strong, low-voiced barks, as rushing me to come on in quickly and be with him.

Ginger and the night in Zichron have welcomed me, and I turned to spend another nice night in my home.

CHAPTER FOUR

PIERRE, THE DOGS AND THE RIVER

The alarm clock was invading my so sweet, heavy morning-sleeping hour and as quick as lightening, Ginger was already in my bed, on my covers, licking my face, waving his tail, tucking his nose between my ear and shoulder and kissing me good morning. Who can have, but warm, smiling feelings with such a welcoming to the day?

Ginger is a bit of an English Terrier, the smartest, kindest dog I have ever encountered and I have been with dogs all my life. When we have lived in Ethiopia, when I was 12-15 years old, we had 2 dogs, Sandy a German wolf, who's kingdom was outside of the villa, in the big garden, and Pounkey, a poodle from Israel, reigning over the inside of the villa. Our luxurious Villa was very spacious and in a very upscale neighborhood in Addis Ababa. One time both Pounkey and Sandy were pregnant and each had 9 puppies. My mother, of a Jewish-German origin, came one night down to my floor to say good night and suddenly she saw that my blanket is moving and popping up here and there. She lifted my blanket and was stunned to see 18 little, beautiful puppies under my blanket. She wanted to let me have it and exclaimed "Daaaanielle!" with an emphasis on the first 2 letters, (only my mother was allowed to call me that way, my name is pronounced with the emphasis on the last three letters) but instead laughed and called my father to enjoy the moment.

So, Ginger is an exception, from all the dogs that I have known. At times I wanted to genetically marry him to some beautiful intelligent female, but it did not turn out.

I patted Ginger somewhat and thought of the day that awaits me. I am going to make it a nice day. I went over to my PC as always to open my email program while brushing my teeth. It was a very nice sunny day at Zichron, like spring although it was already October, and fall time. While heating the water in the electric kettle for my coffee, still in my robe, I looked at the beautiful green garden, and went outside to the gate to collect my newspaper. It was my new pleasure, now days, after getting up every morning for over 30 years, between 4:30-5:30 to attend my two very demanding careers, to drink my morning coffee slowly, with no rush, no deadlines, and read the newspaper. It was already for some times that I was having this pleasure, but nevertheless its wonder did not fade away. I loved my new morning coffee ritual and it was as important to me as an egg boiled for an Englishman.

When I was working on my PhD, my instructor used to tease me that in my veins, there is coffee that is flowing, rather than blood, since at those days I used to drink around 8 cups a day, each cup with 2 spoons of sugar. Now days, I drink only 2 cups in the morning but they are quite significant for me.

I was sitting, under the pergola, enjoying the sun rays flickering on the luxurious lounge chairs, and looking at the well groomed garden inspiring tranquility and peacefulness. I sipped my coffee slowly and gazed at the flourishing roses I have planted several years ago, about eight bushes, each with a different color, each located at a different place along the house.

It was time to have my second cup of my morning coffee, this time while reading my email. I smiled seeing Pierre's mail. So consistent, appearing each morning, loyally to bless my day.

Thank you Danielle for writing back. Your writing style is much better than mine, believe me. I have published many books in my field of Psychiatry.

I liked Pierre's candidness. I also liked his little mistakes; it made him human and closer to me although the whole Atlantic separated us.

Your field, Molecular biology is as important to Psychiatry as to cancer research. I am actually very intrigued by your field of expertise. I read routinely about research in your field and in cancer research but my knowledge is very limited as I have to be up to date in my area of medicine.

I kept reading although this was not the first time, and I still enjoyed it. He had a way of writing that made me feel like he was here at my den actually talking with me and telling me all this. Pierre, I concluded for not the first time, appears to be a warm man. I liked warm people. I could relate to them. I felt they were more open and I felt that Pierre is actually helping me to get to know him and is quite free with me. That also felt good. That also gave me a feeling of familiarity, of closeness and ultimately of belonging. Yes belonging. *I longed to belong.* I longed to be a part of. I laid back again, in my big leather chair and wondered whether Pierre was like that, was so open with me or does he employ the tools of his trade to open me up to him, to put me in a more vulnerable position in a more of an accepting position. Well, I am smart enough to be aware of that and for now I can enjoy all that I received from him through this media of E-mails.

My general practice of Psychiatry, is fun overall. I like helping people and I get a lot of satisfaction once a patient is balanced and well off, emotionally, mentally and overall. Since I like my work, although I am financially secure, I think I might maybe just slowdown in the future years but never really retire.

That is good Pierre, I was beginning to talk with him in my heart, semi enjoying it, semi aware of this new development and it's possible consequences-me getting attached to him. G-d, I haven't met the man yet. I haven't touched him yet. I haven't been kissed by him yet. I have to be more careful and not allow myself to get attached to him so quickly. I have to take a slower pace, although Pierre's most attractive character, his sense of humor that was peeking now and then was quite capturing for me. Pierre's plans were getting along with my own plans for my own future like a glove to a hand. I would like a mate that is busy with his world. I have a world of my own and would like to go on and enjoy it. I need with me a man that harbors his own interests as well as our joint ones, thus letting me have my space, enjoy my research, my writing, my hobbies and letting me do my own thing. After all I am a very independent woman, a very successful and accomplished one, and even when retied I would like to be involved with my own newly developed areas.

I gave Pierre a small little lavender point in my mind. Lavender is my favorite color, thus Pierre, without knowing has gained quite a bit with me, and was evaluated quite high at my judgment ladder.

My life in Savannah, Georgia on the river is a pure pleasure. The river is clear and beautiful and every day is colored with another tone or shade of green. The kids are playing in the water and I enjoy boating in it with my different boats. There are days that I like to sail, there are days that I just like to roam around the different places and marsh with my motor boat and there are days that I like to row and listen to the serene, peaceful sound of the water and the birds.

Wow! That is the kind of life that I want. That is the kind of life that I need. That is the kind of life that I so yearned for and so hoped for. The kind of life that revolves around nature. It was like Pierre was residing in my subconscious and was knowing exactly what buttons to push. How to run me. The magic word was nature. I was suddenly getting carried away and imagining my life on the river, every day, every week, every month, not only for a limited time for a vacation or a breakaway from my so immensely tensed work life. Wow, that is something that I knew I wanted so very much. To live on a river. ON THE RIVER. On Pierre's River.

Maybe it will be. Maybe it will happen. I thought in my mind, with my heart being the dominant role player. My heart continued to read with a warm pleasing feeling, smiling while encountering his delightful light sense of humor.

My 4 dogs, Pal, Petunia, Sweetie and Jacob are a playful bunch and bring a lot of fun and pleasure to my world. I like to walk them in the forest nearby. Sweetie is a real female and knows how to extract pets and cookies out of me whenever she feels the need.

I stopped to breath and think and process what I have just read, for who knows how many times, after I have reached this part of his letter. The more times I have read it, the more of an appeal it had for me. If only he knew. Maybe he does? What could I have wanted more? The man also likes dogs. No, he loves dogs, and has 4 of them.

My home on the river was designed and built by me. It is my second hobby, and it is built in a warm and comfortable fashion with wood being dominantly used in all 3 levels. It is connected to my dock which I have built as well and so it is very comfortable to enjoy the water, whether just to read a book on the balcony overlooking the river, or to go about the house from which every window, the river and the dock can be viewed, or to return from my various excursions on the river strait to the warm, wooded home.

I was feeling that I am beginning to fall in like with Pierre. I wanted time to pass. I wanted him to be the one. I wanted to be over with looking for the right mate. I wished Pierre and I were already over the getting to know each other and already in the together phase.

His letter manifested so many prospects.

Yet, a cloud was there, his last letter. His so open of a letter, letting me know everything regarding his health. What a brave man. It must have been difficult for him to spell it all out to me.

A happy Simchas Torah and Succeth to you,

Pierre.

So I wrote, letter number 1: *Good morning Pierre,*

Your thoughts about molecular biology are very interesting and I definitely agree with you. I remember during my PhD schooling and shortly after, it was difficult for MDs to perceive it that way, especially for those who originated from psychiatry and psychology. Genes were some strange animals and could not be attached to manifestations of mental disorders. Today people are much more open to the idea and the facts that have been discovered during the last 2 decades and I liked to read it in your mail.

In addition to my career at the medical center, I was very busy for over 20 years with my career as an assistant professor and lectured 4 full frontal courses each year, 2 for each semester, which was a very heavy teaching load. I was considered, much to the envious feelings of my colleagues, as a "gifted lecturer", and each year, poor them, I always received the highest grades from my students. I got reminded of this, because one of the courses demanded a lecture and seminar work of the students, and I took it upon myself, to relate psychology and psychiatry to molecular genetics, and they have turned in beautiful works and seminars regarding genetics and the latter disciplines. It was enjoyable.

Your house sounds fantastic. So Serene, and harbors both nature and enough solitude, but still safe. It reminds me of my long quest for a place on the oceanfront for myself, until I found the one in Myrtle Beach SC, which I am so happy with. Which 5 Hurricanes were you there? This is a phenomenon that is quite frightening for me. I know how to handle a situation of a suicide bomber, or war, but such nature manifestations are new to me. Do you live there all the time, or like me divide your time between the city and the river? By the way, your mail caught me a few days after I have returned from Myrtle Beach to Israel, I still am under the influence of the Jet lag.

How do you manage with all your dogs? Do they come back and forth with you in your car? Who walks all of them? I remembered them this morning when I woke up, since Ginger is always watching me, when I wake up, and when he feels I am awake, is jumping to my bed and licking my face and waving his tail happily and kissing me good morning. I imagined what it must be like with 4 dogs, 4 lickings, 4 kisses- nice to enter the day that way. By the way, which one of the two gentlemen in the picture is you?

Well as to your question, of living in two cultures, I have been exposed to different cultures since childhood, when living in Addis Ababa, Ethiopia for three years ages 12-15, in Cincinnati, Ohio participating in an exchange program for excelling students in high school, studying classical ballet in Santa Barbara, CA for a year at age 21, after the army and *before plunging to the science schooling, post doc in England and then spending every summer and some of the winter with my husband in the US and in Europe. I enjoy what both cultures can give me, and these are quite different cultures, and there is a lot to enjoy. The sense of freedom and privacy is different, the weather, the attitude of people, the warmth or coldness of people, and so much more. If one knows to take the best there is, and one has the ability to see what is offered, I would say I have the best of these two worlds, and I do enjoy them.*

Regarding my retirement that is actually just starting, after getting up every morning at 430-530 AM, and running around in a fashion that every minute counts, living in a world where sharks prosper, and I, a woman, a sensitive one, has to be always intelligent, beautiful and elegantly achieving all that is needed for my lab and work, in a way that will always leave the doors open for me and with a smile, I am happy for once to wake around 700-800 AM and read the newspaper under the pergola, in the garden with Ginger, while drinking my first coffee for the day, with no deadlines waiting for me.

Then there is a big list of wishes that I would like to engage in. I would like very much to write. I was thinking and planning it for many years, and now I would like to do it, in my den/office, while listening to some good classical music, both here in Israel and in Myrtle Beach. I would like to have more time to read, and think, which I did not have much, until now, and I miss it. I would like to spend a lot of time in nature, after being for too long, in the lab, in the lecture rooms, in meetings, in conferences and such. I would love to cultivate my garden, and spend more time in the sport activities that I enjoy, swimming, hiking and such. I also intend to spend a day or two, managing a project, whether at the nearby college-thus science oriented or in the nearby Jewish community.

And there is learning to paint, and the list is very long, I think I would need to construct a genetic twin of myself. Most of all, I would like to invest a lot of time in my new relationship, should I find it, in my new friend for life.

Where have you studied, Pierre? Are you close with your children? Do you enjoy your work? What in particular? How does your day go? Have you always lived in Georgia? Where do you see yourself in 5 years?

Some guests are arriving, so you are saved by the bell,

Hag Samech,

Danielle

And then I wrote letter number 2: *Good morning Pierre,*

You are in the midst of your pleasant dreams, about me, and here I am, in Zichron Yakov, on the mountains in Israel writing to you. I am writing to your personal mail address (let me know if I have the right one and that you have received my mail), as you offered, but I will negotiate it with you, in return I would like to receive some current photos of you, your home, the river, the dogs, and don`t tell me that you do not know how to operate the digital camera and hook it to the pc and send the photos, because you can always recruit your grandson to your help, and the new generation boy will undoubtedly be able to do it within 2 seconds. So, I am waiting, and to show some good faith I will send you a picture of me with Ginger, and Bobby, my father`s dog, in my garden, before my one hourly-morning-walks. (2 additional ones as a bonus)

I was invited last night to dinner at a friend's house, in their Sukkah, and it was quite hot so I decided to braid my blond hair that has grown long somewhat, and it felt good. When I arrived, they have not seen me for about 6 months, they both said I looked like returning from a vacation. The point is, that when I came back home late at night, I found your first mail, and it brought a smile to me when going to sleep.

However, this morning, when I woke up, and was having one of my finest hours in the day, drinking my coffee, in the garden, under the pergola, with no rush, I found another mail, a very nice personal one, that brought another whole smile to my face. Maybe even two smiles.

Yes, Ginger is a male, a very loyal, affectionate, highly intelligent one.

And I do have time; my schedule is very laid back, as I built it since I have retired.

I am happy you are more at ease concerning your son Anthony being in Iraq. These are very difficult situations, and it is hard to have a loved one, far away and in danger. Although this is a routine in Israel, one never gets used to it and to the loss of life. It must be quite difficult for your daughter in law. Is he due to come home soon?

So to your numerous questions; Hag Sameach is Hag-holyday Sameach-happy thus a happy holiday, the 2 words that are most abundant these days in Israel as every person is wishing to his neighbors and friends and family. As I walked today with Ginger, along my path, almost every house hold had a nice Sukkah in the garden. It was a pleasant sight.

And to your second one… "Are you as intense as you write, or is there a playful part to you? What would you do with a country bumpkin like me, who watches bats at night for kicks?"- Well I am both. I am intense, very intense, when my profession is considered. When I am working. Personally, at home, with my loved ones, with my family, I am a very warm, feminine, vulnerable, playful, smiling, happy, satisfied and an affectionate person.

What would I do with you? For some nights I would watch the bats with you, for other nights I might tempt you to go skinny dipping at night, in the river, when all your neighbors are fast asleep, well in dream world, with us accompanied by the stars, the night`s silence and 8 little eyes, attached to 4 waving tails. And there are the days as well, that may be spent boating in the river, stopping for a picnic lunch, and lovemaking in nature where only the birds (your bats may be asleep then) can see us. There are thousand and one things that I could do with you, the serious ones, as reading together, going to the Opera with, gardening, hiking and the more serious ones, like the latter above. Life is full of them.

The third one.….I did not understand the situation about your home. Are you painting it? How many years are you living in that house? Are you upgrading it? Do you like it? I love to upgrade my home, one of my hobbies is interior decorating, and some years ago, my husband surprised me with a subscription to the British journal "25 beautiful homes", which I love to read, and implement some of the ideas I learn from them. Our

*house here in Zichron is decorated on the classic side, and has accumu-
lated quite a few compliments from guests, friends and family members.*

*Do you still teach at the university? So are you a doctor for the 2
legged and also for the much nicer and lovable 4 legged? What made you
choose these areas?*

*It is still Succoth here, so I will still wish you a Hag Sameach and a
happy Succoth,*

Danielle

Pierre was a psychiatrist, and one could notice that from reading his
emails. Pierre was asking frequently for my phone number, but I felt that
it is too soon, and wanted to get to know him as much as I could, from
his mails that were quite long, before talking with him. Unlike Brian, with
whom I felt, this would not do, and who insisted repeatedly on us talking
on the phone, Pierre seemed to be satisfied for the time being, with our
mail exchange.

Brian's mails were very short and, not getting to any deep areas, while
it seemed that Pierre was an open book for me, and was willing to share
with me even more than I have asked for. It was very interesting to correspond with him. He was totally infatuated with me, which helped a lot,
and boosted my self-esteem, and it was obvious that he was regarding me
as his, for sure, next long term relationship. He was hungry for every piece
of information regarding me, and it seemed that he would read my mails
several times and address each issue presented, in his mails back, at different times during his day, my night.

Pierre was from Georgia, living in a beautiful home, which he knew
only too well to use as a tool to attract me further to him. A riverfront
wood home, and to top it all, with a pier to the river, all what I have dreamt
of for a future home for me and my future to be mate for life. Thus, Pierre
had a lot going for him, concerning my feelings, my dreams and intellectual needs.

"Danni," I read in our chatting room, this was his new nick name for me, he felt Danielle was too harsh and wanted to make me more feminine and soft for him, so he invented Danni, well, why not.

"In January I'm going to South Florida, the Keys, for a conference. I already scheduled everything for me, but if your schedule is free I would like to get you a plane ticket and a room if there are any left." This gets riskier and riskier.

I smiled, how daring he was, I liked that in a man, he was willing to take chances to get to know me. He was in the midst of his morning sessions with his patients and we were chatting along nicely. What do I answer a strange man that I have never met in my life, only have seen pictures of and exchanging mails with, who invites me to come over from Israel to Key West Florida. Not bad. Not bad at all. Winter is coming to Israel, and I could use a bit of a summer, a bit of some sun shining days, literally and emotionally.

Now, the break up from Jan-Paul, who I loved so much, and who drained me so much for the last three months, that seemed such a disastrous situation much undeserved after losing a husband, seemed all of a sudden less of a major tragedy in view of my possible new Gene, and Pierre's invitation was very tempting considering all that I was passing now a days.

It was so much easier communicating with Pierre, than with Brian, that I actually tended to reply with a "Yes" A big, nice "Yes." But, I should make it sound a casual, nothing out if the ordinary "yes."

In my hesitation to answer, Pierre went through to his next subject, his next need to share with me of his so capturing, wonderful, new feelings for another person, another woman. Also, as a professional psychiatrist Pierre knew better than to push me, the woman that he perceived as so bright and smart and attractive and accomplished-he would let it sink, and let me process the idea.

If only he knew that my mind was already made up, very quickly for the yes option, I wonder what he would have thought. I wanted, I needed to be admired, caressed, looked upon as a miracle, by a man, these days.

Not every man, but Pierre will do, for now, and maybe for a long, long time. We will see how things develop.

"Well, Doctor, I need some advice from you. I am afraid I'm suffering from an addiction. The name of my addiction is Dannie!! I meet almost all of the DSM IV (Diagnostic and Statistical Manual of Mental Disorders) if I don't hear from you I manifest withdrawal symptoms, and most of my waking thoughts are about you, and I am a bit embarrassed to admit that some of the sleeping ones too.

So, could you please treat me for this affliction?"

I smiled.

"I would like to let you into my plans. When we meet at the airport, and I will look into your big, brown eyes, and melt seeing your smile, I will pull you to me and kiss you so deeply. We will go to our hotel hugging each other, while I will get intoxicated from the delicious smell of your perfume and the caresses of your waving long hair; slightly flowing in the breeze."

This was nice. It was getting nicer and nicer, since he had succeeded in reading me, I thought, and understood that I like matters to be delicate, classy and never vulgar. After all he was a psychiatrist.

"When we will arrive to our hotel, I will carry you over the threshold and when inside I will make love to you. No, first I will slam the door shut with my foot."

He continued to write and his very developed sense of humor was showing. I liked his sense of humor. It was an intelligent one. I could relate to it, and frequently it brought a smile to my face. Pierre seemed to be a very strong emotionally person. A man that sees reality with a smile, a joke, a light attitude, very different from me. I was an extremely serious person, although I understood humor and after the last few years, was craving for it to light my life. My husband was also a kind of a person who would see all things very lightly and none threatening. For him everything was work-able, dealable and feasible. For me as well, mostly regarding my careers, but it seemed, that I was a bit buttered emotionally lately and I would welcome a happy positive light yet deep and intelligent man in my life.

"I will kiss you all over and....."

I could not read more.

This was a bit too much for me. I could not imagine what he was writing now. I don't know the man how can he get so intimate so quickly? Maybe this is a difference between men and women? NO, this can't be, I was married to one of the former and such images never occurred.

Maybe time has passed, and it is today's fashion and I am out of fashion? Maybe I am too conservative? It was hard for me to relate to, so I decided to ignore it, and let it go.

"Where are you now?" He concluded.

"In Zichron, in my den."

"Where ever you are, Danni, is seventh heaven by definition."

I smiled.

"When you want to talk with me e-mail me and I will explain to my patients that it is you, they would understand. I promise to converse nicely."

I was beginning to understand that Pierre's way of communicating with me right now was via humor. It was his shield, and his tool, and it was a nice way, a soft way, a way that pointed out that Pierre is actually also a vulnerable man.

"How was your rowing getting along yesterday afternoon?"

"I was rowing for an hour, the river was so peaceful and I enjoyed the work out, especially when I was thinking of you too.

I need to go now, my patient has just entered,"

Love Pierre

Love?? Love Pierre??? That is very quickly, too fast. But, well, why not, let him feel the way he wants and needs to feel. I will be myself and true to my feelings and honest with him.

CHAPTER FIVE

MUTATIONS, GENES AND DNA

Germline mutations in the TP53 tumor suppressor gene are associated with Li-Fraumeni syndrome, which is characterized by a spectrum of neoplasms occurring in children and young adults that predominantly include early-onset of breast cancer, a variety of sarcomas, brain tumors and adrenocortical tumors.

I started writing my current paper.

It was a hard paper to write. It was of a very young woman, 23 years old, who passed away due to cancer. I was writing this paper, while the work in the lab was actually still going on, to find out, what form of cancer this woman had died of. This was an unusual situation. But it was crucial to find this out as soon as possible, what was the kind, if any, of a mutation harbored by her, since the woman had 3 young children and 2 young sisters, approximately her age. Taking into consideration the young age of her death, a factor that might represent a profile, in this specific family, we took it upon ourselves to establish if possible, the cause for her cancer related death, And the sooner the better.

The family was waiting for our results and we were anxious to be able to give them an answer, hopefully one that would put their mind at ease.

This young woman was with no family history of cancer and she presented bilateral breast cancer at the age of 20 years. Twenty months later she developed malignant fibrous histiocytoma of the right clavicle and another primary left breast cancer.

We thought she might be harboring one of the BRCA genes, and thus we carried out molecular testing of mutations 185delAG, 5382insC in BRCA1 gene and 6174delT in BRCA2 gene. This was done in my lab, performing multiplex PCR and separation on a denaturing polyacrylamide gel.

The results were obtained yesterday and my technician showed me the autoradiograms. I was sorry to see when analyzing the results, that she did not harbor the latter mutations. This meant, that we still don't know, what had caused her cancer, and what kind of a cancer causing mutation, if any, did she harbor. On the other hand, I was glad that I could not detect the latter mutations in her DNA. This meant that she did not harbor these so horrible mutations. Women that were found to carry these mutations were at a hard spot. A very hard spot. Don't I begin to know it myself? Since the risk for having ovarian cancer, which is very hard to battle, and the dramatically high risk of up to 50-85% of having breast cancer, are so threatening, many women are opting to undergo a total mastectomy and oophorectomy.

This is a tremendously hard decision, to undergo the later procedures, since, naturally we are talking ovaries and breasts, such important and representing beautiful organs of a woman.

So, she did not harbor either of the BRCA genes. What should her DNA be tested for? I was trying to concentrate and see the whole picture. She had NO family history, yet she manifested several forms of cancer. I was beginning to think about a possible gene that when mutated, might manifest such a presentation-the P53 gene. It was a very long shot, and 99% unrealistic, but for the remaining 1 %, and for her children and sisters, I decided to go along with it and test her DNA for the possible existence of a mutation in the latter gene. Mutations in the P53 gene are extremely rare, and usually show in a family with a heavy history for cancer, so probably we will get a negative result.

Unless, unless, the mutation is a novel one, a new one, and was formed in her DNA, thus she did not inherit it from one of her parents, hence we do not see a family history of cancer. Yes, Yes, we will do this test, although finding a new, a novel mutation that has never been found before, that has never been revealed before, well, again, a very long shot. But we must do it.

"Regina, do a DNA test for P53 mutations for the L girl", I said on the phone to my assistant. We called the young woman the L girl for the Lovely girl, we all felt for her, for her suffering and for her dying so young.

"But why a P53, it is for sure not the mutation and it is a waste of money and time" Regina confronted as always. She was right as to the price-around 3000 dollars, and it was time consuming, we did have other patients and other samples to analyze, but I pulled out my authority-like voice, and said "do it Regina, I want us to know and eliminate this as well, or maybe find out that she is a P53 mutation carrier."

"But there is no family history, Danielle" Regina insisted. I was sometimes tired to argue with her. She was a PhD, but did not like to put an effort to thinking, or even working too hard. She was married to a dentist, a sort of a man that needed mothering at all times, and she actually came to work, to relax and rest from her demanding wifely job at home. I disliked it, but that is the manpower that salaries given by the government allowed me to have.

Regina's imagination would not even consider, yes the farfetched of a possibility, that maybe we are dealing with a novel mutation, harbored for the first time by the L girl, and hence no cancer family history.

"Regina, why don't you start the test tomorrow, so we will have the results next week, OK? Let me have the autoradiograms next week on my table, Regina, and be prepared to our weekly staff meeting for tomorrow afternoon", I concluded. I hung up the phone thinking I am getting too tired and too fed up to work with such mediocre people. But, as always, the goal stood out loud and clear in my mind, I have to put every effort, and more, for this family, and try and find out of a possible cancer causing mutation existing in the L girl. The L girl. I liked her. I liked her very much and, a bit unprofessionally, I felt so much for her, I wished I could do something for her. But, she is gone. I will do something for her sisters. I will do something for her children. I will walk this extra mile and do more than my best, for this girl, the L girl.

CHAPTER SIX

MY DEAR EDEN

"Hello my beautiful, how nice you look this morning", Eden said when entering through the garden gate. I stood up lazily, not fully awake yet, dressed casually with my short khakis, to welcome her. It was a lovely October noon time and my friends and my father were invited for brunch for Shabbat. I liked dressing simple and casual, it was my rebelling from the week long dressing in power suits for staff meetings, and my smart dresses for my lectures. I was known for my taste in dressing, and looked quite lovely, and almost as a strange phenomenon in the environment of the Medical Center and the University, for appearing always so well dressed and taken care of. My jewelry always fitted my clothes, and my perfume always fitted my mood, the time of the day and the season.

People liked to look at me, some admiringly and some with a jealous attitude. I liked myself, and liked to plan my outfit a day ahead. I also enjoyed my clothes shopping, to which I could dedicate time only when being abroad, with my husband, either in Europe presenting research data, in a conference, his or mine, or in the States again lecturing or attending some business meetings.

So, it turned out that most of my time I was dressed as in Vogue, and on Shabbat I rebelled and wore my torn jeans or some other simple faded shorts, but still, always, very becoming and as my husband used to say, doing justice to my figure.

I smiled happily to Eden whom I loved deeply.

"What did you bring this time?" I peeked towards the bowl she was carrying trying to see what kind of good food did she prepare for us all. My friends knew me very well, and when they were coming over they knew they better bring some delicious food, because I am a lousy cook. So, each time they were gathering in my garden they all pitched in and brought some good cooked food. I was offering the nice garden, the nice atmosphere, accompanied with some classical music in the background, some Bach or Albinoni, beautiful table cloths and porcelains, in short the whole production, of which I was famous for among them. They were always staying in my well planned, nicely organized and handsomely decorated gatherings long after due hours. We all enjoyed so very much those gathering. "I prepared some delicious Cuscus, with some lamb, the way you like it, my dear," she said smiling.

I came to know Eden under very sad circumstances.

When I was sitting Shiva, mourning my husband, one night, under the pergola, which was one of my most favorite spots in the garden, surrounded by visitors, hardly feeling I existed, in came a woman, a woman I did not know. She was very tall, projecting confidence, yet full of compassion, looking at me strait in to my eyes, saying, Shalom, I am Eden, I am the cousin of your late husband's passed away first wife!

I looked puzzled, trying to process the information, hardly succeeding, with my heart devastated and actually gone, and my mind numb and dead as well. Cousin, first wife, my husband, the words kept dancing in my mind, and I could not comprehend the meaning. What does she want? Who is she? I looked at her; she was standing there near the table where all were seated. I raised my head to look at her eyes, and I saw the warmest brown eyes, the most hugging brown eyes, I could get lost in their affection and care. My God, she is a relative of my husband former wife, whom he had loved so very much and lost years ago, before marrying me. This woman, who is from my husband first wife's side, came to pay her respects to me. She came to convey her condolences to me.

Slowly the meaning of her being in my home, in my garden entered my subconscious, and went right through to my heart. I felt so warm with gratitude.

I was grateful and thankful for someone from my husband's first wife's side to acknowledge my pain. To be there for me.

So, I was overwhelmed with Eden's gesture, which made us friends from then on. After that encounter, she took me under her wings and cared for me in my hard times. We became very close loving friends.

Soon the garden was filled with smiling relaxed friends, and their soft voices conversing with each other was mixing with the birds singing and Bach that was still playing. With time, some small groups were formed, and were scattered in the numerous nicely planned seating areas. Some were seated under the pergola, around the big green table that was now covered with lace detailed table cloth. It seemed that most of them were the men, the husbands talking about politics of the hour, very important...Very important indeed. On the other side of the garden around the anciently engraved stone table with its matching stone engraved benches, some other friends mostly women were chatting happily, and I found myself, in between going in and out of the kitchen bringing more food or drinks, and joining later some of my close friends, that were sitting around the Morocco table, which I was proud of its checkered blue, green, yellow and purple little stones.

"And you Danielle, what are you doing in terms of housework?" Peleg asked as they were complaining each of all the hard chores they were caring out, during the week. I smiled somewhat embarrassed, since they all knew that I was holding two very demanding careers, and when my husband was with me, he did all the grocery shopping and he quite enjoyed it. We also had a lady that came once a week to clean the house, and a lady that cooked for us. The taking out of the garbage was also my husband's job. Thus I really was left with very little, mainly the laundry, that I sometimes was sending out, and the instruction giving to the Gardener, the cleaning and cooking ladies and to my husband what groceries to buy. They always made fun of me, my friends, and were lovingly laughing at me, the big housekeeper.

"To tell you the truth, I still do give all the instructions" I said with a small embarrassed smile, which harbored a mix of being lucky of always having such a support system around me- feelings and a little shy and ashamed of doing so much less then they all did. They all roared with laughter, but a nice supporting laughter. They all knew that now, that Michael is gone, my father is helping me with whatever is needed, so I can go on with my so much of a demanding life.

"You look so lovely Danielle, come and tell me what have you been doing with yourself lately", Arik was asking warmly while I was passing by him on my way to the kitchen. I smiled and tilted my head towards the kitchen, as duty calls right now.

Everything seemed so calm and tranquil in the garden, they all took a small vacation from their hectic lives. I felt so secure with them around me. They didn't know of my new troubling news. I was not going to share it with anybody, until things will clear up, and I will know where I stand. It was a heavy secret to carry, even when it could be a false alarm. Part of me wanted to just be hugged by my friends, share with them the awful possibility, and discuss with them my plausible future options. No, I will not do that, I will let everyone escape to this happy garden gathering, and also allow myself, not to think of anything serious, just enjoy the now. Just enjoy the present. Do I know how to do that? Well, I will have to learn to do that. This is one of the new characteristics that I will have to adopt, that I will have to get accustomed to. Enjoy the now and the moment. This will be my new, for now, motto.

The sun was setting down, Ginger was trying his luck for some food, each time with someone else, looking so sad and desperate like he was being starved to death by me, making quite a success with every one, and having a feast as well. The atmosphere grew even more relaxing and quiet, and no one showed any signs of planning to leave. Luckily, Agam prepared a very tasteful cake, and it was time for some coffee and cake in my beautiful PORCELANS. "Who wants tea and who wants coffee," she asked loudly so all in the different corners of the garden could hear. While she counted the orders, Selah said he wants neither. "Oh, Selah you should, the cups are so beautiful", I explained. He looked puzzled and everyone laughed.

They all left later on, full and satisfied, reluctant to go back to reality, to their lives, to step out of the gates of my home that symbolized a little piece of heaven to them. I could feel that the day was a success.

"Did you ever think you would feel like a teenager again? And blush again? I didn't, but I am. Are you getting ready to sleep? What are you wearing for bed?" I saw Pierre's chat when I entered my den.

"Well I am wearing my shorts, a blouse colored lavender, my favorite color, and Nike socks right now, since I was in the garden till now and of course my panties. But for bed I usually wear a man's T-shirt, a big one," I pleasantly answered thinking that chatting with Pierre, will give a nice ending to my so pleasant day.

"You must be the only woman in the world, when asked what they are wearing in bed say: Nike socks, Danni. The tight panties part was nice though, I was interested in that. And also the garden. I am declaring Lavender as my favorite color from now especially if you wear it. Did you think about me today?"

I smiled at his very delicate, sexually touched, inspired remark, mixed with affection feelings towards me.

"I had a wonderful day with my friends; we spent the whole day in the garden and enjoyed some very good food, accompanied with some very nice guests. Did you have a nice day?"

"Danni, you could be a great diplomat, as you are the best person at avoiding specifics that I have ever met. Have you thought of taking up professional poker, you could buy half of Israel and all of Myrtle Beach with your winnings, and your poker face. When the dealer asked if you wanted a hit or not (another card) by the time you were through with him, he wouldn't know if he was playing canasta or cribbage.

This must be how you deal with the high powered men in your career, with the sharks, poor little loveable creatures. I will write you tomorrow afternoon and Sunday when I come home, I will do my best to never miss a day writing you, it means too much to me, and you too.

Wow, will wonders never cease. You have become so important to me.

May the stars sparkle with sufficient brightness to light your dreams and thoughts to the heavens. Love Pierre"

I sighed comfortably and bid him good night. It was nice chatting with Pierre. One could feel his warm personality come through, and as always his humor and mind were appealing to me. It was also nice to read the linkage he made with my two homes, the one in Zichron, Israel and the one in Myrtle Beach South Carolina, the oceanfront condominium that I have purchased and where I have been spending my summers, since Michael died. I have just returned from Myrtle Beach a month ago, and my body was still very much tanned and toned showing the vast amount of time spent walking on the beach, on days I did not lecture in the local University. I was quite a mystery there for the staff members, being such a "gifted lecturer" as they have put it, and thus the reason they were courting me to join their department, and being severely addicted to the beach.....

And so the next day I wrote to Pierre: *Good morning Pierre,*

Your dock sounds lovely. Your home on the river sounds lovely. You must possess quite a will power to leave all that nice nature every morning and drive to your practice. How far is it? Is Savannah far from where you are living or working?

Zichron is about 25-30 minutes away from the Medical center that I have been working at, driving almost every morning on a beautiful road on the shore, listening to some classical music and drinking my third coffee of the day, and looking at the sea, its colors and waves. When coming back home late at night, busy with my-business- phone calls, talking with my husband, and with my father.

My mother passed away at 1989, it took me about 10 years to get over it, she was my best friend and I loved her dearly. My father, who is a phenomenon, is my best friend now, a man I admire and look up to, a man I hope will be with me here on this earth as much as possible-I am quite selfish in that respect. I am very lucky with the people I am/was surrounded by, my parents, my husband and my friends.

Zichron is beautiful and not dry at all with very pleasant temperatures, very similar to Myrtle Beach, laid back and quiet, and that is partly why I have chosen both places to live, and Myrtle Beach after a Doctorate on the internet searching all over the world and almost purchasing something lovely in Australia in the Gold Coast. Have you ever traveled outside of the US, Pierre? If yes, when and where to and what did you like most? What impressed you most?

My other career as an assistant professor, was as lecturing some in the medical school here in Haifa, and at the University of Haifa and some at the University of Tel Aviv, but mostly in the Academic College in northern Israel, on the border with Lebanon, 2.5 hours driving each way, from Zichron. Quite difficult but at the time rewarding. You mentioned you were teaching at the local university, what were you teaching? Did you like it? Why did you stop?

The pictures you have sent me are lovely. Brenda, your daughter, is a very lovely bride, and Bethany, her daughter, has the biggest, nicest, smiling intelligent eyes, ever. Your son in law looks like a very purpose-

ful serious man. Your semi smile is matching your semiserious eyes, and some more pounds will only do you good. I wonder what your dock looks like, your boat, and you rowing.

Have a very good morning, and look at your dock for me, I would love to drink my first coffee there,

Danielle

"Good morning, Brian."

I decided to top my nice day with a short phone conversation with Brian. He was asking, no, demanding for quite a while to have my phone number. I did not feel yet that I wanted, but agreed to talk with him as he was so insisting. I did not want to lose him and felt I could compromise on that, with me deciding when we can talk, with me phoning to him and still having my privacy with my phone number unrevealed to him.

"Danielle, so nice to hear from you," his voice projected a cocktail of surprise dipped in his metallic tone. I never quite felt welcome by him, when talking with him. Only later, in an occasional email, in between the lines, I would realize how so very much he was attracted to me, and from that I draw the strength to continue and interact with him. Otherwise, his cold attitude, was putting me off. Strangely enough he regarded himself as a warm person, and was looking for warmth in me.

"Well, I thought I would bid you good morning Brian, and let you say sweet dreams to me."

"Thank you, and thanks for the morning mail and additional pictures. You remain attractive. I will send other photos to you when I get home tonight as well as answer the same questions I posed to you. Good night Danielle and thank you for calling," his tone was a very much of a busyness tone.

That was it. So much for Brian toping off my day.

I went to pour myself some wine, and spend some time with my self, to reflect on the day passed, when I heard a mail coming through.

Danielle,
Thank you for phoning. I'd be happy to have you call "collect" the
next time.
I have to go to work now, but have one more theoretical question:
If you and I still think auspiciously of each other in four weeks, would
you be willing to reflect upon meeting (perhaps Western Europe). I have
some vacation time-interval then.
Hope to talk to you shortly,
Brian

Now this was better. Much better. With this I can go to sleep, and have my sweet dreams. Good night, Pierre and Brian, I said in my mind, tucking myself in between the covers.

"Good night, Jan-Paul, my love."

I closed my eyes and fell sweetly to sleep.

CHAPTER SEVEN

PERGOLESI, YAEL AND OUR L-GIRL

"Dr. Goldbear, Professor Tal would like to speak with you, is now a good time for you?" The lady in the phone said. A good time for me? It is never a good time for me. I was way over loaded with work, with everything seeming urgent and everyone wanting and needing a piece of me. "Yes, absolutely", I answered warmly yet authoritatively. "Good morning Danielle, how is our L girl? Have you made any progress?" Yael asked.

She knew so well to accommodate herself to the immediate reality. She was the head of one of the most prestigious Cancer institutions in the country and the world; Hadassah Medical Center and when she wanted something, she got it. I was drinking my third coffee of the day in my favorite cup, sitting in my office, which I have planned and decorated, with Pergolesi playing softly in the background. "We have Yael", I answered in my still authoritatively voice, but this time well dipped in warm tones.

Yael approached me a year ago to help her diagnose our L girl. Her L girl. She summoned me to Jerusalem, to a meeting to get to know me. When I entered the meeting room that was full with her staff members, she sat there, a woman well taken care of, with her eyes looking me all over, showing her appreciation for the pride my image has, as always, projected. Nevertheless she bombarded me with professional questions, in front of her medical staff, while everyone was quiet and attentive. I could see how she enjoyed the way I stood up to the seeming "attack" of hers, which ended with her saying, "Well Danielle, now that I took your full anamnesis, I would like to work with you!"

One could hear the respect and warm feelings in her voice towards me and there was a moment of sisterhood there in the air. I smiled still detached and professional, when I just said "that would be fine." I always felt an equal to my superior in rank, and mostly with the talented unthreatened professionals, males and females it bought me many good points. She liked my attitude and professional achievements, and thus we were collaborating for almost a year now.

Yael was a very beautiful woman and a strong one. She knew how to handle herself in "The Boys' Club". She wore her long black hair flowing to her shoulders, emphasizing her femininity, while her voice was authoritative, semi commanding and a total contrast to her hair. The latter cocktail worked well for her as the CEO.

"She does not carry any of the BRCA genes that we have tested for Yael, but we are carrying our assays on"

"She does not??" Yael sounded so disappointed. She knew too well, that this was our chance to find a mutation in the L girl. These genes presented an opportunity, although so threatening, but still an answer, and maybe a way to develop a follow up strategy for the L girl's sisters, for her children. There were no other realistically candidate genes for us to look for. Yael knew the L girl personally. It was extremely important for her to arrive to some sort of a solution, of an understanding of what has happened to this so young, full of life and beautiful L girl.

"You are sure you tested every possibility in the BRCA genes?" Her voice was sinking but as a professional she was beginning to feel that if there is nothing that could be done, then that is it, and she will have to let it go. "Yes, Yael" I said confidently, "but I have another idea, a farfetched one, but I would like to try it, and that is a possible mutation in the P53 gene". The line was silence. I could visualize Yael thinking. She was caught by surprise. "How come the P53 gene?" Her tone was professionally confronting the rightness of this idea, but one could hear her rising hope.

She knew how rare the mutations in the P53 gene are. She knew there was no cancer history in the L girl family, a characteristic of the P53 mutations. She knew it was almost unrealistic to find one in the L girl, but she liked the reality-daring decision, the creative decision, the "out of the box" decision. "Good, Danielle, that will be something else if you will find a mutation in that gene. That will definitely be something else."

"Let me do it Yael, let us see, I should have some preliminary results early next week."

"OK, keep me posted!" The line went dead. That was Yael's way, no goodbye no nothing, she was already in on her next case.

I was still sitting in my big leather chair, with my eyes gazing around my office, heavily filled with books, but I was not really noticing anything since my attention was focused inward, to my thoughts, my planning, how will we run all the DNA diagnostic tests for the L girl. I have to push Regina into doing more assays, and quicker. That for itself is a big project. I summoned all my patience and all my forbearance, went out of my office and into my lab with, as always, my cup of coffee in my hand.

"Good morning Regina," I said cheerfully, "how is the first analysis of our L girl going?"

"Danielle it is a lot of work and I am sure that it is for nothing," her tone was complaining, as usual. "Is that your last autoradiogram? Good work, Regina, it looks quite clean and sharp. Why don't you repeat it next week, and proceed this week with another panel of assays?"

She looked puzzled, and appeased at my complimenting her work, and said "yes it turned out to be quite a nice autoradiogram, I decided to expose it for a longer time, so the radioactivity of the P32 in the DNA tested would allow the appearing of the black bands representing the DNA sequence to be seen better."

She looked at me, like a poodle thanking his master for noticing him.

"That is good," I mumbled while fully focused in examining the results presented in the autoradiogram. We continued to talk and analyze the current results with me balancing my way between letting her feel how important she is, how important her input is, and delicately drawing her commitment and enthusiasm to proceed the work in a faster pace, letting her feel that she is making some of the major decisions, the important decisions, and there is a heavy responsibility on her shoulders.

We concluded that Regina, with my un noticed help at working on her calendar and specifying the work needed to be done for each day this week, will be actually done by the end of next week should everything go well on the technical side. And, as a thought was running in my mind, should her husband just let her be for a while and let her concentrate on her work while being in the lab, instead of phoning around seven times a day, to enquire about his lunch, his clothes and their bank account.

Kinder gardening, was a major part of my job, I was thinking, regarding my own staff members, as well as working with the higher hierarchy, my superiors in rank in the Medical Center. But, that was the only way of getting things done. It was part of my every day work, I was thinking while hurrying to a high-management meeting, in which I was planning to demand and get some more money and manpower for my lab. Demand and get, I laughed in my mind. I wish it was this easy. I wished I could just show them how over-worked we all are at the lab. How, almost every Medical Center in Israel is choosing to work with us. How so frequent I am being invited to present our work, in international conferences. I wished that all the facts regarding my lab, the reality which is so transparently clear and obvious would be noticed, acknowledged and appreciated, by the way of supporting my lab in the so much needed more manpower. But I knew this is not happening on planet Earth. Maybe it is happening on planet Earth, but not on planet Rashi.

So, I had my own developed strategy, which almost always worked.

A busy voice of men talking dominated the room on my entry, I was the only woman attendee and most of them raised their eyes when I walked in. I knew this meeting is crucial, and I chose my clothes last night, with all coordinating jewelry and matching high-heeled shoes. I felt very confident with my tight ankle long black skirt, and my tight yet very respectful gray shirt, toping all the somewhat masculine colors with delicate feminine, long antique-pink colored earrings with a matching big ring.

I could feel David's eyes running very quickly all over my image, with the others, noticing my femininity as well as my professionalism, conveyed by their standing up to shake my hand, or nodding their heads welcoming me in respect. I was not fooled by the welcoming attitude. I knew and felt their respect and even some admiration for me. But all that was put aside when the undercurrent war of competing for resources would begin. Not to mention, that jealousy also took part of these men's decisions, and some of them would do whatever it takes to deny me my professional needs, and even hurt my job, my lab, and all accompanied with a very warm smile. Men needed tending, nurturing, and I was very busy doing that all my career's life, for the time I would need their help, their backing. For the time I would need to harvest the fruits of my efforts.

I woke up feeling very cheered up this morning and decided to drop Pierre a short teasing smiling "good morning" to place a smile on his face, before getting along with my day.

So I wrote: *Good morning "my like",*

This is just a very short good morning, before I have even walked with Ginger. I was in the midst of drinking my first coffee under the pergola, and was thinking of you, how come you are not here drinking the coffee with me.

I hope that now, that the week has begun for you, you will still be somewhat relaxed and able to enjoy our correspondence.

Part of me flew over for just several minutes, to your home on the river, and I was quite confused, until I found your bedroom, but I did, only to look at you sleeping, wish you pleasant dreams till the morning of Monday and make my way back to the pergola.

Good morning.
Danielle

After my early brisk walk, I could not resist but write him another letter before heading to the Sharks at work…

So I wrote: *Good morning again, I liked the picture that you have sent me, it projects some of your characteristics which I like, like humor and intelligence. But you are not off the hook and I am waiting for new pictures of you at various places and various sizes. Do you ever wear jeans? I think you would be very attractive to me in a pair of rugged jeans and a simple T-shirt. I try to imagine you in that way.*

I have returned a while ago from my daily-hour-walk with Ginger, which I love. It is a time for me to think and also enjoy the view of Zichron and the surroundings. I also enjoy the way I can control my body, and the physical aspect of hiking/running/walking. In Myrtle beach I used to do it on the shore/beach which was also lovely, and enabled me to hear the waves and smell the salty air, and after my hike, I would just take of my shorts and Nikes, and walk (with my bathing suit on) to the water and enjoy the difference between the brisk walking and the slow bathing, letting the water caress my body and just surrendering to their touch and slight movement. In winter time I have to settle with my treadmill, at home, in the special safe-room/shelter where one is spending time when missiles are falling around. It is a nice room with a window to the garden which can be closed hermetically protecting from gas and missiles, and has a TV for me to be somewhat entertained when walking on the treadmill.

The dogs are Ginger, the bigger, with a touch of brown, standing, and Bobby, smaller black. Ginger is a bit of an English Terrier, the smartest, kindest dog I have ever encountered and I have been with dogs all my life. When I come to the US, Ginger lives with my father and his friend Bobby.

I am happy that you like coffee. Do you drink coffee in the morning? I will wait for you to make me these delicious styles of coffee that you were writing of.

I would love to sail with you for a week on some yacht, and wear a whole week, just my bathing suit, and maybe some short old torn jeans, (what a change it will be from my usual power suits, that I have been wearing for work) and be for a whole week barefooted, just you and I and the ocean. It can be near Main, or the Keys in a safe place and season, or the Caribbean, with occasional snorkeling and skinny-dipping and reading and just enjoying nature, and each other.

So, do you have an interesting case at work? Do you see the same patients, once a week? Like 5-8 patient a day? Tell me about your work a bit? When and how do you drink your coffee in the morning? In a rush or you take your time? What do you wear usually to work? What kind of a car do you have and is it a long drive to your office? Do you have friends there or just colleagues? Where do you eat lunch? When do you come back home?

Regarding Florida, where is your conference exactly and when would you like me to come?

Have a pleasant day, Pierre, what a lovely name, a name that I rather do like,
Danielle

CHAPTER EIGHT

PLAYING WITH THE SHARKS

"Danielle, as you know these are difficult times in Rashi Medical Center and we are in the midst of a manpower redundancy procedure. You will have to let go one of your assistants" said Yonatan, the CEO of the medical Center. He was a man of a short height, a professor, who respected me being a scientist and doing research. He was always very a matter of fact man, when talking using very short sentences and to the point, and I liked that. I could deal with that, because it was pure business, no other motives, unlike most of the other members sitting around the huge brown oak table, all with very serious like facial expression, like we were discussing World War III. I was sure each of them was paying very little attention right now, when I was the issue, and were occupied with their own concerns.

"Well" I said very pleasantly, agreeing with Yonatan, "I understand the reality"

He was stripped immediately from all the guns and ammunition he has prepared for battling this over with me, and sat more deeply and comfortably back on his big leather, brown arms chair, replying in relief "so you are willing to let go one of your assistants?" His relief was projected by his voice as well as his body language.

"If this is what you want and think I should do, then this is what I will do" I said softly.

"What do you mean by that Danielle?" David attacked me coldly "you should be thankful for having 2 assistants until now at a time when everybody else had only one assistant and you know how expensive this manpower is?"

David was my primary superior, and the only one in the room with no academic rank and thus always harboring somewhat inferior feelings. Even I was a professor, I, his subordinate. He was from one-side proud at my achievements, because they could be attributed to him as well. On the other hand, inside, deep inside, he was angry at my success. He was furious at my accomplishments. He knew that everybody was aware of the fact that my success was due to my talent, and it had nothing to do with him. He was happy to attack me there, when his intuition led him to feel he could succeed at it and have the support of the majority present in the room. Most of them sat full of confidence and self-respect, checking my face, and waiting to see how this will develop. Some felt a bit uncomfortable and took great interest at pealing their apple, God forbid it will be done the wrong way.

Also all knew that one of David's 4 daughters, was a scientist that ran her lab two floors beneath mine.

David had an agenda. His own private agenda.

He wanted most if not all resources channeled to her.

I knew better than to wait for help. I looked David straight in the eye, and said with a very relaxed, low voice projecting self-assurance yet respect for him, not wanting to alienate him further. "You are right David, it is very expensive, but I have brought over today, a chart that shows how we have developed and that all major hospitals in the country are referring to us and to us alone"

I began distributing the colorful, short but to the point chart.

They were overwhelmed. They did not expect this kind of a reaction. Yes, a tear or two, maybe some pleading but very quickly folding down, enabling them to get on with the really important matters, their matters, who will head what department, who will be promoted to what degree, and such.

"Chart is paper, Danielle, we are talking reality" said David harshly, throwing the colored chart away, on the table, in disinterest, not knowing he is sabotaging his own reputation, because, still, my success was his success, not to mention the hospital success, not to mention, the client, the patient success, and thus enriching the hospital.

"Wait a minute, I want to see this, I want to understand Danielle. You are saying that Hadassah Medical center is referring to us and to us alone?" Yonatan's voice was full of surprise, questioning with interest, partially already proud, wanting and anticipating the answer to be yes. Hadassah Medical Center was the most prestigious hospital in Israel and among the best in the world. Yonatan was a smart man. And here my strategy was evolving. ***Business should always be good for and benefit both sides***. Yonatan realized that in my short presentation. He saw HIS benefits.

Clinicians did not have time for long explanatory presentations. One had to be very innovative and present the facts in a minimalized fashion so they can be grasped within seconds. And that is what I did. He caught on to the large profits the hospital may have, should I be allowed to keep my second assistant, not to mention the prestige and publicity that HIS medical Center would have. Rashi will be the talk of the town, analyzing DNA samples using state of the art methodologies developed in my lab. Rashi Medical Center will be famous. Very famous, and so will he.

Professor Mayer who admired me, felt this change in the atmosphere, and felt it was safe to balance the weight in favor of keeping the second assistant- "Why don't we let Danielle keep her assistants, it seems she is doing a very good job, it is important to advance our diagnosing techniques" he said thinking why not help me, when it seems for sure that the wind is blowing towards my maintaining my assistants, and with his little push, his little help, I, the blond, beautiful, talented researcher-woman, who was an enigma to them all, would be in his debt in the coming future.

"I for one am sending her quite a few samples monthly and it is a pleasure working with her. In fact we recently operated on a very young teenager, only on the basis of her analysis which turned to be very accurate. He had colon cancer and harbored the gene that was causing it, and we saved his life. Danielle felt in the first place, that his DNA should be tested for this gene, and the clinical approach for treating him was leaning on her findings" Mayer felt he could, thus kill two birds at once, having me in his debt, and more importantly, being there for Yonatan for making the right decision, and scoring a good point from Yonatan later in time to be appreciated.

I sat there quietly listening and letting other people do my work for me.

I saw Ravid, the head of the Blood Bank in the Medical Center, a full professor already and a PhD like me, a researcher that respected my work, looking at me smilingly, with his eyes showing he was hoping I will succeed in this pursuit of mine. He knew how hard it was for a PhD to survive, not to mention succeed in the world of the clinicians. David moved his huge, big, tall body in his chair, looking very uncomfortably, with his green eyes casting harsh looks and his blond hair moving every time he nodded fiercely.

But he said nothing. My eyes shifted from Mayer to Yonatan, with the latter sitting quietly listening and I could see him evaluating and re-assessing the situation. If he agrees to let me keep my second assistant, he will have to cut down somewhere else. It is not that simple. He will have to confront someone else. Politics were involved. Additionally, I was an easy target; A Female in the world dominated by males. I had no protector. I had no mentor. I only had my talent, my achievements and the data to prove my argument was right.

But mainly I had my secret weapon, my strategy, which is mainly making my need, my want, appearing as a benefit for the decision maker and thus extremely appealing for him. I had presented the reality as it is showing how he, Yonatan, could benefit from it personally and professionally. Moreover, the client, the patient will benefit, and the bottom line for Yonatan was indeed the welfare of the client, the welfare of the patient. He was short in height, but definitely big in his vision and understanding the needs of his medical center and how he can advance the institution he is heading.

"After re-evaluating, Danielle, I think you are right. Way to go, Danielle, I will let you keep your second assistant," he said smilingly, when we both knew other labs had to let go the first and only assistant they had, due to the recession and hard times in Israel and in the Medical Center. I felt so good. I felt so relieved. I wanted to come across and give him a kiss on his cheek, a big one, but remained seated there very restrained, not showing any signs of what I really felt. Let them pass to the next topic in today's agenda.

I looked thankfully at Mayer who remained serious, but I could see his eyes, sending me a fraction of a smile, as to say, we made it this time, one small battle won, lets continue with our work.

I felt I accomplished a week's work in this latter hour, and elegantly poured myself a cup of coffee, not wanting to be busy peeling an apple while the discussion was now focused on who will be running the biochemistry unit, now that the current head of the unit is retiring.

My mind was already busy with my next project, and when hurrying back to my lab, at the already late hour, I was pleasantly surprised to see that Regina is still working.

Some days at work, I thought with satisfaction, were indeed enjoyable and worth the extreme effort needed.

Entering the driveway at home, always felt so good, such a relief. The whole day was beginning to wash away with its worries, huge responsibilities and stress vanishing as I stepped out of my car with my lips smiling when hearing Ginger barks of excitement. The mask wore by me during the day, presenting a strong detached career minded woman, was slowly fading away to an enjoyable, softer entity. It was good to be home. It was good, although these last days, when coming home, with my mind free to wander somewhat away from work, a new immense and quite stressing load, was floating there in the space of it, my possible DNA results.

I sighed deeply and went to my computer to look for some relief, some optimistic positive rays of happiness that might be found with my other projects, my pursuit for a new mate for life. This was not an easy task to say the least. It was draining by itself, but the prospects and possibilities energized me and gave me hope, dreams and power to go on and invest so much in now 2, selected out of many-new gentleman friends, Pierre and Brian.

My heart slightly accelerated its pace when I saw Pierre's mail waiting for me. Now, this is a way to end a good day at work, with a smile and warm greetings from my new courting man, Pierre. I sat in my leather brown hugging chair at my den, with my eyes roaming all over my neatly placed books, most leather bounded, some burgundy-colored, some deep green colored, all distributing an intoxicating smell of luxurious leather and inspiring a pricy, professional, classy yet cozy feelings. Filled with confidence and warmth I was all opened up to Pierre, ready to throw myself to his reality and be captured for a while in this other world.

And so I read: *When I receive your letters, Danni, I feel so near you… my body yearns to learn you..do you also feel that way?* He wrote.

I answered:

I am a woman, I am different than you. I crave for your affection for your care for your feelings and respect. Also, I am slower than you. But I must admit that with time, lately, I do want to be in your arms, sometimes, and I do want to make love to you. This comes, personally with me, from being attracted to your personality and your intelligence. I am an emotional person, and my lust depends on my feelings.

Your Danni- And I like your own invented nice nick name, for me- that makes a new feeling, a new world, a new beginning and a personal one that is unique to you and belongs to you, I am your DANNI

I pressed the send and my letter went on its way.

As I was laying back on my seat, I was in a mood for answering some more of his questions, some more of his enquiries, I felt I wanted to open up to him, a bit more, thus my heart began to murmur to him while my hand was typing.…

And so I continued to write him:

I do have a smile with my coffee, and I like being a Danni for you and to you.

Thanks for the pictures, although I did get only one new-that of you and Elizabeth, which is lovely, you both look so nice and happy. Are you emotionally available, Pierre? What do you think about the term and the possible need for a "transition" relationship, or a rebound relationship? Who were you with before Elizabeth? Was your marriage with Elizabeth a good marriage and what made it good?

As to your questions and my part in our nice bargain:

I had been with my husband, Michael, for over 25 years of which for 5 of them he was trying to make me pay serious attention to him, until I finally did, totally ultimately and exclusively.

Michael was a professor at the Hebrew University of Jerusalem. A very well world-known scientist. When he passed away, his colleagues all over the world mourned him deeply and conferences were held all over the world, in memory of him, and reviews and papers were dedicated to him. For me, naturally, it was an extremely hard period, and the first international conference that I was invited to lecture about my work at that time, was at Nice France, and I have accepted the invitation, more as an exercise to learn how to live again than as a professional venture. I remember, it was 3 and a half years ago, and I have lectured about my findings on Breast Cancer, and among others, a very famous scientist came to hear me, Finch, after whom a syndrome is named, and he was concentrating at my lecture nodding his head all the time, and look-ing very serious and respectful. I later on encountered him and others who complimented me immensely at my work and lecture. They did not know, how emotionally hard it was for me to do all this at that time. Off course, for a long period, my papers were also dedicated to my husband as well. Today, I look at that phase of my life, as a beautiful phase, and as written in my profile, am in search for another beautiful, lasting phase.

I am, fortunately a very healthy, intelligent, optimistic in nature and extremely capable and developed emotionally person. Thus, I assume it has happened intuitively, as a result partly from the above characteristics, that I have spent, not being aware to it, 3 years, dealing with my grief, the right way for me, a slow process, that led me to today's reality, of an emergence of a looking forward person with the love of life, the energy to enjoy it and the eagerness to take a good part in it. I look at my life with my husband as a beautiful phase and nothing clouds it any more. I consider myself very lucky to have experienced such a good marriage, and I am healed, with scars, that have transferred to be a positive motive for life ahead. Thus, I feel healed enough to risk a new "friend for life".

Yes, our marriage was a very good one. It was for me a natural, built in way of life, sharing with Michael, everything, from intellectual aspects as to my/his research, to the political power struggles in my 2 work places (which were extremely aggressive, since I was working with the top people, and was much envied because of the mixture I harbor, of being extremely intelligent and also quite an attractive woman. Luckily, with my own intuition and way of handling things, and the presence of few, but very counting and important/high on the power ladder, intelligent unthreatened, self-secured figures, I have always succeeded in getting more than I wanted), to the way I would like to redecorate our home, or which other tree I wanted to purchase for our garden (on which he always said that we need a second floor of a garden for me), or will these earrings match me more than the others. And vice versa, I enjoyed sharing, listening, advising on all subjects, with Michael. My life with Michael was based on an extremely mutual respect and equality. I think the key words are friendship, respect, a lot of compromises that do not feel like compromises, because you are so attached emotionally, and of course fantastic chemistry.

I have an array of perfumes, some for the summer, some for the winter, some for the day time, some for the night time, some for work, others for pleasurable moments, intended to tempt, at night. And it also all depends on my mood. What kind of delicate smell would I prefer at that time and place. All these are also being taken into account as to what I would like to wear (if at all).

I like my perfumes.

As to the smell of my hair after I bathe, we will have to wait for a while, unless you will surprise me so nicely and tell me that you have managed to extort a small little nice vacation from your cruel employers, and you are going to come to Israel, next month, and then I can also smell you, feel the strength of the back of your head, be in your strong masculine arms, and maybe forget my self there, for a while.

By the way, maybe it can be my birth day present, which is today, I have turned 52, and expecting many more nice such days to come.

I do speak French, since in Ethiopia I have been attending the French school "Alliance française", but I would need a few weeks in Paris to refresh it. I was in Paris around 2002, was invited to lecture about my work on colon cancer in institute Pasteur, and my husband accompanied me as always. At night, when we were going out, my French was quite helpful. Additionally, I was a consultant to a French biotechnology company, and they did not know of my mastering their language, it was quite helpful as well to hear them discussing business so freely around me. Naughty me.

A very good morning to you, Pierre and Pierri,

Danielle

And I continued…

I went down to prepare some coffee, but then I came up to write to you. The house is so clean and quiet, the curtains in the bedroom, see-through butter-off-white-colored with some light brown additional curtains on them, are slightly moving, with the light breeze, and everything is so serene.

The lady that is cleaning the house was here today, and I love it after she is gone, all is so neat, clean and in place. She comes once a week, and was supposed to come tomorrow, but tomorrow is a holiday eve. so she came today. In fact, my father brings her, for years. Without the help and backing of my father and my husband, I would not have been able to be so successful and enjoy myself through the way. Nowadays, I do not need my father to help me, but it serves several aspects to let him continue. My father is a very busy man, we would always have to coordinate our schedules as when to see each other.

But he made it a rule for himself, that his daughter comes first, and in the last 15 years dedicated to me a whole day of help. Nowadays, since I know that every day that I still have him, is a miracle, I love it when he comes and if I am home we drink coffee together. Plus, he is such an intelligent man, that it is a pleasure to talk with him and also to consult with him. So, he is still feeling needed which is very important to him, plus he sees his daughter, of whom he thinks quite highly, plus he feels as my protector, as he always felt for the whole family, and always was the rock and the stability symbol for us all. He is now finishing writing a story about his running away from working camp, in English and in Hebrew and hopefully he will publish it soon. I love my father.

To another totally different, but also of importance, your message today, was also so very nice, and I could feel your warmth and softness, which I so liked. I am quite a serious person (who loves to laugh and appreciate such a wonderful sense of humor as you possess), and I do not take lightly my emotional time and energies. Thus the fact that I am in such a constant, continues and intense touch with you, means that I like you. I like you and am attracted to your personal characteristics, and am finding myself being drawn to you physically as well. Thus, you are standing near my chest in that arena.

I have grown accustomed to receiving your mails, every day and every morning. So, this Friday and Saturday I would have to control my withdrawal symptoms? Speaking of Control, I am not a controlling person, neither a power struggle oriented one. I find it serves nothing. As long as my basic needs are met, I am quite like a soft, milk-lapping kitten. So you are asking yourself, in a tense fashion, what are her needs? A needy person?! No- I need, as I wrote to you once, a blue sky and a smile. A pleasant loving atmosphere, affection and consideration. Yes and respect. (What a long list) Well and a few other nice things.

The sharks will wait till tomorrow since we are dealing to night with some kittens.

Danielle

And I felt I wanted to go on, thus I continued:

A few clarifications from our conversation of two nights ago; I do not wear Nike socks to bed, I was still dressed in a "homey" casual way returning from being in the Garden (oh, the famous garden). Additionally, let me return the compliment to you, as to mastering a conversation; you excel in it, in fact it is part of your skills, your job, your profession, and I could certainly feel it from time to time. The tight thing was my **shirt**, *a very small sleeveless tight shirt-miscommunication, or a very vivid developed imagination? But truth to be told, in bed, when I sleep, I either wear a big men`s T-shirt or sleep in the nude. How about you?*

So, is it common to have a private retirement plan of one`s own like you? What does a person have to aim to, financially, in order to retreat to retirement enjoy it and be secure, in the US? Is it a closed plan or one is free to use it as one see fits? This is a different situation that what is currently found in Israel, and in fact Netanyahu, when presiding as chancellor, wanted to change the Israeli system and employ the American one, and was quite un-liked for that and lost quite a bit politically.

You mentioned you have been to and liked Greece. I too have been many times to Greece and several of the islands there. I enjoy the nature aspect, the architecture and the people. After my husband passed away I flew over there rented a villa with a private swimming pool on the beach and spent a week there just being and enjoying the surrounding, swimming in the nude in my living-room-attached small beautiful pool, and boating on the Mediterranean. It was lovely.

I also was invited several times to lecture in international conferences in Crete, Greece. Since some of my work is clinically related, and the clinicians excel in choosing the most exotic places in the world for their conferences, I usually accept their invitations, and enjoy both the conference and mostly the place and the nature aspect it has to offer. I have been invited 3 times over there, twice as presiding as a chairperson-head of a session, which is an honor, and it was so like our conversation of the British and their small talk about the weather and the garden, as in the morning I was very serious, a scientist, a chair-person, and giving my presentation and was terribly smart and assertive and attractive, in my power suit, then in the afternoon, I would meet one of the lecturers, with whom a discussion was developed concerning some scientific findings in the morning, in the water, with me being topless as in Europe (when in Rome..), and us talking very intellectually about the nice place and the warm water, with his eyes, kept very modestly and respectfully on my eyes, and my eyes only.

This specific time I was accompanied with my husband who waited for me on the beach. The other 2 times I was already by myself, and must admit that after my duties were over, I attended mostly the beautiful pool and the beach. It was even somewhat embarrassing, that a cancer MD researcher from NY that was trying to make a pass at me (they always try) and suddenly saw me after 2 days that I was not to be found (was laying in the swimming pool and walking on the beach) was so happy to find me at last and I had to smilingly and somewhat embarrassingly reveal that I was sun bathing enjoying the fishes' company. He laughed and said that for sure that must have been more interesting. I totally agreed.

Good morning, to all three of you, My-Like, Pierre and also Pierri,

Danielle

It was already morning and of course just a second after sending my last mail to my like, I received a long, loving, lusting, yearning, wishing, wanting mail from him.

And so I answered:
Dear Pierre,
It was nice to receive your long soft letter this morning, and read it before coffee and drink my coffee with a smile. It is not that I do not trust you, I just am slower than you. Your suggestion of coming to Israel was a very good one. I would have accepted your invitation to come to Florida and stay for 10 days and your offer to cover all expenses, but to endure the hard trip, which I did this year 4 times, is a bit too much. I could easily do it, with knowing the man I was going to meet, and have I known you, and was so happy to meet you,

I would not have felt it is a hard trip. Thus, maybe you can come in the near future, and I could then be with you in all those places in Florida, restaurants, beach and so forth? I would wait for you in the swimming pool while you are very seriously listening to important lectures, reading my book or my Journal "25 beautiful homes" and sun bathing with my new bathing suits.

Your idea to come to Israel, will allow us to get to know each other deeper. There are nice hotels here at Haifa, some on the beach, that you can enjoy, and if you would not mind me sneaking to your room till late/ early morning, until like 3-4 AM, and maybe later on, maybe spending the night, the whole night with you, and while I take a quick shower you can order some coffee to our room, so we can have our morning coffee together, that could be enjoyable. You may want to divide your time, as to see a bit of Israel, there are professional guides for that who know their way around the best places, and to be with me. If you would like, I can also join you in seeing Israel. You can plan your time as best as you see fit according to your wishes, and I would devote almost every minute to you, should you come and should you want me with you.

If we still like each other, than I would not have a problem, accepting your invitation, and come over, to Florida, to Savannah, to where ever you are.

Good morning, to all three of you, My-Like, Pierre and Pierri,

Danielle

And I continued to develop the idea so embraced by Pierre
And so I wrote:
A very good morning to you Pierre,

For me after flying too many times for the last 20 years, being saturated with the hardship of flying, I have become to quite dislike flying. It is quite hard to sit in one`s chair, when on the right a fat ugly smelly man is almost sleeping on you, and on the left a sweaty snoring man is falling all over you, and you have to relax for 12 hours and try to pass them sleeping. The long *flight, containing a connection, with all the 9/11 security hassles, and herds of people crushed one on the other, when doing repeatedly, and not only once a year, has become, quite disliked by me. That is why, I and colleagues of mine, men, in my age (thus it has nothing to do with age, rather with a somewhat saturation due to too many flights), fly business mostly.*

When you will come to Israel, you would not have neither to rent a car, nor to fly to Haifa, I would have my personal taxi driver pick you up and bring you straight to the hotel of your choice, in Haifa, or Caesarea (about an hour and a half of driving), which ever you want, and in time, I can book it for you.

If you wish, later on, you could rent a car. But we will have my car to drive around Haifa and Caesarea, and I may be your personal driver in the day time, and, if you wish and have time to see Israel, there would be professional guides, which would also have to be booked in advance. Coming before Christmas and going back after New Year's Eve sounds terrific, the only drawback, is that it sounds like only for a week. By the way, flights and hotels may be over booked, thus you might want to check the situation. But only one week? It seems that it will be I who will tuck you in, but I can certainly take turns with the guide. The weather in the end of December and the beginning of January are similar as to your area, so mostly winter clothes should be packed.

Your fantasy of us dancing is not necessarily far from reality, since I dance quite nicely, having danced classical ballet from age 8-30, and a whole year at a school in Santa Barbara Ca. Assuming you dance nicely as well, we could certainly draw some attention, (which is not new to me, I was invited to dance on top of a table this January in San Diego in a Hard Rock Cafe, when they played YMCA and only the waiters and waitresses danced. But it seemed that they liked me mostly, and asked me to go on top of a table; imagine, a serious scientist, a published molecular oncologist, dancing on top of a table!-I said no, smiled, thanked them for the compliment and danced away.). But most importantly, we would enjoy ourselves. The thing is that I would not know where to take us in Israel, since my life in Israel was on the serious side, no night clubs AT ALL. So it will have to wait to be in your territory, in GA. (Florida could have been good for that).

How about going to the Opera with me? If we are together, would you do that with me in the US? Another thing that I would like, in due time, is to go back to cycling....Taking small little trips to nature with some lunch and maybe some coffee, via cycling. Do you think you would like to share this with me?

Who is Muri? How was your time on the Farm with your granddaughter? What did you do? Did you both enjoy yourselves? Your home sounds very lovely, warm and nicely built. I am waiting to see the pictures. I am also waiting to see and feel your thrown rugs in the Library.

Danielle

His answer came shooting like lightening, not accompanied by a thunder: *I am coming on Christmas!!*

And then the rest of his letter went on describing his home, and making soft love to me with his words on paper

And so I answered:

What a lovely home you have, Pierre, truly lovely. All the greenery around and the pier to the water, all seems to inspire tranquility and serenity, the right dosage of solitude and people, for our days, thus safety and nature combined; absolutely lovely. Tel your friend M. that he has done a good job, not only the house and the surrounding are projecting calmness, but he has succeeded in including you in a combined so flowing way. You look happy and proud of your kingdom, and so you should.

The wood in your home is so heartwarming, when you say that putting up the wooded way to the dock was a hard work, do you mean to say you did it yourself? I liked to see that there is some sun in your lawn, where, I can imagine myself lazily laying on a sun lounge chair with one of my new bathing suit (so not to give you a bad name, by your neighbors-thus with a bathing suit)-stretching out like a contented kitten having finished lapping the milk, and surrendering myself to the caressing rays, lightly brushing my body, from top to bottom, and from bottom to top.

Good morning, Pierre, look out the window for me, to caress with your eyes, the imaginary figure of me lying there;

Now I can picture you rowing, and understand what a magnificent way you have found yourself to relax and wind down after a stressful day at work. It is like for me, walking and swimming, which are so important. I would walk Ginger, at winter time when it is all dark at 500AM (you just got me very distracted with your erotic yet delicate, suggestive yet so soft, loving and tender, cleanly described thus why so arousing poem-I was there with you every minute-and so enjoyed the heights that were achieved, all due to the so very elegant, nearly there, nearly touching, not a trace of vulgarity, thus so much ever more tempting ...making me wish I was there with you...) and Michael, my husband would call the Mayor, from Jerusalem, to put on the lights in the streets so it will be safe for me, and Michael could get any one do anything for him, thus the lights remained on for 2 additional hours, only because Danielle needs to walk the dog before work. When I would come back home, the same thing, for an hour, thinking about the whole day, the research, the findings, the power struggles with the different departments heads and the CEO of the Medical Center and his deputies, of whom some adored me, and my staff and so on.

We were considering at one time installing a swimming pool for us to enjoy, and for me to swim in. I still sometimes think of it, although in my other place at Myrtle Beach there are about 7 swimming pools.

I must admit that I am very attracted to your more mature and serious side, with your nice jokes, and your rare ability of humoring a situation, as a sense of humor is to cherish and yours is a gift, so intelligent, so sharp, so challenging, and makes me smile so frequently, and is there at all times. Got distracted again, not as pleasantly as before, by you, and your so appealing poem, but from my new gardener, who came with a crew of 3 to get the garden going again as I had to let go the previous gardener that neglected the garden to a poor state.

Back to you! Can you make Christmas come sooner? Can you make these months go quicker? If we were together, how would you see our lives on a daily basis? That is besides spending most of it loving each other? So what book are you reading now, or is it hard to read while so pre-occupied with patients and the stress of work? Are you in touch with Elizabeth's son? Did you happen to travel with Elizabeth or was very busy with work?

A very, but very, pleasant morning to you, Pierre,
Danielle

I went to the kitchen to prepare a good orange juice drink and came back to my den to see a reply.

Danni, - I have booked a flight to come over, but I need to share with you a few matters, of my lesser aspects, concerning my past:

Regarding my previous life partners, my health and my character.

Well, how nice of him, I thought. What an honest man. I like that. Everybody has some "lesser aspects" as Pierre has put it so beautifully. I too. But till now, each and every man I have encountered had only bothered to tell me of their virtues, and sometimes overly exaggerating their good qualities, to say the least. *I* read on;

As you have come to know me, I lead a full life enjoying my work, and have raised my children, being all throughout my adult life an insulin dependent diabetic, in addition to overcoming lung cancer, twice. It was tough, radiation and chemo but I got over it. It was seven years ago. It then returned two years ago, but again I received some aggressive treatment and I am well, now. I do need Viagra some times.

My heart sank. My God. I felt numb suddenly. It takes so much work and a miracle to meet someone that is fairly compatible on the shallow level, not known yet personality, and here is Pierre, that I counted on, that represented for me a life saving vest now days in my new genetic reality, not to mention a good candidate for being a real close friend if not a mate, a lover, a husband maybe? But now, with this ton of bricks falling on me, I suddenly felt so empty, so disappointed. Why did this have to happen? All the effort that I have put in, the intensive emotional work, and now it seems that it all was for nothing. I also felt angry. **Why is this happening to me?** I felt that fate presents me quite frequently with seemingly so appealing opportunities, and when I send my hand to reach them, they suddenly reveal their real nature which happens to be unfit for me at all or unobtainable for me at the larger picture. I am not to have another mate for life, another love. I have had my chance, my love, was very fortunate, more than most people. I was privileged to be loved by a giant of a man, my husband Michael, which I loved so much. I had more than 20 beautiful years with him and in fact I can't complain.

Most women do not experience such strong emotional bonds such great love that strengthen with years like an aging wine, only getting better and better.

My husband was all for me, my friend, my lover, my mentor, my confident and my companionship. We evolved together and it was always interesting and refreshing to be with him. When I returned every Wednesday night from the University up north after a long day that started at 430AM, driving in to our street seeing my husband's car in the drive way, my heart would always miss a beat, being so happy to know that he is waiting for me and we can be together for the rest of the week.

My thoughts roamed in my mind in reminiscing of my husband that I longed for so much, with pride to have known him, love him and be loved by him, with a deep feeling of content to have achieved that, giving way to strength and confidence that were drawn from these memories that were all dipped in some sadness.

Yes, I was very fortunate.

But still, after three years, I longed for a loving relationship. Nothing wrong with that. I will always love Michael, and he will always be part of my heart, my life and my feelings and thoughts. With this giving me strength for ever, proud and confident, I want to meet another man.

My thoughts went back to Pierre, thinking, it is not all that bad. We are all not 18 years young, and we all have our histories. I have just discovered a possibly new reality of possibly carrying this gene, this cancer causing gene, My possibly new addition for life.

Yes, but still I might be just a carrier. I am not sick with Cancer. He was sick. Do I want to fall in love with a man that had cancer already twice? Not to mention diabetes? Do I need that right now in my life, especially after losing Michael when fighting for his life for 6 months in the intensive care unit?

Well, one could marry a young healthy attractive man and loose him to a car accident the next week, or to a heart attack the next year. There are no guaranties. I should give it a chance. Pierre might be suitable for me, after all he seems to be sensitive, and he having experienced all this hardship might equip him for a possible future of me having to encounter my own destiny. My own fate, health wise.

I kept on reading, becoming more calm and serious;

My wives, I have been married 3 times.

When it rains, it pours, I thought, what other surprises this man has for me.

1. to Claudette, Eleanor's mother. I met her when I visited Belgium and the marriage did not work out. I was too young, she wanted to live in Europe, and in the end we divorced. The divorce was bitter. Eleanor did not get good parenting from either of us. Claudette lost custody and I moved back to the US with our daughter...,

Part of me was reading with a growing disappointment; realizing for now, that this man might not be for me, after all, he is way too immature, and made some careless decisions in his life. This has become to be heavier and heavier for me. Another part of me was getting interested in this novel-like story. More importantly, my subconscious craved to give this man a chance. The stable solid analytical side of me decided calmly to go on reading and then address each and every aspect by itself before arriving to any conclusion. My emotional hopes and excitement were no longer there; all this needs to be considered very carefully.

2. Later on in life (Soon after Claudette and I separated,) I went to a party, looking to meet a woman and met Brandy. I was working very hard and raising my daughter and knew it was not a good time to commit, but I did. I was not mature enough and did not think things through....We had our son Anthony and life was difficult.

He knows he is or was an immature person, I wonder if he really matured. I am an extremely mature woman, I would like at my side a mature man, well, I kept reading-

I tried very hard to make it work but we both knew it was not the right time for us. We were married for 10 years. But it did not last. I got custody of Anthony and raised him with Eleanor.

My eyes kept on swallowing the lines, racing to finish and be done with all the bad news, so I could process it in my mind and arrive to a safe shore regarding my decision about Pierre. My emotional entity already started to process all this new information, it so wanted Pierre to be the right candidate for me, at least for now, until further developments. My emotional entity could not give him up so easily, this man who saw me as a wonder, as a princes, who was intelligent and kind and suddenly all his health problems just matured him for me and gave him this additional experience necessary for today's life, as I have experienced, so hard with my husband.

The lines danced before my eyes;

3. Elizabeth. After being a single dad for a while, I met Elizabeth when I was invited to dine with some friends. I fell in love with her the minute I saw her. We dated for three years and she lost physical interest in me. I was very hurt and I left her.

I respected that. I liked that. Pierre suddenly appeared so vulnerable before me, and actually very strong to reveal all this before me, a stranger.

The lines kept on, .

But then we met again and the old flame came so strong and we got married. We had ups and downs. She helped me when I needed her. After 4 years she found out that she is dying from cancer. Breast cancer. I was there for her until her last minute on this earth.

Her death shocked me and it took quite a while for me to return to my routine and normal life.

I was speechless and overwhelmed at the tragedy conveyed to me by his simple words describing his reality and by his total openness and honesty manifested.

My heart was heavy and my emotions were mixed as were my thoughts when I read his last line; *I used to have a bad temper, but it seems to be quite tamed and under control now.*

His last line did not mean anything to me. I was already well saturated and could not have absorbed or internalized any more.

My eyes danced through his poem,

I am humble

Kneeling before you

Open like a book,

Don't close those brown, big eyes of yours on me

Let your heart open to my soul

I read and was semi touched, semi so very tired. Tired that I had to be confronted with this. Tired that I had to make big decisions. Tired that things could not go smoother and easier.

I decided to lock all this in a distant chamber in my mind and think about it at a later time. For now, Ginger smiling eyes caused my lips to break in a smile. I petted him comfortably, clinging to him for bringing me back to my own warm, nice and cozy reality at my safe home.

CHAPTER NINE

BACH, 6174DELT AND THE GREAT BARRIER

Bach was playing in the background and I sipped my coffee, unable to enjoy the view of our garden that always had a calming effect on me. I knew I had to pull myself together and dial THE Number. A number that had so many consequences for me. I had to call Mayan. It was time, they should have an answer for me. Am I a BRCA carrier or not.

Ginger was sitting at my feet feeling through his instincts that I am quite preoccupied and somewhat distressed. He looked at me with his warm brown eyes and pushed his nose and head to my hands to be petted. I couldn't pet him, I was so closed in my world and with my hidden well tucked fear. I couldn't give at that moment. I needed every ounce of my energy to face what this call will bring. Intuitively, my mode of action has changed to automatic, with my sense thus protecting me and enabling me to shut the emotional part of me and open a cold analytical element within me to address the needed phone call.

I took the phone in my hands, and dialed Mayan's number, waiting calmly for her to answer. This was not a time to be in a panic. The only way I could encounter the coming conversation is by being detached from my feelings and from my emotional world and handling whatever she has to tell me with cold calculated fashion, like a business decision; what has to be done next. "Hello" her cheerful voice answered

"Hi Mayan, it's Danielle" my voice struggled to sound as calm as possible, although my heart started to beat so fast forgetting all the decisions I have made about being analytical and detached.

"Oh, Danielle, hello, how are you?" Her voice became too soft manifesting too much of a concern. I did not like it.

"I am fine, how are you?" I forced myself to continue the small talk although already gathering what her answer might be-she was way too soft to me and way too concerned of me.

"I am well, just returned from the US yesterday". She would not shift the conversation towards my results. Maybe I am way too involved and misinterpret her, maybe she is just nice to me because she knows and respects me maybe I am well and do not carry the Gene?? I had some hope rise in my subconscious, but my voice still remained steady and calm. I decided to plunge in; "I imagine you still don't have my results, Mayan? It is surely too soon?"

"No, Danielle you were found positive" There was silence on the line.

"You mean I am a carrier?"

"Yes, Danielle, I am afraid you are".

As a scientist I know that these results are checked well and done in triplicates, but still my voice pleaded "are you suuure?? There is no mistaaake??"

"No, Danielle, we checked it several times and you appear to have the **6174delT** mutation, thus you are a BRCA2 Gene carrier. As your friend Marian is."

I could not say a word I was feeling as all is closing on me. Part of me wanted to ask a million times whether she is sure. Surely they have made a mistake. It is so hard to believe that I, Danielle, the scientist the molecular oncologist, the genetic counselor who has counseled so many people as to them harboring a cancer causing gene am a BRCA carrier. I, the fragile so sensitive blond beautiful woman am harboring such an endangering Gene. I wanted to say, scream, so many things. As a scientist I wanted to reason with her and find a mistake in their work. As a frightened person, a woman, a woman who has just suffered the loss of her beloved husband,

I wanted to tell her that this cannot be true, I do not deserve this now, I am just recuperating from a three year-long mourning period. I needed to make her understand that she should re-examine all the results again and maybe repeat all the diagnostic tests.

But, as a woman that is so strong, my voice came out calm and tranquil "so I assume this is it Mayan. What do I do next?" I looked for some guidance from her.

I gave this guidance so many times. To other people….To other families….To other women. I was strong and professional with my help and guidance. Now, I needed some from her. I could not make the first steps alone. My mind was still shocked….Still refusing to believe this new information….Still unable to cope with this new situation.

Danielle, let me give you a name of a good onco-gynecologist, you must, but muuussst have your ovaries out as soon as possible. Call him and make an appointment, he will take you from there.

I knew this all too well. My mother whom I love so much, who was my best friend died from ovarian cancer. I knew too well that the BRCA gene puts a woman at up to 54% risk of having ovarian cancer, 50-85% risk of having breast cancer, and a risk of having uterus cancer and I also knew that the ovarian cancer is so aggressive, I saw my mother die. Remembering how we fought so hard for my mother and couldn't help her, how we saw her succumbing to cancer, brought me back in touch with my emotional part.

And I remembered….

"Daneily" Her voice was like bells, ringing delicately in my ears. In my heart.

Still is. Only she called me by that nick name and I allowed only her, this pleasure. All other, I insisted, will always call me Daniel.

Her voice as her deep honey-brown soft big eyes, always caressed me, also when teaching me a lesson and giving me a piece of her mind when I needed to have it.

She was my safe harbor, my total and absolute secure world.

We were like one. We felt the same, in the same moment, in the same instant. We only had to look in to each other's eyes, and we would understand. We would know. All.

We were like two peas in a pod.

I looked at us, from outside my body. From outside of my being. From the door way. She was asleep on her back and her arm was lying across the bed with her hand holding mine, like forming a bridge, an imaginary bridge, one that is eternal, one that is forever. And while I was asleep on my left side, holding her hand in mine, I was trying with all my power to transfer my energy and love to her so that she would conquer that illness that as a scientist I knew from day one, will soon take her away from me.

She was sick for nine long months, saying she is going to the Hilton, whenever the time came for her Chemotherapy, always with a smile.

They all said that I am her Gibraltar Rock.

That I am her future, her strength, her power to go on and fight. Because I never wanted her to know, and for all those months I talked with the full confidence that she is going to get better, to heal, to be healthy, because for us there was no other option. And she believed me. She followed me. She needed me. And I was there for nine months.

Like she had carried me for nine months.

You look so alike, people told me in the funeral. I didn`t know how to react. I smiled. But cried in side deep in my heart.

It took me ten years to accept her passing out of my life.

Now, only now in the last years, I was able to forgive her for leaving. And I love her, so much, again.

She. Her. My Mother.

And now, I felt so much fear from the unknown, from the huge threat.

I felt longsome for my mother, I felt so small.

Mayan's voice reinforced reality on me and I intuitively shut this emotional path and listened to her dictating me the number and name of the recommended doctor for me to see. I hung on to the little left from my strength at that moment and calmly thanked her in a still professional, yet soft manner and hung up the phone, not knowing what exactly I should do now. Should I call Marian to tell her I too am a carrier? Should I call my father, who since the death of my husband has become my closest friend? Should I make myself a cup of coffee? Should I read the newspaper? I was totally lost.

A Bach concert which was still playing but could not be heard by me due to my deep preoccupation with the event at hand, was suddenly sounding so irritating, but funny enough, it brought me back to reality. I am going to draw a flow chart like I am used to, I decided while walking to the CD player to turn Bach off. Suddenly, I was full of strength and energy. I always tackled problems and future realities with flow charts. They made me realize what is needed to be done and helped me *focus on doing rather than on fear.* They made me focus on details which enabled me to go through a needed reality rather than be intimidated by a huge mountain that is needed to be climbed on. I felt there is a way I could handle this, and the mere act of chart building, the mere act of plans making gave me hope. My father has always taught me that *hope is always there* and hope always had a relieving effect on me. Hope was good. *Hope was my alliance, my friend, my source of strength.*

I walked to my den full of confidence, drew out an 8 x11 sheet of paper and sat down in my brown leather chair, thinking what would be my first steps. My hand began writing decisively and with cool-headedness the name and number of the onco-gynecologist drawing an arrow down from his name to the next step I should be making, looking into my health insurance policy and coverage and getting in touch with my personal family doctor and events will take me from there.

Yes, Suzan will probably help me. Suzan will probably be there for me. Suzan was a nice family doctor and a nice friend.

The day looked young and the morning fresh and the future was not as threatening as an hour ago. There is a lot going for me right now, so many promising projects, my research, the L girl, my students at my lab and those so intelligent young full of initiative and drive at the university. My mind was regaining its normal vitality and my stomach muscles were beginning to relax somewhat. I sank a bit deeper to my engulfing leather brown chair, leaned backwards and thought about the so many nice events that are waiting for me, including the interesting and challenging project of finding a mate for my new life. How will I be able to go on with all these projects, part of me feared a little but then I was calmed by the idea that all can continue at a slower pace than I am used to and all these projects will actually balance themselves against each other and might charge me with positive energy and allow me to sort my new status as a BRCA Gene carrier. I was ready to plunge into Pierre's reality again and answer his last mail. I decided to stay at home and indulge myself with a quiet day, occupying myself with Pierre, Brian, all the men in my life and my dog.

I looked at my brown fur-colored dog, and my eyes were petting him and he, understanding my need for warm attention, watched me with his almond-brown, so intelligent eyes, and waved his tale smiling to me and reassuring me; I am at home, my cozy, beautifully self-decorated, nice home and reality can be handled, not all is terrible. My confidence returned for now, for today and I began thinking pleasantly about Pierre. I liked him so far. I remembered one of his first letters and I decided to re-read it.

While finishing reading I already knew what I have to do. I can't throw away this so appealing for now relationship. I should give it a try. I should go on and get to know him better. After all, everything that he has written to me of can be either understood or handled. So he had three wives, Yes it shows of poor judgment, but he was young, he is aware of his mistakes and hopefully he has matured. So I wanted to believe. Yes, he has had cancer twice, but that also shows what a strong man he is, and how positively he has fought it. Who am I to reject a relationship on account of this when now I am bearing this new gene of mine? True, I am just a carrier, and hope to stay defined like that, and he has been sick and still is not completely out of the woods regarding his cancer, but as a molecular oncologist, I know that there is hope and prospects for him being well.

I started responding Pierre, decisively,

Good afternoon Pierre,

I have received your letter headlined "Decisions" and am trying to absorb the information, process it and put things in perspective. Had I not formed any feelings for you, at this stage, I would be somewhat threatened from the portrayed reality, and would not have found it difficult to convey to you, that it does not work for me. But the reality is different, and I found myself not wanting to let you go, without further thinking, processing and talking with you, openly, about everything. Health wise, I have just finished mourning my beloved husband and I do not feel I would like to enter a relationship that statistically already is somewhat bothering. What is the prognosis for your cancer? I assume that these 2 cancer incidents are not connected but rather coincidental or was it a relapse and a metastasized form of the first manifestation? What is the prognosis for your insulin dependent diabetes as years will pass?

It seems that I have grown to like you, and if all was going to go well, I know myself, I would fall in like with you, and thus, I would be devastated to lose you, should this horrible situation will materialized. On the other hand, I might get a heart attack the next morning we commit ourselves to each other; there are no guarantees in life.

You having three wives is also bothersome to me. Maybe you are not equipped to give a woman what is needed for a long lasting and loving relationship? On the other hand, you did solve some of your problems, and if Elizabeth would not have passed away, you might be together for many, many, years.

I am very aware of life mishaps. I am aware that our time on this earth is limited. I am a sort of a person that does not wish to pursue thousands of dates and relationships; I perceive it as a waste of my emotional time, which is very valuable to me. I would like to meet a man, whom I feel I am attracted to, intellectually, emotionally and physically. Live with him for a while, say around half a year, and if I still like him, pending he still likes me, I would like to be married and go on with life enjoyments together, with my mind's and my emotional drawers free to invest in him, in us, and in our life-no more wasting time dating exploring, meeting, experiencing and so on. I am a woman who is very much sought after, by various men, scientists, MDs, judges, CEOs and such, but that world is of no attraction for me, and of the latter type, there are so few, that really appeal to ME. I find myself being attracted to you, which is as I mentioned rare for me and thus of much value. I find myself drawn to you.

Having said all that, I would have to know your feelings, about my thoughts described above, and how do you see us, if we are married, after living around half a year together, at your end of the world because of your present commitments, financially getting along? What is your financial situation? We are not 18, and one needs to be aware of that angle as well before making any commitment. For me to say let us try it, does not work, because if we will go ahead, whatever kind of form it will take, knowing me, I would get more attached to you, and fall more deeply in like with you, because as I explained there seems to be some basic characteristics of you that I have come to reveal and learn of and thus am attracted to you. So, I would not want to find myself attached emotionally to you and find-ing, after I have worked all your decision letter information and come to terms with it, we do not fit in our expectations, financially and commit-ment wise. I need to know about this and any other important issue that you think is crucial, before I can go on and make up my mind.

This letter might seem very confused to you, but I tried to be as open as I could with all my inner thoughts, sharing with you, and am thanking you for being honest and open at this stage of our knowing each other.

Your answer will provide me with some additional tools to process, understand and decide.

You have become somewhat important to me, and I do not take this lightly and thus would like to see how matters can be worked out.

Yours,

Danielle

Thus I finished my letter to Pierre with an emotional satisfaction and a small smile was resting upon my lips. This is good. This is an opening of a window to a possible new and promising future. I sat back deeper into my brown-leather big comforting chair in my den and let my mind run free for a moment, feeling more secure than before. *There is nothing like taking action and control over one's life,* I thought, *that provides strength and hope.*

While feeling a bit better, my thoughts drifted away slowly to the past. Jan-Paul. Jan-Paul my love. What an intense love. Like from the movies, like from the stories. When I first saw his picture on his profile, I did not really like it. It portrayed a very cold and strong man. A man that is incapable of being considerate of a woman. A man that is rough and selfish. But I thought I should be more mature and get to know him more, looks might be deceiving and are not the most important factor in forming a relationship.

I may be misjudging his traits as seen by me from looking at his portrait picture. I was magnetized to his writing. What a beautifully, appealing written profile. The man really knows how to write and through his writing I could see the personality he presented. An extremely intelligent, highly creative, deeply thinking man. He was very well read, according to his profile and I liked that a lot. I like men that are reading classics and history books; it reminded me of Michael, my husband. The husband that possessed my entity, charmed my being for over 20 years, and always fascinated me, until he died. Actually well after his death, because I talked and shared my feelings, and heard his advice when I felt emotionally strong and secure to enter that path, the path of remembering my husband, feeling my husband, seeing, imagining and smelling my husband, all this without a burst of deep sorrow and being stricken with grief. Only then, would I allow myself to indulge in my husband's memories whatever manner they took. These were very seldom times, and for very short periods, since still, after 4 years, my heart was terribly aching and broken and could not be mended, neither accepting the loss. Thus it was nice to read Jan-Paul's profile and feel engulfed and captured by his manifested personality. I remembered how I started corresponding with him, with actually a feeling of immense bliss whenever I got a response from him. He was actually a very tough cookie.

He was attracted by my profile, and was much complimented that a woman of my caliber would take interest in him, but played it very secure and kept it remote from his heart. He did not really open up to me. I could feel his distance from his letters, and there was a big gap between my warmness and openness to his closed and detached letters. I was ready, then, as actually am ready now, to fall in love, with him? With love? I did not really analyze it then and was so yearning, to fall in love with a man I thought I could, or to maybe to actually, just love again. Just love. When I questioned his distant attitude, he responded quite frankly with the so logical and acceptable reason, of the thousands of miles that are separating us.

I actually agreed to his reasoning and named it "the 5000 miles Great Barrier". Yes, the great Barrier, of 5000 miles between my country, and his. I, being a cosmopolitan career oriented, independent woman, who has spent her life living in different continents, who was invited to lecture about her research in international conferences all over the world, felt the world is really but a small village, and distance is not in any way shape or form a Barrier, if the Right love is found. I, that am a secular and was so happily married to a religious man, a fact which is thought upon as almost impossible by many, felt that *if really and strongly wished by both sides, we can make it happen.* We can form a relationship, and I was very eager to prove it. I remember the mail I have written him, the 5000 miles Great barrier mail, it was always nearby so I could re-read it. My eyes looked to the closed folder, my brain saying no, my heart saying just a little and my hands as having their own autonomy, opened the folder. My eyes started racing over the lines of this letter written a year and a half ago, while my heart still ached;

Dear Jan-Paul,

It is Tuesday and I have been thinking of you, rising with you in the morning and going to sleep with you at night.

I need the man besides me to be among other things; intelligent, kind, warm, respectful and a friend and you seem to harbor these qualities in addition to a bonus of being physically very attractive to me. I do not take it lightly because as I told you I rarely am attracted to a man as I am to you. This is why 5000 miles are not a barrier for me. True, it might slow the evolving of a relationship, but since I need to go slow, and need my time to get intimate with another man, it works with me as long as the relationship is somewhat balanced emotionally.

Yes, I admit I would much rather have a cup of coffee with you and learn about you through a string of enjoyable encounters, but things can be achieved with the 5000 miles barrier, and also may have an angle of uniqueness and a positive longing. The latter can be overcome with both our minds put to it, if we care to and wish so. If things continue, after exhausting the possibilities of a phone communication, you might consider visiting me in South Carolina, and if we wish, I might consider visiting you in Washington and go fishing together, we might want to meet in Europe and go to the Opera or a Ballet or whatever together, and still later on in the future, subject to our wishes. The sky is the limit and as for me, my future plans are very flexible, and I am willing and capable of relocating for the right relationship and the right man.

We, human beings can never find exactly the right specific "package" that we want- purple eyes, tallish, with green hair and living around the corner-thus a "5000 miles barrier" will exist for the both of us wherever we turn in a different manner- she might be beautiful but have 18 children 1 to 7 years old which preoccupies her, she might be very attractive but somewhat shallow and too dependent. He might be all I thought I wanted, intelligent, well read, a man of the world but very cold and unpleasant. He might be very kind and warm and happy but uninteresting- Thus every woman that you will meet and every man that I might meet will manifest their own "barriers"- This is why I do not take it lightly that I have these unique feelings for you, that I am drawn to you and feel I have a chemistry with you- so the 5000 miles barrier is an acceptable and welcomed barrier that I can cope with and have solutions for, which I do not for the other "barriers".

As for men being attracted to me- I share your feelings in respect to you and also have my fears. Here I am deeply in "like" with this man Jan-Paul, and he is exposed to 80,000 beautiful women in JDate and probably corresponding enjoyably and consistently with 10,000 of them and I am here far away, with only my dreams of him. You are a very strong man. I am a very sensitive woman. But if I want to be in touch with you I have to take a certain chance. Otherwise I can remain at home, will never be hurt but will never have a chance of meeting someone to my likings. Granted it is easy to write and very hard if one is ended hurt, but of the little I know of you, I am sure that you will do everything within your power not to hurt me. Then, if a relationship does come along- there is trust that builds up, and both parties are usually so fulfilled, one with the other, so they do not see or need another party in their life.

I too, am glad that we are "talking" about these things. I enjoyed reading your thoughts and feelings Jan-Paul, while you have opened slightly, and I must confess there are some sentences that I reread twice and three times and smiled pleasantly.

I wish you will open to me and to us, I wish that you will allow yourself to fall in "like" with me, I wish that you will consider being more than my friend,

> *With droplets of "like",*
> *Danielle*

The moist nose of Ginger was brushing against my knee, bringing me back to reality. I was startled for a moment, and then looked smilingly into his brown warm eyes, of which their smile was enhanced by his waging tail, looking at me so innocently and lovingly. Ah, what a blessing to have him, I embraced him, kissed his forehead and walked to the kitchen to prepare myself a nice cup of coffee which always seemed to lift my mood, with Ginger following me faithfully. The aroma of the freshly prepared good coffee filled the house, and with my cup in my hand, which is a trade mark of me at both my work places, the University where I lectured and the Medical Center where my research and diagnosing cancer involved genes in tumors and families took place,

I returned comfortably and longingly to the past and my den remembering The 5000 miles Great Barrier Letter.

Remembering how skillfully I have convinced Jan-Paul to be more open, more drawn into a relationship with me. *When there is a need, there is a capability* I thought. And of course, Jan-Paul was drawn to me, not only because of my persuading letter, but also because I represented to him all that he will never encounter and all that he was so drawn to, far places in the planet, different cultures, mystery and a very, but very dissimilar world than his. Jan-Paul was born to a French mother and a Norwegian father and was living in a 2000 people small village in the middle of nowhere. Since he has had the taste of the Big city and all that comes with it when being in college and university, and in the beginning of his extremely successful career being a millionaire, he wanted, now that he has chosen a smaller world to live in, to taste some of that cosmopolites, through me.

CHAPTER TEN

SWEET, INTELLIGENT SHACHAR

The sound of my phone ringing got the attention of both Ginger`s and mine, with him raising his brown silky hair-covered ears targeting the phone with his intelligent questioning eyes and while I reached my hand to answer, my voice displaying the annoyance of this disturbance. Who is calling on my day off, at home? I am not a brain surgeon and I felt that in view of my so few taken days off, and my so demanding hard schedules I deserve to be left alone unless it is an emergency.

"Hi, Danielle," the young warm and vivacious voice of my favorite graduate student, Shachar, was there. One could note the slight questioning in her voice as to disturbing me, she knew me so well, mixed with her admiration and respect for the woman, the instructor, the mentor and the scientist, she thought so highly of.

"Hello Shachar, how is your writing going?" I asked her, with my voice fully reflecting my warm feelings towards her, yet also manifesting a small distance and authority.

"Danielle, I hate to disturb you at home, but my presentation for tomorrow is not working well and I need your advice." I was helping Shachar with preparing both her written dissertation and her lecture presentation which every graduate student had to go through. The presentation was quite important since there will be some colleagues, some scientists from various universities in the country as her judges. Actually we were prepared for the whole lecture hall to be not only full but over booked with people sitting on the steps and stairways.

My students, which I handpicked very carefully, the best of the best from a long "waiting list", as my colleagues would say, had been famous for giving challenging, interesting and highly innovating lectures, thus attracting quite a vast audience of researchers.

"What seems to be the problem Shachar?" I enquired, all of me now a scientist, a professional. I invested in my students, in their research which was actually always part of the research that was going on in the lab, with them, according to each with his/her own capabilities, contributing to its advancement. Shachar has put a lot of effort and time, and the latter, mixed with her being highly intelligent, resulted in very exciting results. We were actually in the midst of writing a publication, summarizing Shachar's work, and I was invited to an International conference in Crete to lecture about it. I wanted to help Shachar for all the reasons in the world, I liked her, I respected her, it was important that the scientific community will be aware of her findings, here in the medical Center tomorrow and next month in the International conference in Crete.

Actually, we have worked together on that presentation for quite a while. I also wanted Shachar to succeed as much as possible, get the highest grade possible, as most of my students got, and be helped at taking her own place in the world, with the best presentation we could create.

"It seems that it might be a good idea to enter the FAP2 family as well, don't you think so?"   Shachar's voice was full with confidence as to her suggestion but also all still warm and totally open to my views. Shachar was always totally counting on me, my decisions, my analyses, but never was a "yes woman/student". I liked our discussions and debates. They were mature, to the point and never about ego battles. I took a long sip from my coffee, with my mind contemplating her suggestion.

"Don't you think it is too early to consider talking about the FAP2 Family?" I asked remembering that the FAP2 family was a small family of four, two parents and two children one 24 years old and one 18 years old. The father of this family was diagnosed with colon cancer. After performing exhausting DNA tests, we have found a very medically important and interesting finding. I tried to recall Shachar's entry for her presentation, explaining that FAP stands for Familial Adenomatous Polyposis (FAP) and that it is an autosomal dominantly inherited predisposition to colorectal cancer. We continued on our abstract to describe that it is characterized by the development of hundreds to thousands of adenomatous polyps in the colon and rectum, usually within the third decade of life. We added the information that mutations in the adenomatous polyposis coli (APC) tumor suppressor gene are actually responsible for FAP. The gene itself is located on the long arm of chromosome 5.

"What would you like to add regarding the FAP2 family Shachar?"

"Well, to date, we know of more than 300 germ-line causative mutations which have been described. We also know", she added, "that as many as 98% of mutations described in APC result in a truncation of the normal protein product resulting in a smaller protein which functions differently than the usual one, the normal one." I heard her describing the data, quite proud with her, my student, my protégé. She continued quoting the literature, with a strong confident voice, "The analysis of a large number of related and unrelated FAP patients demonstrated that the severity of the clinical phenotype of the disease and the extra colonic manifestations are in many cases correlated to the position of the mutation." I heard her breath. "So", she deducted, "everyone knows that it is quite important to find whether a person harbors a mutation, whether he transferred it to his children, but not less important is to pin point the exact place of such a mutation."

We both knew that we found a new novel mutation in the father of the small nice family FAP2. We both learned in time to like this family, I as a human being exposed to the suffering of another fellow person and also from my interactions with them on several genetic counseling sessions. Shachar grew very attached to them during her endless efforts and the huge amount of time in a very rushed and urgent manner to diagnose them under my supervision. Shachar, our lab technician Lucy, who was in charge of such work, and I have spent days and nights to resolve this specifically illusive possible mutation harbored by the father of the FAP2 family. This meant a more thorough work of analyzing, not just through linkage but actually finding the exact place of the latter possibly excising mutation and thus dictated more sophisticated state of the art technologies that we, at my lab, were implementing.

"Shachar, we have not yet fully localized the mutation as to its accurate specific place, we only know approximately as to the region it resides, and also there is the young son of 18 years old to be still analyzed, don`t you think it is enough for now to report only of the new, novel mutation?" I asked while my voice is stating and almost negating her suggestion.

"Well, Danielle, data on the clinical phenotypic manifestation of disease caused by mutations in the region on which the FAP2 family mutation was found was reported in the literature previously and those mutations are expected to result in a milder clinical presentation and phenotype. The clinical phenotype exhibited by the father is an aggressive form of FAP, thereby differing from previous reports on the general region of the gene. Thus I think it is quite important and actually urgent to state, lecture and publish the manifested difference of this aggressive medical condition linked to the region where we have found our novel mutation in the father," she almost declared this, and I could hear her sigh out of effort to explain to me. I could notice that she was under stress, both from an ethical point of view, wanting the medical and scientific world to be aware of this finding and also she wanted to do her best in her lecture tomorrow.

A light delicate ringing sound from my computer indicated I received a mail. While still contemplating her suggestion, I opened the mail and read that Josef Mayer was notifying me as to Simcha`s condition getting worse, and please could I get in touch, since my line is busy. I expected this. Simcha, the father of FAP2 family, was very brave, but neither science, nor medicine could do anything for him at this stage. This is why I felt that for now the most urgent and quite important thing was to find whether his young child of 18 years of age was harboring this new, novel mutation, that was found by us to be in both the father and the older son aged 24 years.

"He is getting worse, Shachar, I just got word from Prof. Mayer." She sighed again, but this time out of genuine sorrow and said, "we were expecting this Danielle, did not we?" "Yes, we did, let me think about what you want, and lets meet within a couple of hours at the lab, I am going to meet Prof. Mayer and then I will see you and we will decide how to proceed, have a nice afternoon Shachar and see you later." I hung up the phone, my mood turning to be thoughtful and serious.

CHAPTER ELEVEN

MICHAEL AND THE SHABBAT

It was a Tuesday and I knew Wednesday was approaching, Wednesday the day I always drive up to the college upstate to lecture, thus I will not be in the lab. I have to go tonight and settle everything, so tomorrow I can be reached but can also give my lectures. Tomorrow is Wednesday I thought and my heart ached for a minute. Wednesdays represented something else in my mind. In my heart. In my soul. Wednesday was a day before Thursday, which represented the great expectancy, the looking forward to Friday, to the coming of the Shabbat. But for me the Shabbat began earlier then for most people. And what a Shabbat. A Shabbat of the religion, of my entity and of my being.

Yes, actually, the Shabbat would start on Thursday morning, when Michael went grocery shopping for us, after his morning daily prayer at the Synagogue. He would hurry home before I went to my work at the Rashi Medical Center, he would hurry up not to miss me, and enter home with a nice large bouquet of flowers, for me, for the Shabbat, even though the Shabbat has not started yet.

This would send me, with a warm smile at my heart, dealing with quite a difficulty, going to work, leaving Michael at home, our Home, in Zichron, alone, more accurately, me being away from him for an additional day as he always came Home to Zichron, on Wednesday afternoon, after a long drive from Jerusalem, from his laboratory in the Hebrew University of Jerusalem.

It would have been so hard for me thus to leave on Thursday morning to my laboratory in the Medical Center, topping the fact that I was actually like a vegetable, a lettuce, so desperately tired from my previous day, my Wednesday, which was always, Tel-Hai Day, thus the day that I woke up at 430AM to walk Ginger briefly and drive to the college upstate, 2.5 hours each way, with a whole day of lecturing two courses, thus about 5-8 hours and attending staff meeting and student counseling, and then returning late Wednesday back home to Zichron.

Thus, actually my own Shabbat would start at the entering to the curve, to our street, all so tired, but my heart racing and anxious, and my foot pressing harder on the gas pedal, will I see my husband's car, Michael's car on our driveway? Has he come? Has he safely made the trip and, at last, I will see him again? And always, but always, I felt this Pang in my heart, and a large smile and burst of new energy would fill me up, Yes, His car is there, quiet and tranquil, MICHAEL is at home.

Thus, My Shabbat would actually start at Wednesday late evening-night, pending on the hour I returned from the college up state, when part of me would become alive again, for four days, until Sunday morning when Michael would leave, leave me, Ginger and Zichron, for another short week that seemed so long for me.

I would barely have patience to park my car safely on our driveway, adjacent to His, like two peas in a pod, two Toyota Corollas, two Identical cars, laying, parking one near the other so peacefully, resting each from His/Hers long way of driving, waiting to be near each other, again.

I would almost gulp the 7 steps home, run to the doorway, impatiently open the door with my key that would almost every Wednesday seem to have some trouble opening the lock and take way too long, way too long to finally open the door, finally enter My World, My Home, away from work, My Haven with my Husband's eyes meeting mine smiling, questioning, caressing and bidding me a very good evening.

My heart leaped to my Husband, to Michael, my hand to caress Ginger who always welcomed me with jumping, licking and crying out of happiness that I am back home.

I always was so happy to be welcomed each and every day like this by Ginger, but nothing, nothing can compete with that welcoming small little moment of Michael's welcoming. Why small little moment? Because Michael was always so stable, a Rock, so solid, so real, thus immediately the moment came to be a normal, routine, ensuring with its evolving moment, thus transforming from a magical encounter to a feeling of peaceful strength and stability.

Reality would buzz in and the awful tiredness would start dropping slowly to our living room with me already asking him to warm some dinner for us as I was already starting my transformation to a vegetable, more accurate a lettuce. Everything from now on to the night would be achieved only through my will power. I was dead tired from the whole week, from the whole day, and on that specific moment from everything under the sun. These two careers I ran were not easy and quite draining, and on Wednesday night I actively was always deciding not to think too much and not to make any decisions, just wait for the hard, always very punctual to visit on Wednesday night, big wave of exhaustion, to go away, to disappear, for a while, even for a small little while.

And it did, with growing and augmenting moments of pleasure, of happiness, being with Michael, My Husband, sharing with Michael, My husband, living with him and breathing the same air under the same roof.

Brushing my teeth and secretly smiling knowing that He is there, downstairs in the kitchen, turning to another side in my bed, knowing that His head is resting there in the adjacent pillow, and getting dressed on Thursday morning after running on my tread mill for an hour, so full of power, so full of energy ready to conquer the world, all from the knowledge of His presence from the feeling of His being near me, from sensing Him.

So, The Shabbat, with Michael, has had several levels of entering our house, our home and our hearts.

For most Israelis, for most Jews it would start on Friday late afternoon with some preparations beginning early morning, but My Shabbat, with My Husband Michael, would start as early as Wednesday early evening/night.

All day Thursday would pass as if though I would be on the clouds. My colleagues would never guess how come I am so smiling, easy to satisfy, always on Thursdays. They would attribute it, to as most people were, being closer to the weekend, already at home in their minds. Yes, I guess it is a kind of a similar feeling, but magnified.

My mood would always be so good on Thursday, that my students knew it was the best day to meet with me, to ask their requests of me, to try and obtain whatever they needed from me. Thursday was THE Day.

The corridors in Rashi Medical Center, when I would be on my way to a meeting, seemed to flow under my feet. Everybody I was in contact with seemed to be so nice and accommodating. And suddenly, the usually dull and grey Medical building transferred to be quite appealing with the noticed geraniums scattered and the art work so carefully placed on the walls, interestingly enough, data that escaped me during the rest of the week, when I usually only saw inward to my professional thoughts and was preoccupied with business, hardly noticing anything else but my professional duties and goals.

Some of me could not wait for the day to be over with. Some of me, a big whole lot of me, wanted the day to end and be on my way home for a long so eagerly waited for, weekend with Michael. Michael, My Husband, My Colleague, taught me how to separate the week days from the Shabbat.

I was startled by the sound of the phone ringing. "Danielle" His voice was a cocktail of immense self-sureness, authority and but one could sense today a slight note of urgency there.

"Yes Josef," I was immediately offering all my professional entity through my voice. I sensed that something was going wrong. Something was going bad, Josef does not phone to me every day, not to mention when I am home. Although we have kind of a dual relationship, a professional one and a semi intimate one from his side, we manage always to carry out the right one according to circumstances.

Josef has made it no secret that he likes me very much. Once, when he "gave" me a lift to an international conference that took place in Tel-Aviv, and tried to court me the whole day with pleasantries like an outstanding lunch at my favorite over the water restaurant, and a nice slow drive home with exquisite, unique classical music on a rare cd that is hard to find today, which at the end of the day was given to me as a gift, he insisted on escorting me to my door, and as a required courtesy that I felt at the time, and could see no other way, I offered him to enter for just a few minutes. The moment the door was closed behind us, I was already feeling his hands engulfing me strongly yet delicately, I looked up to his eyes, semi questioning, semi smiling, not knowing exactly what to do how to react, not wanting neither to offend him, his ego, his huge masculine, professional emotional ego, yet, nor did I want to enter this path with him.

My intuition told me and led me to be passive and very slow, take no action. I am working with this man and did not want anything I did to ruin our so good professional relationship. Yet, No, No! I did not want to be involved with him, neither emotionally, nor physically. I was all captured with my belonging, magically drawn to my husband, I was filled in all possible areas with calm yet stormy engaging satisfaction, from my so special interaction with my husband, that there was no need or appeal for me to be put in this current position at home. I did not see other men. They did not exist for me as men. I could only see my husband, as a friend, as a colleague, as a lover as a mentor, as a companion, as All A Woman needs, always.

Yet, my intuition caused to me stand still. Wait. I felt his strong hands lifting my face so his eyes could pierce my eyes. His eyes looked so serious, but very soft, I have never seen them like that. He kissed my forehead and murmured softly, "you are a miracle that has happened to me, you are a miracle..." I said nothing, letting him enjoy His moment of great need of displaying for the first time his feelings towards me, vocally, although I suspected so. And so have, I think, the whole Medical center watching how he always was there to take care of my professional interests. He kissed me again on my forehead and left.

From that date we were exchanging with our two modes of relating to each other, surprisingly with no difficulty, according to the reality and situation at hand and thus his phone call today was all about business, and as such I would respond.

Josef is usually very busy running his department, the latter being one of the best Genetic Disorders department in the North, and all his other appointed duties, at the University, being the deputy CEO of Rashi Medical Center and its representative abroad and many other, thus his call caught me somewhat surprised, even though we shared some interesting moments..

"We are going to lose him, Danielle, I need you to get me some results as to his son, and to the exact location of the mutation, have you had any progress with that?" His voice was a bit impatient. Josef wanted his demands carried right away. No actually not right away, not even immediately, but yesterday or better last week. And Josef was used to always get his way.

"We are working on it day and night, I am going to meet you in an hour, I am coming over" I said, my voice betraying my devastating feelings. I liked Simcha so much, and I felt so helpless, not being able to help him. "There is nothing that you can do here Danielle, just get me those results, so we might be able to help the boy in time." His voice was short and as always, he politely but coldly said "thank you", and hung the phone. He was not waiting for a reply, he just wanted to put some pressure although he knew that we were doing more than could ever be expected, more than he would ever ask for, since we were very professional in our work but also very concerned with this lovely family.

I knew that he was right and there was nothing in specific that I could do to help Simcha. But I could not stay at home. I had to be doing something that is connected to Simcha. I decided to hurry up and drive over to my lab and see where things are regarding the work on Simcha's son's DNA and have a talk with Shachar.

While driving over to my lab I ran through the results in my mind. My finger pressed the fast dial on the car phone, automatically without noticing the view or where I am at, all my entity preoccupied with what is happening at the medical center and at my lab. I was trying to catch Shachar at her working table at the lab.

"Shachar, I have thought about your suggestion." I said with my voice projecting the relief of finding her, yet harboring within the made decision to refuse her request and suggestion. Shachar knew me so well, she got it from my tone and without me further explain she asked quite warmly "Why?" She was aware of the difficult emotional situation we are all in, we were all sad that Simcha is not going to make it. It was not easy for us. We all got attached to this family. This small family of four of which the mother was a nurse at our Medical Center, and not once or twice but many times we invited her to the lab, talked with her and bonded with her. We were all there with her frequent visits to the medical center for the treatment of Simcha, her husband. Moreover we were all there when her 24 years old first born son was diagnosed by Josef`s staff and went under colectomy because of so many polyps found in his colon, one of the characteristics and diagnostic features to FAP, this hereditary Colon Cancer.

"Well Shachar, I feel that it is not ethical to present the data of this family, because we are not done diagnosing them. Now we are going to work even harder for Josh, we need to find the exact location of the mutation for him so we can save him in time. This is what we are going to do."

We both knew that Josh, the 18 years old son of Simcha and Judy is now enjoying himself in a long trip in South Asia. We have already found that he has inherited the mutation for FAP from his father, but he did not want, under any circumstances to come to a session of Genetic counseling. That was very disturbing, since he was over 18 years old and the law prohibited us from giving the results, the devastating results, of him positively found to carry this hard Gene, this colon cancer causing gene, to his mother, or his father, or any one in that respect. The results of his DNA analysis are to be given only to him.

He living all his life experiencing the hardship of his father, taking part of the distress and difficulties, emotional and physical his senior loved and adored brother was going through, made his young heart closed and blocked to anything connected with this disease, with this so threatening reality.

"You are right Danielle, I feel the same way, maybe we will be done fast enough to help Josh, and maybe it will be soon enough to present it to the world in the international conference next month in Crete." Her voice was calm and intelligent, accepting and already moving on to the more important matter, the localization of the mutation.

I knew I could count on her. This is why I liked and respected her. "See you in a while" I concluded and while hanging up the phone, realizing for the first time that I am already actually entering the parking lot of The Medical Center, and about to enter another difficult reality.

I put on my "mask" my "armor" my "The Medical Center" face and being, and started my way to the fifth floor, to Simcha, first.

CHAPTER TWELVE

THE MEDITERRANEAN SEA HAVING TWO THOUSANDS AND ONE FACES

"My poor sweetie" Gal said when I presented him the letter bearing the news that I am a BRCA2 Gene carrier.

It was a Thursday, and while driving back home from the college up state I have decided that it is time to go forward with my "to do list". My so detached automatic-mode to be carried out check list as to my new Gene. I have decided that in order for me to cope with all array of impacts, this gene bears on me, I have to accept it is a part of me, and of a good part of me. I have to understand, focus and enlighten the possibly good aspect of having this gene. No, The Good aspects of having this gene.

"Actually, I am very lucky to have this Gene" I told Eden on the phone, not letting her respond to my News. She did not know how to respond. She could not respond, she was in shock. In utter shock. I did not leave a minute of silence in our phone conversation, and continued on, interpreting the new reality to her as well as a started campaign, for myself, persuading myself as to the actual benefits of having such a gene.

Intuitively, I knew I can cope, or try to cope with the reality of living with my Gene and the horrible threat it poses on my every week, every day every hour of facing cancer, only from a positive strong source within me.

Additionally, it came from my mother.

My mother that I so loved, so missed, so needed to share life with, successes and failures, my mother who I so respected.

Thus, I cannot hate something that I have inherited from her. No.

"Now that I have it I will have to be under a very strict follow up, a half yearly one of MRI, Mammography, Ultrasound of the breasts, a routine clinician checkup and Ultra Sound of my Uterus. Thus, since every 1 of 7 women will have breast cancer, this strict follow up regime, will actually be of benefit to me and I will be exposed to a constant monitoring, unlike other women."

"Yea," she responded with a small weak voice. I could sense and hear her being lost. What could she tell me? What could she offer me? She was confused, devastated, frightened, for me, for herself, when sympathizing with me, from Cancer.

"This is actually an advantage, see Eden, if I am monitored so closely, should there be a tumor, it would be discovered very early, thus giving me a great chance that other women don`t have, to discover it in early stages, thus treat it in early stages. This is good?" I stated, half with complete confidence and some of me pleading for her to agree that this is actually Good.

Eden followed my lead and said supportively, "Yes, you are right Danielle".

But no more. She could hardly process what was going on. The overwhelming news I have just thrown on her.

"See, today, if discovered early enough, there are very high chances to survive the treated cancer "I added with more self-persuasion then assuring her that I am in a good position...

She collected herself, combined both her kind, considering personality and her profession of heading the department of Social Help in the northern county, and softly offered, yet in a more stronger calm voice "it is very good Danielle, that this is the way you look at it. It is brave, it is strengthening and will help you through your new Journey."

I could hear all her friendship, all her love towards me invested in these few sentences that provided me at that time with so much support and confirmation as to my chosen outlook at my New Gene.

She gave me a new peace of mind. I was calmed down somewhat and felt that I have made my new ally, my new friend and the first one, to start with my first steps in public and in my own inner world as to walk my new path.

My conversation with Eden gave me the courage and the ability to talk and share and tell of my Gene to a selected group of friends. Close friends.

Not to mention, my father.

Well that is another story. That is not so easy.

How shall I tell my father, who had lost his beloved wife to Ovarian Cancer, that now, today I know and understand that it is due to the BRCA2 gene my mother have harbored in her DNA.

How can I tell my father?

Has not he suffered enough?

My father, The Giant, became my best friend over the last 10 years, and I shared almost everything with him. He has always been The Rock of the family, and was my Rock, my personal Rock, especially after I have lost my husband, not to mention during the so difficult, so horrible 6 months of my husband being in ICU with all my entity and efforts to save His life; that tragically and devastatingly for me, did not succeed.

I felt quite torn between my wish to protect my father from this new situation and what it will materialize into, as I would have to be operated on as soon as possible, to undergo oophorectomy, so my ovaries will be out and not present this dreadful danger of having ovarian cancer, which is still, today very hard to treat.

Thus how can I tell him of this.

But part of me, a big part of me, felt I NEEDED to tell my father. I can`t bear this information without him knowing. Is it still the child within me? Is it still the daughter within me. How come I don`t have the strength to shield him and walk through this alone? Am I too selfish?

I could not address these questions at that time. There were too many things that were laying on my shoulders and I felt that I could not relate to some of them.

"Oh, my poorest sweetie" Gal`s words pierced my world, my thoughts, my memories.

He was sitting there at his big mahogany wood table, in his expensive, classy looking office in his clinic, looking at me, seizing me up, yet trying to offer some sympathy.

He was my Onco-Gynecologist.

I did not like to hear his offer of sympathy. I did not know what exactly I wanted to hear from him, yet I knew this was not it.

I looked at him detached, and closed, and actually wanted to be done with him, roll the ball and have my oophorectomy scheduled. I knew all the medical facts, I needed just his technical expertise, and I knew that I can cope with this huge new thing in my life only through my brain. Should I open my heart and let him console me I would break down and I could not afford this, I have a very long way to go.

"You know the tremendous risk, Danielle, you know that it is quite difficult to treat Cancer of the ovaries today."   He offered his voice still somewhat soft, but turning to be more a matter of fact, more professional. I liked the latter attitude, it helped me think, evaluate, and make the right decisions for myself.

"We have to remove your ovaries as soon as possible, how old was your mother when she was diagnosed with Ovarian Cancer?"

"58 years old and she died 8 months later still being 58 years old" How young she was I thought, I am only 52 years old and Marian is only 55 years old. Now unlike when I was 30 years old and lost my mother, did I fully understand how YOUNG my mother was when dying.

"Yes your friend Marian is scheduled to pass the operation within 3 weeks, let me get in touch with my secretary I would like to squeeze you before that maybe within 2 weeks, if possible, will that be OK with you?"

Here came my connections in the medical center into use, he is going to squeeze me in, even when it is almost impossible to schedule an operation, for such a short notice, not in Rashi Medical center, not in a governmental medical center. I was thankful. I was grateful, for him offering that and doing that without even my request.

"Yes, I will accommodate any date you find to squeeze me in, Gal, and the sooner the better, I want them out, they terrify me"

"Let's take a look at them why don't you go behind the curtain, get undressed and let me check your breasts and your uterus"

I went in a robotic way, not feeling anything, just doing what he said, in very slow motions, all focusing and concentrating in folding my clothes nicely, and battling and fighting very determinately any possible thought that might be crawling to my mind regarding this checkup of his, and the possible immediate consequences.

His hands felt very cold to me, and his voice was heard from very far away, by me, like in a fog, form a mile away, reporting to me all that he is doing, when entering my uterus, checking left, checking right, looking for my ovaries in the ultrasound, and telling me what a nice lovely uterus I have.

I could not say a word, I could not react to any of his comments, my mind was waiting for the bottom line, very anxiously, very on edge, being ready to any kind of diagnosis.

"Well, your ovaries look OK, they look fine" He said in a cheerful voice trying to cheer me up "we will just need to remove them, but they look like 2 little twins, nice and fine" I was somewhat relaxed to hear him say that although I did not give it any credit, I knew, I knew so well, as a scientist, that until they are out, until they are checked in the lab, I would not have the almost definite answer as to their malignancy. So, I took his finding with a grain of salt. I could not wait for them to be out.

"Why don't you get dressed and get prepared for my breasts checkup, take your blouse and bra off and call me when you are ready, OK?"

I did not even answered vocally, just went ahead and did that and called him, continuing on this small first mission of mine, being checked for the first time by my Onco-Gynecologist, for my new reality, harboring an armor, a very strong one consisting maybe from 80,000 walls to protect me, learning with this being my first step how to proceed, weeks, months, years to come, with my new discovered, personal reality. I felt encouraged from how I was doing, from how I was getting along. It gave me strength. It enlightened, and as time went by, confirmed as to the strategy chosen by me, for me; to be closed emotionally, to plan each step, to make my decisions from my mind, not to cry not to pity myself, hell not to even go this road, I did not have time for that road, just to flow with events and needed steps to be taken, all from my mind and brain aspect-no emotions are allowed, yet.

His, brown soft kind eyes were smiling at me, trying every trick in the world to ease this situation on me. In less severe situations, I as a woman have always found it hard to undergo these checkups....These routine checkups. Today, it was even harder. These checkups are going to be a very central part of my life, I was thinking when his voice suddenly sounded somewhat alarmed" There is a small bump here, in the right breast at the 12 hour on top of your nipple." My heart sank.

"But I think it is just something hormonal, we should recheck that after the oophorectomy, it could be that you are due to have your period and it is just a normal bump" I adopted his offered theory very quickly. I could not face now any other issue, any other problem. Don't I have some ovaries to be taken care of? This was all that I could deal with at that time. And alone. I just removed his comment out from my mind, also knowing and thinking, that I really am not hiding, and will have plenty of opportunities to re-visit this discovered possibly new "bump" in the weeks to come, when being checked numerous times before my oophorectomy. Nothing was that urgent that I had to react today.

"My secretary would get in touch with you as soon as possible and we would take care of your ovaries within the coming days" Gal said seriously but still softly when ushering me out, going all the way to his door office, manifesting all the respect in the world, and all the support he could, by walking with me all the way out of his clinic escorting me well outside to the outdoors, with his secretary and his waiting patients eyeing us surprised, seeing us both, him so trying to protect me, me walking "chin up" as my husband would say, all proud and beautiful.

As always, when in stress, I would stop on the way home, at a deserted place on the beach.

The view from my car window, at the sea-front road is so peaceful and never boring with the sea, the Mediterranean Sea, having two thousand and one faces.

I just sneaked a small quick look and I spotted a whole school of dolphins passing by and biding me good evening. There were big waves surrounding the dolphins, which were like a magnet for one's eyes, colored with a mixture of deep green/blue and grey and some white teasing, appearing here and there and disappearing.

I was fascinated. I was as always very taken with the sea, and part of me began to calm down.

Water, water, water I thought - I am addicted to water, and apparently there is no cure, not that one is needed. I have been in the water since the age of 3 when we moved from Jerusalem where I was born, to Haifa, Israel, and was swimming on the back of my father, at the age of 4-5, with my little tiny rubber sea fins, for kilometers.

In fact every weekend we would be on the Mediterranean beach which was a four and a half minutes' drive away from home, and all summer, when in high school and in Israel, the only place I would be found at is the beach from early morning to late night. My parents knew, that I am gone for the whole 2 months of summer vacation and could be found on the beach.

So, Water is in my Genes, my Blood, my Spirit and is part of me.

Thus, there are very good Genes that I harbor. Very good ones. I like my Genes, all of them.

"You know you have the possibility of removing both your breasts as well, Danielle, "Gal's voice echoed in my mind." There are a lot of women that choose that over being threatened and fearful of having breast cancer, all their lives. After all there is a very big chance of a BRCA gene carrier having breast cancer" I was aware of him depersonalizing this data this information and not linking it specifically to me. "You know that up to 85 % of BRCA2 carriers will develop breast cancer, and IT IS a big burden to carry each year, no each half year, when you will have to undergo your routine checkups, for your breasts." He wanted to let me have all the pos-sibilities, and let me feel that each and every decision I make, is backed up by him, my doctor and by women, by medicine, by what is done out there in this so new world for me. New world emotionally.

It was hard to think of removing my breasts. My ovaries is one thing. I am not that attached to them. They do not represent for me anything. They do not represent my womanhood for me. But my breasts? That is totally another issue.

But then, to live so fearful, so threatened…I would have to give this a lot of consideration.

CHAPTER THIRTEEN

THE WAVES PLAYING AROUND US AND WITH US, RISING AND FALLING

"Should I put this slide of FAP before describing the family?" I was thinking at my desk at my den at home, starting to prepare my presentation for the international conference next month in Crete.

Yes, work was a blessing for me now, this evening, after spending the afternoon with Gal, and walking for an hour at my favorite spot at the beach. Let my mind, my subconscious, my emotional world process the information, the need to be done list, the "what is" before me, for now. I have to preoccupy myself, and I always enjoyed preparing my lectures and presentations. They were so colorful yet very classy and solid and professional, using all the up to date techniques to pass my messages along, my findings, interpretations and analysis and thoughts.

I liked Crete. I remembered the last time I was invited to lecture at the international conference on Oncology in Crete. I was appointed to preside as a head of the session, thus sat there on the podium to present the different speakers, and had to know some good questions to be asked, after each and every lecture, before presenting mine which was the last. I did a good job, people, scientists were interested in the discussion I established after each lecture, and when all was done, quite a few had a need to wait and congratulate me on a well-directed and interesting session.

I came a day before the conference began, on a very tiring and long flight, wanting to reach my room as soon as possible, to be by myself. By myself and the beautiful view from the suite, that I knew I would have, this not being the first time in that resort chosen for the conference. I loved the place, and in my heart, deep down there, I knew, that there was a small percentage that consisted my accepting the invitation to lecture, that was a cocktail of me being so drained and tired at that time from still mourning my husband, that lured me to that resort. Not to mention the nice memories I had from that conference and resort from a few years ago being there with my husband.

Then too, I was a chairperson. I was actually very proud that I was asked and invited to preside as a chairperson. My husband too was very proud of me. I always accompanied him to his international conferences, and he always accompanied me. Thus it was hard in the last years to fly alone and experience all by myself, my successes, the nice feedback to my lectures and the scientific respect that I was gaining. I had a very good time with him when we were there together.

I remember the morning of my lecture, I dressed in my power suit as always before my presentation, he prepared me a cup of coffee, made sure I took all my necessary cds and papers for my session and bid me success with his serious, yet smiling eyes, semi green semi brown I could never figure that out, letting me feel and know, that he is absolutely sure I would do well, and that the truth is, it is not that so very important, get my priorities straight, it is not the most important problem of the world, thus making my anxiety lessen. I knew, we knew I am good, very good, but I was always very self-critique and self-judgmental expecting the best and only the best from myself.

I went to the lecture hall two hours before my session, the session which I was heading and was to give my lecture at as well. I sat there just to breathe and get the atmosphere of science again. Be a scientist, not a wife, nor a lover, since I have spent the former days enjoying so much the beautiful rocky beach of the resort with my husband. I needed a few hours without him, alone, to return to another entity of mine, and be a serious scientist. I never let him accompany me, never let him hear me, though I have a feeling, a good feeling, that once in Geneva, he sneaked to the full lecture hall and heard me, I think for the first and last time. I saw his head peeking in. We never discussed it, but he was very high spirited that night and his eyes were very bright and I could feel he is all full of pride and admiration for His love. He being one of the most respected scientists in the world. **The World**. I was just a small butterfly compared to him. But, in my reality, I had my place in the world and he was full of pride for me.

When sitting there in the lobby that connected all lecture halls, that morning, before my session, there sat a young Italian scientist, that while making some small talk with, I learned that he too, was going to preside as a chairman for another session, at the same time that mine was to be. He offered his apologies for not being able to hear me, since it appears he had read some of my work and actually wanted very much to listen to my lecture. All of me was already very professional, and I smilingly politely responded that there will be other opportunities.

"Maybe we can meet later on and discuss some of your findings?" He offered with his eyes, deep brown colored, checking my face closely. Luckily it was time for me to go in to my lecture hall, and I said causally "maybe," smiling. I for some reason did not like so much to mingle with other scientists in a conference, although this was naturally one of the important goals; to meet, discuss and exchange data, I did not really like it, but I always defined a time to do it as well. It was also important. But it was not that important to me at that particular conference. Maybe I felt subconsciously that I will not have my husband for long? Maybe my intuition led me to spend every opportunity and every time possible with him? Not enough though. I wish I had devoted more time to us, to him. But, at that time, I was engaged with my career, and He, being so famous, was also engaged with his career. Actually we were both very satisfied at the time, with the way things were being, with the way we led our lives. We were so happy. We were ON THE TOP OF THE WORLD.

I could not run quickly enough when my session was over, with my nice gray high heeled shoes and my tight ankle long skirt, and tight gray jacket, to see my husband. I ran all the way from the hill, arriving to the sandy beach, all dressed up, beautifully looking, with my clothes, my jewelry, my figure, my blond, long hair letting the slight gentle sea breeze blow it somewhat. I did not see any one, and had only one goal, to let my husband know I am done, it went great, I got a wonderful feedback from my fellow scientists, and now, most importantly, I am all his. No actually, now he is all mine.

I arrived to the steps leading to the lower part of the beach, where all the people were wearing their swim suits, and laying on their lounges, and I spotted my husband, there, near the water, two steps away, reading his book; a mix of seriousness and power, so attractive, with his tan tall body, there on his lounge chair. When I called him, he lifted his eyes and I saw what delight spread on his face accompanied with a smile that shined from both his eyes and his lips, that were still holding his pipe, his forever trademark, his brown expensive, full of aroma, pipe.

"I will be right there," I called, "I am going to change to my bathing suit and be right there" I said full of enthusiasm. A woman who sat nearby looked at me smilingly and kindly. It must seem strange, a thought passed through my mind, seeing me all dressed up in this beach haven where all were seminude. She saw my child like, innocent glowing happiness and she understood. Even though she did not know our language, she understood. It was nice, I liked it. I went to our suite, walking a bit more as a scientist then a woman-child so carried away with enthusiasm and happiness, trying also to remember that my colleagues are all around.

The sun was so soothing and caressing my body, along with my husband's eyes, when I was laying on the lounge chair, two feet from the water, I felt so safe and content, and was encaptured with my book, the sound of the waves, the smell of coconut sun screen and my husband's nearness to me.

The waves called me very soon, and I took of the upper part of my bathing suit, as most women on the beach were, and paced proudly, knowing that my husbands' eyes are accompanying me, to the water. I always enjoyed the touch of the water. It always washed away all my worries. It always liberated me of all unnecessary baggage. I was, always was, in love with the sea.

"So, how did your lecture go?" my paradise was invaded for a moment. I transferred my look from my inner world to my side, and saw the young Italian scientist that I have met this morning. "Oh, well, and how was yours" I asked, as we both were very careful to look to each other's eyes, only eyes and nothing else. As much liberated as I was, it was somewhat funny to meet him in the morning being well dressed with my power suit, and encounter him now in the water, in-between the waves, wearing only my lower part of my bathing suit, with the waves playing around us and with us, rising and falling, rising and falling, and defiantly revealing my breasts. My breasts that were then so pure, unthreatened and immensely and so beautifully feminine, I thought.

"Well it was very interesting" He answered, his eyes still hooked, magnetized to my eyes, forced, I could tell...

"What a nice day" I said

"Yes a lovely day. So, can we maybe talk some science tomorrow, will you be there to attend some meetings? "He asked, waiting very patiently and so polite, like a real well-mannered European that he was, for my answer.

"Why don't you E-mail me, I have so many previously scheduled obligations, we could talk and discuss things at leisure this way"

"Yes, I will do that" he said, and understandingly offered, "Have a nice rest of the day" as I was backing out of the water, towards my husband, collecting my towel to dry myself and redress the upper part of my swimming wear.

Yes, we were in Europe, yes there were all these other women with their upper part of their body revealed, but I felt more comfortable with both my bikini parts on, when the water was not there to caress my body, to semi hide it, to let me enjoy its nudeness in my private world, not for all to see.

Yes, we enjoyed our stay there so much, I thought while sighing and passing to anther slide for my future presentation in Crete. How different it was from my last stay there, I remembered. The only thing that I wanted was to be in my suite alone, protected from the rest of the world. I enjoyed being alone, these days. I needed to be alone these days. I had so much to process in my mind, my heart my subconscious. All was quite difficult for me to come to terms with. All being, the loss of my husband. As much as I was and still am a goal oriented woman, a career woman, ALL was actually my husband, I discovered. Not really, I think I felt it, I sensed it, but it became more evident, I was more aware of it, since I have lost him. Although I saw some familiar faces while waiting for the connecting flight to Crete, I tried to remain by myself, and buried my face in my book and papers. There was this short, round figure, dressed with a dark blue suit man that eyed me from time to time, but I did not pay much attention.

I was glad at last to land in Crete, and walked briskly to the taxi stand to take my own taxi, no sharing to the resort, where the international conference took place. I already knew the way the routine and was longing to face the reception clerk, be assigned a suite and get some rest. And yes, most importantly walk the rocky shores, get semi hypnotic and totally absorbed with the calmness and peacefulness of the area, the swimming pool, the geranium filled village that was the resort.

I literally snatched a taxi before that blue suit almost joined me, and we drove to the hotel. I was glad to see that there were no people at the reception desk and I walked my professional walk all proud and business-like to the clerk representing myself as Dr. Goldbear. Although he met so many doctors and professors, I needed all I can recruit at that hour, with all my exhaustion from the long tiring trip, to get the suite I wanted, The suite I was with my husband at. The suite that he prepared coffee for me each morning. The suite where each night we would sit on the large balcony, which served as a roof to the cottage beneath us which possessed a beautiful garden and watch the sun set, on the calming Mediterranean and the surrounding rocky beaches and so well taken care of gardens. It was laid out as a village, with five swimming pools each serving a different area, and all buildings were just two floors, two suites, facing either the sea or the court yards which were of the architecture as ancient Greece was. One could walk in the numerous paved paths and get lost in history, in architectural beauty, in one's world.

And I was planning to do that. To get lost in the beauty of that village, and maybe absorb some of the deep calmness it offered. Yes, I would enjoy presenting my lecture as well, I would enjoy briefly the science encounter as well. I would enjoy presiding again as a chairperson of my session. But at that time, I longed most of all, to forget myself in one of those almost vacant, pools, decorated with huge big ceramic pots, filled with flowering bright and colorful Bougainvillea, having the sun caress me and my body. I was thirsty for the warmth of the Sun and the different world of silence and peace.

"Yes, Dr. Goldbear we have kept the B4 suite for you" He said smiling his professional smile meaning nothing, hardly seeing me and already on his way to tend his next task.

"Could I see the manager" I tried to master my most authoritative yet polite still demanding voice. He was surprised. He did not expect that. Not from a woman. Not from me. He actually seemed to me to be a man that was threatened by women. By strong women. Not to mention strong and attractive, a cocktail he did not know what to do with and how to handle. He appeared offended, looked at me and started to object, but seeing my piercing look and the determination on my face, he backed and called in Greek for his superior.

"What can I do for you, Madame?" "Madame," I thought? Here in this international conference, he is calling me Madame? Is that good or bad? I looked at his eyes, they offered the same professional, polite yet meaningless and artificial smile, his face projecting his impatience, wanting to get rid of me the current obstacle as quickly as possible.

"What seems to be the problem, Madame?" His voice sounded well mannered, but cold and short, he was in a hurry. But I have done my homework, and was ready for that.

"Hello Demetrius, how are you?" I said with my warmest possible voice, smiling as cheerful as I could after being dragged on two flights and a ten hour long connection. He was confused and baffled, his eyes became more humane and warm and he studied my face carefully, then cried, "Dr. Goldbear, how so nice to see you". This time his voice projected genuine warmth. He was so proud I have remembered him. I have remembered him from last time, and we actually became quite friendly, then. He learned to respect me, know me a bit and like me.

"Let me see if your last suite is available" He said immediately backing to the computer, starting to work it so quickly and efficiently. I wanted that suite. I wanted that specific suite so much. Please, let him find it for me. He called his assistant, I saw them whispering to each other, him working some more on the computer and at last he approached me with a light on his face, I knew he got it for me. I was so grateful. He made a strong hard gesture to the man on the far corner, threw some orders around in Greek, and smilingly and efficiently told me that Argyris will be taking me in his cart to my court yard, my Greek lovely court yard, where my suite is located.

I thanked him warmly and turned to see that my suitcases were already being loaded on the cart. I walked to the driveway to climb the cart, already visualizing myself sun bathing in the roof-balcony of my suite, when I heard a deep warm kind and friendly voice saying "So we meet again?"

It was the blue suit from the airport, he managed apparently to get a taxi right after me, to reach the hotel right after me and to be helped with his living quarters, right after me. They scheduled the both of us to ride together in this so large a village of scattered beautiful Greek cottages.

"Ming", the light sound of an e-mail arriving to my inbox was bringing me back to reality. I rushed to open my mailbox, deserting my slides for the forthcoming conference in Crete. I wanted some refreshing atmosphere. As good as it was I wanted the now and the present. The now and the present consisted of some harsh aspects, thus I was so welcoming an e-mail so late at night. It could only be either Pierre or Brian, and oh, I so wished it would be indeed one of them. Nothing hard, nothing needing debating, just a smooth, engulfing, warming mail that would recharge my energy, refill my "present" cup.

I have learned through the years that *life consisted actually of different circles*, all busy, all going and happening at once. Rarely, a person is satisfied with all. Rarely. I have had a period during my last two years with my husband, in which all was totally satisfying. I was happy with my marriage, with my work, with my family with my friends, with my home and house, with my dog, with whatever my life consisted of. But a person has to be real lucky to have that. Or real wise to know how to perceive matters in life, how to regard events and how to prioritize wishes and wants. I thought of today, tonight, my small reality and sought to find *my Good Circles*. Do I have good circles? Yes, I do. And a lot of them. Maybe most of them even. Most of the events and things in my life, I felt at that moment, were working for me. I am coming to accept my Genes, all of them, those that are addicted to water, to the sea to the Ocean as well as the one which is exposing me to Cancer, the one who is making me prone to cancer, but is also presenting me with the knowledge, awareness and choice of defending, protecting me from cancer, thus actually putting me there on the safe, on guard position, luckily.

My work is very satisfying to me, my father proved to be the most supporting, ever hard solid rock to lean on, my friends and colleagues showed their utmost understanding and love, what else could I wish for?

Not to mention Ginger, dear loyal friend, my shadow, at my so cozy, safe and beautifully interior decorated by me, HOME. Yes My Home, My Garden, My den, My Master bedroom, all that was there in the back ground of my life, providing me with a solid, stable environment.

And now, this new window, this new circle that was developing and offering me another angle of life, vividness and support; Pierre and Brian.

Not Jan-Paul, though.

CHAPTER FOURTEEN

BRAHMS AND BRIAN

The light and delicate sound of a mail coming in startled me.

I did not feel I wanted to communicate with any one right now. I was grateful to the barrier of my PC, thus no one could know whether I would check my mail or not. No answers are required immediately. I needed to be within my own world, my new world, the one, in fact that I was creating, every minute and every hour and every day for myself.

I have learned lately, such a fascinating new thing, new outlook on one's life, I have learned that *Life* Is a *PROCESS*, that phases are important, that things in life have their own timing, their own need for evolving, and that one actually, cannot very well enhance it. One might try, but maybe it is better to let the PROCESS take its place and time. Right now, I find myself in a process, a very important one, a very challenging one, of building a new world to myself. What a new world, it consists out of so many aspects, so many parameters. Not only am I learning to build my life without my husband, but now, I realized I am very preoccupied to build my life with my New Gene.

So, there were moments that I wanted and needed to be with myself and MY chosen other people, persons and entities, according to their input, suitability and accommodating ability to MY own Process.

I pressed the inbox button on my mail box and there appeared Brian message. "It seems that he read my mind" I thought smilingly. I definitely was welcoming his mail.

Danielle,
I am working but my mind has its own will and is drifting to people and places far away (you and Israel).
(Don't get alarmed, I won't ask you to marry me for another week or two!)

Wow, I thought, Brian is opening to me, Brian is getting somewhat brave and revealing his feelings to me, maybe he is not as cold as I thought?

I kept reading with my eyes running along his mail, and my heart wishing for some more, some attention, some binding, and some attachment to someone. I wanted and needed someone to be close to me. Someone to share my news with my world with. I wanted to be, for the first time in a very long while, WEAK.

Yes, I am a human being I thought, and I wanted to be weak, fragile, just for a moment or two, just a glimpse of a feeling that there is someone who will protect me, who will be there for me, in this unknown future that is being unveiled, step by step, day by day.

But, the more I get to know you, the more I want to meet you... as expected (with the exception of appearance of some data that makes me think that we are not well suited).

Your view?
Brian

What appearance? What data? Is this his emotional safety net, in case I would reject him?

Before I had a chance to contemplate on this, another mail came and manifested the feeling of a rushing message. I felt he wanted to reach out to me, yet to remain on a safe terrain.

I always thought that if *one does not take chances, one does not reach any of one's goals in life. Calculated chances though.* I felt that life would be very boring for a person who did not take chances. Maybe he IS boring as I thought previously for a few times. Maybe this is why it is already 9 years since he is divorced and has been in not even one committed or long term relationship. Actually he has had NO relationships at all since HIS wife divorced HIM.

"She did not even try to live with me." I remembered how he told me of a possible lady friend of the past that did not even try to come and live with him and actually rejected him right there, right then.

Danielle,

I feel you should know that the contract I have signed here at Washington DC, at the Medical Center, with the Trauma unit, is for 6 years and I enjoy my job. Additionally my divorce and putting my 4 kids through college have set me back somewhat. Thus it is improbable that I can/would move from Washington DC for the next six years. After that moving may be conceivable. That said, I have accumulated quite an amount of vacation time, but I am looking for a relationship in which I can cohabit with my partner the majority of the time.

Have a wonderful evening,
Brian

I was speechless. He is stepping two steps forward, wanting to be with me, and one step backwards, still on guard for himself. Well that is very sensible. He looks like a sensible man. That is also very natural. My mood was elevated slightly, all in all the man would like to get to know me better, leaving an open window for himself to get out in case...

I appreciated his openness and candidness regarding his future and plans. I liked him as a father helping all his kids through college.

I leaned back on my nice comfortable brown leather chair, closed my eyes and tried to envision him. He was quite tall quite attractive as seen from the pictures he has sent me; his eyes though were quite cold and closed. One could not penetrate his soul. He had a poker face. One could not really feel him, get closer to him. Apparently he DID keep a distance. My eyes opened to the repeating sound of another message coming in. It was Brian again. "Brian, I thought, writing three times within an hour? Be careful Brian, you might fall in love with me?!" I semi told, semi asked him, semi warning him, or maybe warning myself?

I read with curiosity, wondering what is there to add to his last rushed messages?

Danielle,
I am beginning to think that I have done something that has insulted you (or you disliked my pictures), as I haven't heard from you.

Oh Brian, this is not like you. I thought. You are presenting yourself as very interested and worried. What has happened to all your defense walls? Are they collapsing so easily?

I continued to read with some satisfaction, glad that as a female, as a woman, it appeared I really caught his attention, and it was a good timing for me.

I rushed to the phone all happy like a small child seeing his new toy and so very pleased wanting nothing but begin playing with it, but stopped, wait I did not finish reading his mail.

I can envision that either my learning of your husband's work on the internet, or my statement that I undoubtedly would not be able to move for another six years concerned you. If so I apologize for the former. I can't easily alter the latter.

Yes, he did intrude somewhat on my privacy, I felt with his search of my husband's name. Not that I was ashamed of my husband. On the contrary. Not that I was hiding something. I was immensely proud of my husband and will always be. I just felt that I wanted to share this or whatever information about my husband in my own pace and time when getting to know another man. I was not ready to talk about my husband with another man, let alone Brian who I have never yet seen or gotten close to and that I always kept in my mind and intuition, that he appears cold to me, and actually, I too need my own emotional safety net. I too do not want to expose what I am not ready to.

I would also understand if you have become involved with another man.

He continued writing, and I smiled, as he was covering almost all possible bases.

If you are willing and capable, could you say a few words as to why you have been disinclined to communicate?

I ask for obvious reasons--you wrote me that you thought I had qualities that are attractive to you. I have learned that you have many qualities, behaviors, traits, characteristics and interests which are attractive to me.

Wow, that is a slight change to the first letter a few minutes ago. Now he is concentrating on the nice, good appealing qualities that I have and attract him. My hand was already reaching the phone, with my mind having no say or control. I wanted to talk with him, I needed to talk with him. Partly realizing that I am acting a bit irrational, a bit impulsive, my hand was still getting there to reach the phone and start dialing his number abroad, in Washington DC. So what I can be impulsive and irrational, I have to feed my emotional needs right now, I long to hear him talk to me, confide in me, Oh God, let him have a bit of a warmer tone, a warmer voice, a voice that will let me feel he cares, he feels and he longs to talk with me.
I was seeing the ending of his mail

Thanks,
Brian

I then took my warm cup of coffee with me to the master bedroom, to sit in my cozy, beautiful, Mary Antoinette, burgundy-colored chair with my heart beating fast.

I heard his metallic robotic voice, answering, "Yes this is Brian"

"Good morning Brian" I said with my almost the warmest voice I could master, yet feminine, mature, and collected.

There were a few seconds of silence. I was the last person Brian expected to be on the phone. I was as always a very quick responder, and not once or twice, but many times, I caught other people in surprise and off guard.

"Wow, Danielle, you do not cease to amaze me" he said a bit more warmly, laughing out of embarrassment and playing for time to catch his thoughts and feelings.

"This is more than I expected and assume thus that the answer to my last letter is that neither of the possibilities really exists? "He said semi guessing, with not so much confidence in his assumption.

"No, Brian, I was just busy and had no time," I said and immediately realized that I did not want to make him feel unimportant and second or third to my job, my career, my friends, I felt I needed immediately to re-built his masculine ego and let him be in peace regarding me. Otherwise I would risk his drifting away from me, his closing up on me.

"But I was thinking of you quite a bit, and lately was almost calling you for a few times?" I quickly volunteered with a soft, assuring and seeking knowingly his approval by inserting a slight semi questioning tone to my answer.

The soft mocha and crème-colored drapes moved slightly responding to the breeze that entered through. My gaze was fixed on them and the soft light entering from the garden but my look was focused inwardly.

"So what have you been doing that kept you so busy and away from me, and what is this sound in the back ground?"

"Oh, it is Brahms playing, I love classical music and it relaxes me, I actually am planning one of these days, it is high on my to-do list, to take a trip to Europe, in a wake of a composer, and visit all the places he grew up in and visited, accompanied with his music, his concerts, you know there are such trips."

My hand was automatically caressing Ginger, although I was not feeling it.

My subconscious needed to feel Ginger, to have Bach in the back ground and to sit in my favorite chair.

I was calm, sipping from time to time some coffee from my cup, enjoying the moment.

The line was silent for a second "Danielle you are so creative" He said with admiration, and then "Please take me with you, Pleeease," He said pleadingly and smilingly, I was surprised to the degree of his openness for a moment.

He was surprised too. He immediately transformed to his safe entity, and asked me coldly, "Who is your favorite composer" Now it was my turn to be surprised and caught off guard. I was not accustomed to such a quick change in warmth, or should I say coldness of attitude. Such an abrupt one. Not when I am at home, and somewhat defense-walls down. At work, this would mean nothing to me. But at home, in my master bedroom, where I felt so safe, it was strange to need my work skills. I tried to lift this feeling, to make him return to our previous atmosphere. God, this is hard. Brian is hard.

"I will take you along, Brian, we can go together, we can even meet there in Europe, as you have suggested a few times, this could be a lot of fun" I said, being warm, but not too much not to scare him and to keep myself safe. Then I decided that it was enough for him for one day, such an exposure such openness, things should proceed in an unthreatening fashion and slowly.

I did not wait for his answer or comment and said in a serious, grave, but with a voice full of confidence and strength. "Brian, there is something that I want to tell you. I have been tested and it seems that I am harboring the cancer causing Gene BRCA2. Do you know what it is?"

And thus I started my new, additional journey of sharing my Gene with another friend, a friend that I did not see in my life, a friend that was courting me, a friend that was a male, and here I am about to tell him that I am to be operated on and remove my ovaries, and am contemplating upon removing my Breasts. Yes, my most feminine organ, as I felt,

My Breasts. I felt quite strong at that moment, confiding with a man, the first man, a man that was attracted to me as a female. I felt I was also testing the ground. The ground with him. The ground with men.

It was not Eden my best girlfriend on one continent and it was not Cherie my best girlfriend at another continent. It is also not my father whom I told and got the most supportive response and felt safe with as a daughter, but rather a MAN. A Strange Man.

"It is a Gene, rather a mutation in this Gene that is making me prone to breast cancer having up to 85% chance to have it and around 54% chances of having ovarian cancer" I continued, I was all mind, maybe 90% mind, very collected, very calm and in control.

I did not let him answer, I was careful not to leave a gap between my conveyed information to him. I did not want to hear his answer yet. I was not ready. I wanted to let him have all the information possible, and maybe process it a bit and then respond to me. I wanted to do it right.

Also, I was not ready for his response yet.

"I am, actually, very lucky to have this Gene as I would have to be monitored very closely" I added knowing he is an MD and thus I don't have to elaborate on that.

"You see Brian, I would have a greater chance of discovering a potential tumor and be treated accordingly," I continued.

I still did not let him have the smallest gap for answering me.

"Women in the US are actually contemplating a double mastectomy, Brian," I explained in my professional tone, in my genetic counseling tone, very detached from myself.

"They remove both breasts in order to live their lives more securely and eliminate the huge fear factor" I offered a repeated explanation, for him. Or maybe for me. I wanted to let everything be clear and out there. For him. Or maybe for me. I wanted to hear his response as to my breasts. His, a man, a male, a gentleman courting me, as to my breasts, my most feminine symbol to me. My Breasts.

The doorbell rang quite aggressively and Ginger began barking like the whole Nato Army is standing behind my door. I was puzzled. The whole atmosphere changed. Ginger raced down the stairs, barking even stronger and I could not hear Bach any more. I could not concentrate any more.

"I will call you later, Brian, someone is at the door"

"Good night, Brian" I added not letting him say almost anything. I did not want it to evolve like that. I wanted so much to talk leisurely with him. To talk quietly with him. To listen to his response, to breath his response. Maybe even to be strengthened by his response. It meant so much to me.

I certainly did not want to hear his so waited for response in such a hurry. I hung the phone up and went, rather upset, to see who was this intruder to my phone call, to my world at that hour at home.

Ginger was barking loudly, waving his tail, looking at me and at the door, all his entity is about protecting me.

"Who is it?' I asked. There was no reply.

I was tired.

I was tired emotionaly and physically.

I smiled to myself and decided to be a bit naughty, thinking, I will just ignore them.

Ginger sensed me and my decision and we both went happily up stairs, each looking forward to the world of sleep, bliss, peacefulness and forgetfulness.

We both slept so well.

The phone ring took me by surprise. It was a nice Saturday morning and I was lazily roaming in the upper floor, with Ginger following me from room to room, and the sound of the neighbor's kids playing in the adjacent garden accompanying me. I was snuggled cozily in my robe which was half open revealing my nightgown.

"Good morning," His voice was so strong, still a cocktail of a metallic tone, mixed with an artificial sound of self-secure, Brian always harbored and manifested to a sharp and perceiving eye. This time it also harbored somewhat respect, mixed with fear of approaching me, fear of rejection.

"Gooood Mooorning" I answered very warmly, still keeping my usual distance from him, and immediately recruiting My Brian walls and precautions. I have to be very much on guard with him, in order to navigate through his questions, his curiosity, his actually testing me again and again. It was almost never fun to talk with him. One had the feeling of always being checked out. Brian left me the impression of being extremely hurt by his relationship or relationships. I really could not tell if he had an additional relationship to the one he had with his wife. I guessed not. I gathered that actually the women he approached before knowing me, rejected him. He was very vulnerable from one side, and could not open and thus his extreme coldness, which did not help at all.

But I wanted him to call. Who do I know right now that I could share and talk with on the male scale of life? I wanted very much to know his response to our last conversation. Actually it was not a conversation but rather a monologue. Part of me was yearning to call him, to confront my questions, my answers, his answers.

"Danielle, I was thinking of you a lot lately. I think you are in the best of hands, in the hands of the doctors in your medical center which is famous throughout the world, and you are now passing some very naturally difficult, times."

"Yes, they are famous, and it is one point that relaxes me somewhat" I waited for him to continue.

"You are right considering removing your ovaries. I have looked at the Mayo Clinic web site and your doctors are actually suggesting the right move and proceeding through the recommended procedure that would minimize your chances of having cancer."

I was all ears. He sounded now totally different than the Brian I knew. He sounded now as a Doctor. As my Doctor. His voice was calm and professional, inspiring assurance and security. It was so good to listen to him. I engulfed myself in his voice. I almost drank his words.

I started to visualize him, as he looked from the picture he has sent me, and unlike other times, I liked what I saw. I related to what I saw.

"There are quite a few cases here Danielle of BRCA2 carriers, and you are not sick with cancer, you are just a Gene carrier." He added explaining to me all that I already know, but God, it was so good to hear it from him...So good. He was a male friend and he happened to be a doctor. These 2 characters were very appealing to me this moment right now.

"You know, my wife had breast cancer" He said in a low voice, making a statement.

I was gasping for air. I was shocked. I was almost happy to hear that. "Really" I managed to say. I felt quite silly, happy to hear that some other woman had cancer, although it was very sad and must have been so hard for her. I felt like someone is sharing my destiny. I was ashamed for my initial gladness and my mature part, my human part took over.

"Were you with her at that time, Brian?"

"No, she did not want to be with me, she was with her then male friend, the one she cheated on me with." His voice was still calm and a matter of fact, just conveying the details.

Part of my mind went on a path thinking about that woman. What happened there that a woman, who is sick with breast cancer, is preferring to have her new gentleman friend with her rather than her ex-husband for 25-30 years? What kind of man is Brian to have his wife prefer someone else besides her in such a harsh difficult time?

"You have become very important to me Danielle" His voice interrupted my thoughts "I would like to be there with you when you are having your oophorectomy."

Wow, I was taken back. I liked his request. God knows I need all the support I can get. Surprisingly, for the first time his voice harbored some warmth in it. So Brian knows how to be warm, I thought.

Having not heard any response from me, he added earnestly "I am a good nurse, Danielle, a very good nurse, I will be there for you in the hospital and at home, I can come to Israel and be with you."

Reality dawned on me. Having him detailing his arrival to Israel and being with me along all this time, all this hard time, yes it is appealing. But no. I did not like that at all. I cannot see him for the first time in my life, at such circumstances. He will be at a new place, a new country; I will feel I have to entertain him to be there for him that will be difficult for me. The more I thought of it, the more I imagined it, I felt that I did not like it at all.

It was so important for me to meet him as a WOMAN, as an ATTRACTIVE woman, as a female.

How on earth could that be done when I will be throwing up and feeling aching and weak. How could I be what I am, an attractive beautiful woman on the circumstances he describes.

But I appreciated his offer, his yearning to be with me, on my side, at my difficult time.

Brian might be a man a woman can count on when in distress.

"Brian," I said with my most serious voice, coming from very down deep in my heart. "Brian" I repeated "this is a very big suggestion. A very big one. I am quite overwhelmed. I am also quite impressed. I tend to like it very much. How would I not want to cuddle in your arms after such a thoughtful suggestion" I felt every word was true and representing exactly what I thought. I live my life, as I have learned *honestly and openly, always honest and open.*

"Thus," I added with a very warm voice "let me think about that. Let me process that." I set more deeply in my bedroom chair, recruiting all the resources to say that, be truthful to my wishes, my needs, my wants, yet be gracious to him without succumbing to the pressure that his voice, his wish and politeness exerted on me.

I also, genuinely needed to think about his offer.

Our interaction was becoming thus more serious, more committing, I can't let him come, travel all the way to Israel, if I am sure I do not want him as a lover as a gentleman friend of mine.

No. This action will bear some consequences and I have to think about it.

"Let me think about it and I will get back to you." I repeated in a calm but decisive voice.

"Enjoy your Shabbat, Danielle, and please remember, how strongly I feel about coming. I also want to meet you. I also need to meet you.

I cannot go on being in a long distance relationship with you, falling in love with you, not having seen you yet. I need to see whether there is something going on with us, I need to meet you and resolve that for myself. I cannot postpone it for another month or six weeks. I need to know whether we are attracted to each other. I need to know whether we are working good together. Then, I can bear the distance. Then I can commute from Washington DC to Israel and back until you can come over here to your oceanfront condominium in South Carolina."

I was shocked now for the second time during my conversation with him. He sounded so earnest. He sounded pleading, explaining, needing and trying desperately to persuade me. I felt a bit cheated. He had his own agenda, his own motives as to come so early, so soon. I felt the pressure on me growing and growing.

The Shabbat magic was long gone. I felt trapped. I wanted all to end, nicely, not hurting him, neither agreeing to his suggestion. I felt my energy draining and decided to end our conversation as quickly as possible.

"I understand Brian" I mastered all the patience I could and added "I will call you soon and we can talk about it further, OK?" I sounded like I was appeasing a child.

"Shalom, Danielle." He concluded and I greeted him back relieved that the conversation is over.

It was neither now, nor before, easy to handle Brian, he was demanding, surprising and unexpected.

Lately, I was thinking, whether I need this additional pressure in my life. But still, it was not only a pressure; it was also a good distraction. A distraction and a possible good friend could evolve from it.

CHAPTER FIFTEEN

DESERT SAND, PIERRE AND JASMINE

Anthony held the envelope in his teeth while his eyes were running like a crazy desperate mouse from left to right from right to left, center, left again, they had no rest. Sand was everywhere. Sand was like a giant engulfing ocean, always yellow. Yellow and no other color. Yes, another color, he could not define it precisely, the color of Dryness. And today, unlike any other day, the color of passion. A glimpse of a memory worked its self to his conscience, and he felt and saw with all his senses, the color of purple, purple and black.

He immediately pulled all his willpower resource and concentrated again in the Yellowness, the Dryness, the ocean of sand surrounding him. With the envelope still in between his lips, held by his teeth his mouth was watering somewhat and the sand that found its way to every little hidden place in his body was starting to itch in his mouth. He knew he had to concentrate and focus on the hills of yellow. He knew this is one of the most dangerous posts he had ever been to, and if he will let go one second, one millisecond, a sniper, a suicide bomber, a killer would be able to penetrate the area and he would be killed. He and his buddies and their commanders and lives would be lost. Anthony was a very dedicated soldier, but his mind kept racing between these two additional scenes that did not let him focus on his mission of today.

He was so tired, so drained, he felt like the whole world and an additional one are laying on his 2 shoulders. There was a flickering move that caught his left eye. Instinctually he held his rifle tighter and his eyes got smaller with an effort to look harder at that cloud of dust that rose to his left. His mind was totally clear, and all his senses were automatically recruited to what was evolving to his left. Oh, my G-d, he sighed with an actual physical ache in his heart and his stomach. What would he give to unfold her again. She was all black again. And her eyes seemed to him like 2 big velvet purplish swans cruising peacefully in a serine bay. "Yalla, yalla, Udrobe.." a yelling vulgar voice, a harsh voice has awakened him from his semi indulging sweet feelings to see her shrinking and running quickly, obeying the commanding sound that violated him and probably her too.

She disappeared beyond the hills and he became a warrior that instant, somewhat shamefully for sinking to this so blissful drawing reality that became a dream, a repeating dream that actually with all its insaneness kept him sane in this crazed reality. "Her name is Danielle" he heard his voice murmuring "She is a scientist and a beautiful woman" He heard his voice continue, "She captivated my heart" "I am hers."

For a second Anthony was confused. Did he get a sun stroke again? Was he hallucinating? Did Danielle have purplish eyes, like two swans cruising in a serine bay? His thoughts were racing in his mind, while his eyes were again running like a drugged mouse all over the Yellow. His hands clutched his rifle tightly and his muscles all over his body turned into a tonus. His lips became strained and he then felt the envelope in his mouth. It was a letter from his father, telling him about his new loved one, this Danielle. His father, or Pierre as he called him in his mind was writing him about this new woman in His life.

He felt moisture…dampness, almost wet…yes, wet…Pierre woke up sweating heavily, opened his eyes and was surprised, relieved, and somewhat sorry, he was at home…safe but far away from Her…his mind was racing with questions and his heart needed to know who is that mysterious woman?

He turned to the other side and immediately fell back to sleep.

Some sweat drops were running along his forehead. It was so hot, that actually Anthony did not feel the heat at all. It was beyond a point of feeling. A small little drop of sweat rolled in to his left eye. A slight feeling of burn was disturbing his eye, and he was blinking. For a moment he closed his eyes instinctively, and then with the use of his brain reopened them, he has to keep alert; He has to keep being on guard. He has to be very alert and watch the Yellow. It is his job this morning to watch over his buddies, over his fellow soldiers, over his mates.

Another drop of sweat rolled on straight to his mouth. His teeth were tightly holding the envelope, but he could feel the mixture of the salty sweat drop with the sand. His eyes itched and burned again and he closed them for a minute. Just for a tiny little minute. What a blessed feeling. What a relief. He looked at her puzzled, all dressed with black revealing only her very deep dark eyes. Her eyes were questioning, inquiring, yet somewhat teasing. She was standing motionless and powerful with her eyes, her deep big dark brown eyes, mesmerizing him. He was enchanted. He was under a spell. He felt drawn to her. Every sense in his body every want in his being was concentrated on her. She bewitched him. She had total control on him. Yet, he could only see her eyes. Her body, although covered from toe to head seemed magical. He wondered what would be the shape of her lips. Would they be full and flirtatious? Would they be warm and seductive? She stepped back to further herself from the window. He followed. Her eyes were suddenly begging, asking, inviting. Her eyes suddenly transformed from the powerful, bewitching look to a feminine, most softly gaze that pierced him straight to his heart, and made his gut ache, ache terribly. He felt his left hand rise and touch slightly her long black dress. She moved back some more, like negating his gesture, yet her eyes encouraged him. They looked fearlessly straight into his eyes. They were talking to his eyes. Her body said no, but her eyes pleaded, warmly, softly, womanly, yes.

He moved closer to her, and his hand touched her back. She reacted like a kitten. Anthony could feel all her body responding to his touch. All her muscles were like a coil waiting for him to unwind. This time her body and her eyes were in accord, and she did not step away. Nor did she step towards him. He pushed her delicately to the old, ragged, ugly sofa that was the only furniture in the room. She let her body be led, being softly placed on the sofa and then tangled her body around him. Captivating him with her big, deep, dark brown eyes, and her long, ever so long lashes. Her body, in its own way followed by. He felt that he was drowning in an endless well of lust. He was powerless and could only follow her nonverbal instructions, obeying her body and her eyes, his hands felt her skin. With the endless Yellow, came the endless softness of her skin. The endless warmness of her skin. His hands were magnetized to her body never ceasing to feel to gulp to invade to enter, and his eyes were her slaves. He could not remove his look from them, feeling with each hand caressing, her eyes, responding, with each invasive move, her eyes getting deeper and her entity opening to him the further he would enter, the further she would open.

They were two souls linked together. No power on earth could separate them. Her lips still covered with her veil, and most of her body still covered with her black dress, but her soul, her entity almost completely revealed to his. They both shared something, unknown to the rest of the world.

He then entered her fully looking into her eyes amazed and bewitched from their transformation. Their seductive, pleading, warm and inviting look changed to two eyes, two purplish eyes that looked like swans, peacefully cruising in a serene bay. They both reached their serene world. A ticklish feeling rose in his belly, he was all water, all sweat. Where is he, he tried desperately to figure out. The ticklish feeling would not let go. He scratched his belly with his hand, stronger and stronger, to help him get rid of this annoying feeling, while still puzzled at his whereabouts. When he scratched for the third time, it was so hurting, he looked down to his belly and saw a red fluid. A red gushing fluid. He focused and immediately was sharp again. He understood that he was shot, when obliviously sinking into his subconscious, into his daydreams of his dessert mysterious woman, while on guard. He almost fainted and his lips kept repeating "Danielle, Danielle." A flash back of Pierre's letter, his father's letter, came vividly to him. "I bought her a boat, Anthony, a boat, she will love it, she will love my surprise for her, she will love me…"

Pierre woke up again, feeling wet and sweating heavily as before. When he opened his eyes he was again feeling a mixture of emotions; surprise, relief, sorry he was not at that magical world he has just dreamt of, but happy to be safe and at home. But then, again, far away from Her…who is she? He hurried to his PC to find a mail…hoping, needing to find a comforting mail from his beloved Danni.

Pierre,
*I am very sleepy as I just woke and went down to have a snack and back to bed, so I could not resist opening the mail and reading your messages, thus will have **nothing** for tomorrow morning, for my coffee, unless you will write to me some more, for tomorrow, for my morning coffee…*
Back to bed,
Danielle

And then a big smile spread on his face and his eyes lit…there is another one, another letter from his Danni:

My Darling Pierre,

I have woken up to a beautiful morning, and had a very long and pleasant time drinking my coffee under the pergola that I want you to see already and be under, with me. The last days are quite beautiful in Israel, and I wish I could share them with you. These moments of tranquil mornings, looking at the colors of the Bougainvillea that I so like, are very precious to me, and I would have liked that you will be here to share them with me, drinking your coffee and being soft and calm and relaxed with me, leaving every residue of cynicism, sarcasticness or rough humor, far away at the bottom of the Atlantic, and enveloping me with your soft feelings, your soft words, smiling so intelligent humor of yours, your rich deep voice, and not less importantly, your arms.

It seems that I have a need to share with you, the significant moments of my life, my day.

Remember, that when you are saying and writing that you are waiting for me for a long time, it is also I who awaits you for a long time.

Your story is unbelievably sharp and full of your humor. You should print these stories for publishing maybe one day. If you wish, I will be your editor. The use of words, sometimes, and the mixed realities are very interesting. I laughed loudly when reading it. You are quite imaginative.

Your poems as well, I would create a folder if I were you, and collect all these nice poems of yours, that each time, maybe without you realizing it, reflect your moods, thoughts, and your feelings.

Your letter reflects a somewhat edgy mood, a somewhat distant mood, a little sad? A little unsettled? No wonder the heroine writes a complaint letter to the editor, she might fear her hero is somewhat distant, and emotionally remoting himself from her? Good thing there is the Jerusalem Post to write a complaint to.

Have a calm, reassuring content day, my darling Pierre,

Look at the river for me, my darling Pierre and A very good night and very, very, sweet, soft and tender dreams,
Danielle

He sank deep down into his comforting sofa chair. His heart was beating hard, quickly but pleasantly. This Danni, this woman enchanted him. She had a hold over him. He was her slave. He was her ….hers. Yes..totally hers…He wondered whether she knew it. Whether she was aware of her powers over him. He was wondering so warmly when the sound of an E-mail arriving from his PC woke him to the real world.

E-mail Subject: No wonder…and don`t leave me alone

No wonder the patients keep coming, the office looks so cozy and warm and you look nice as well, how about more close ups of you for next time?

I was listening last night, at semi full volume to the nut cracker, by Tchaikovsky, and was so taken by the melody.

If I am there with you, and you leave me alone, and I listen to such encapturing classical ballet music, you might miss me dancing, which sometimes I do.

Thus….don`t leave me alone..my darling….

My wake-up kisses are on the way.

Good morning and a sunny day is wished for you.

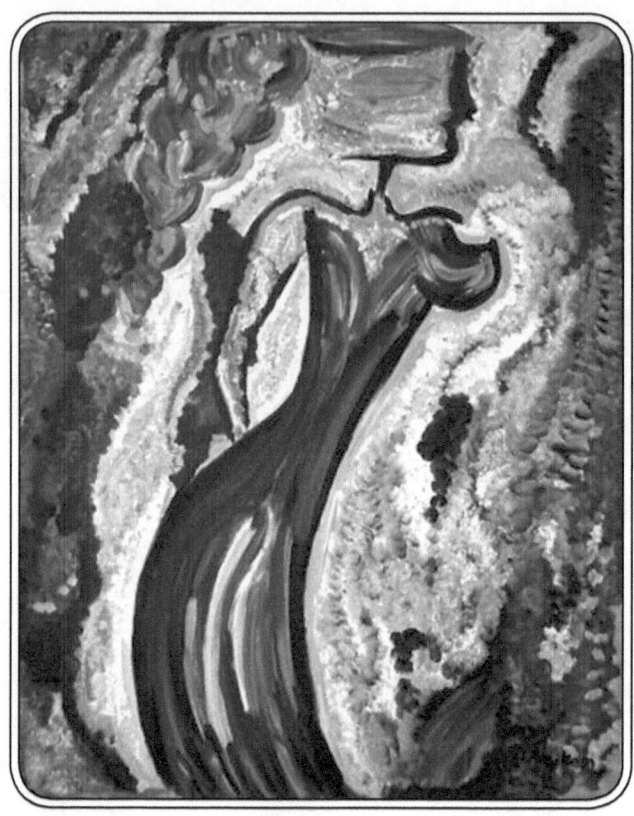

Yes, he sighed, he was definitely hers and the more he got from her the more he wanted. The more he learned of her the more curious he became of her.

A strong smell of detergent mixed with the pleasant odor of fresh linen were invading Anthony's conscience. Intuitively his eyelids opened a crack. Everything around him was white. The Yellow changed to White. It was for a minute somewhat refreshing, offering a sense of security and Anthony felt confident enough to open his eyes a bit more. He scanned this new environment that was engulfing him, being still partial as to his liking it. All was White. Actually a strong White. A blunt bold White. The White evolved with every second passing to a threatening dominating color, and accompanied with the almost coughing-causing smells surrounding him he began to feel threatened.

The White was closing on him and hurting his eyes, and the strong odors of detergents were hurting his throat. He began to shrink in his bed, understanding that he is in the Army Hospital, on the grounds of his camp. He knew this Hospital all too well. There were endless visits here and he hated each and every one of them. He always came, to support and look after his buddies. But the truth to be told, he did not like to enter this place, this hospital. He was afraid he would end up being there one day. They all knew that it was a package deal. The war came with the hospital. He always tried to repress these thoughts. Today, he did not have the time and the wants to face those thoughts. He did not wish to face this reality of him being helpless in that bed he was laying in. He would rather, as much as the sheets smelled so freshly, lay in the ragged old ugly Sofa, with Her. She did not even tell him what her name was. She did not tell him anything. He never heard her voice, that day. He called her, Her.

Suddenly the Yellow was so tempting. The Yellow was so promising and protecting. He missed it. A sharp pain woke him to reality again and he looked at his belly where it originated, it was all red again. No, he did not like the White surrounding him, neither the Red. He dozed off to his choice, the Yellow. He felt safe there. He could almost taste the strong taste of the black coffee he was served. He could certainly smell the warm delicious aroma, of the black Turkish coffee that contained some hel, an ingredient they use in these parts of the world. They were all sipping the coffee, from these small ornamented and decorated glasses, with which they were served to, by the women. It was very quiet around the small, low, old and scratched, wooden table that stood in the center of the big room. They were all men. Local men, but him. He was the only American and he knew it was an exceptional event. It was very rare if at all that the local people here, would invite a foreigner to drink coffee with them under their roof. There were many reasons as to why, among them their fear for being considered as cooperators with the foreigners and thus a possible death sentence might be declared for them. He thus, appreciated their hospitality, and wanted to make the best out of it. It was very important to him to be accepted by them. It would be his ticket to Her.

But, he was not deceived by the good aroma of the coffee and the delicious taste of the Hel in it. The bare walls were more presenting their feelings towards him. They did not want him there. They did not need an intervention in their so comfortable routine, their unthreatened expected life and tradition. He was symbolizing a possible change, the unknown, the unfamiliar future.

She came in, all in black, with some other women, family members, all carrying beautifully decorated tin trays covered with some more coffee and a variety of food. They all walked around the room soundlessly, like nymphs of the sea, almost floating, dancing around, and very careful to keep their eyes down. Their long, black so feminine lashes covering, like shutters, their whole entity. Yet, with only these long beautiful black shutters shown, it was a teasing sight. These shutters, these lashes screamed volumes of womanhood. These lashes moving somewhat up and then quickly down, screamed volume of control. Of strength. This so fragile feminine organ represented Her, and actually he felt the led one. She was deciding and he was following. She knew how to play with her lashes and he was their prisoner.

He tried so hard to focus and concentrate in the ornamented coffee glasses. He already knew every curve and scratch the old little table carried proudly showing its old age. But, his eyes, sometimes, as having their own will, as obeying her long beautiful lashes, were raised for a split second, trying hungrily to catch a glimpse of Her. To catch a glimpse of Her eyes. How he longed to see them again. How he longed to validate his lust, his love, his almost uncontrollable attraction to Her. And of course he so necessarily, so urgently needed to feel that she is still magnetized to him. That she is still dominating him. That she is still so softly, so bewitchingly, wanting to share her womanhood with him.

He felt that he does not exist unless she would acknowledge him with her long avoiding lashes.

His teeth were grinding the rice and without realizing it he had already finished a whole bowel of well-prepared white rice with some lamb meat. He looked down at his bowel embarrassed a bit, for maybe seeming to anxious, too hungry, but knowing that it was a good sign for their hospitality, to be a grateful guest, a satisfied guest and empty his bowel, he smiled very faintly to himself, not wanting to intrude on the serious, very serious and quiet atmosphere of the room. A tantalizing smell of Jasmine, just brushed his nostrils. A strong flash of memory, the pleasant memory was flooding him. He felt he was turning red in his face. He felt all warm. The light Jasmine smell came nearer to him, while reminding him of their stormy encounter on the old ugly Sofa the other day. Yes, it was also then that he smelled this magical smell of Jasmine, dipped slightly in the odor of Her sweat, the odor of the harsh black material that covered Her from his eyes, Her dress, all mixed with the variety of smells coming from the Market, outside the door of that Room. A cocktail of smells so unique, forever theirs.

Funny, he thought to himself, how little he knew of her, how little he saw of her, and how much, so much that he shared with her. He raised his head slowly as to not offend anyone, and managed to breathe so deeply to suck as much as he could, this Jasmine scent, her entity, her being into his, when she was exactly bending to serve him with some more rice. With his lungs full of scent, full with her, he was all tense and ready for her and she responded, as she decided, as she wanted, with a small quick flickering of her black lashes, allowing her eyes to draw him with passion.

He melted. He felt he almost disappeared almost evaporated. She had total control over him. She was one of the strongest women he had ever encountered. *With her Burka, with her Veil, with her long black dress, she was a strong woman...*And he let himself be led...led to his beautiful, magical, mysterious Jasmine...

Again, he felt that moisture...that dampness, again almost wet..yes wet.. Pierre woke up again, sweating heavily as before, opened his eyes and was surprised again, relieved, and again somewhat sorry, he was at home...

safe but far away from Her…he wondered who She is. He hurried to his PC anxious to find a mail…a soothing loving mail from his beloved Danni

And he found one:
As one…

Just finished listening to Emma Kirkby opera-like songs, and now Leonard Cohen is in semi-full volume singing "Dance me to the end of love" Where are you? Can you Dance? To the end of love? If you were here, I would cling to your body, we would be as one, dancing to the end of love, every inch of my body would be feeling yours, and your hands will strongly go slowly over my back, until the song will sadly be finished, and reality will strike-you are not here, I open my eyes, and you are not here, but the next song starts, I can dream a little bit longer, what comfort, the soothing voice of Leonard Cohen and your entity, your body is engulfing me, almost swallowing me, moving to the rhythm that mine moves, and again we are as one, so close, emotionally and physically, as one…,

God bless there is Leonard Cohen, he is still singing…
And I continued:

So, It would have been nice if you were here, now, since some friends came over, and brought with them some delicious Shawarma and Falafel, (since all my friends know that I do not especially like to cook and my plans to learn to cook and enjoy it are for when I will be 65) from one of the best places around and we have just finished eating this delicious food, under the Pergola, in the garden. I would like to take you to the place they sell it, so you can try it, it is not a fancy restaurant, but one that serves a lot of soldiers, army people and everybody on the road, from south to north and we people around the area sometimes drive especially over there to buy some good food to take away or to eat there.
It is a nice day here in Zichron.

As to your question my father's name is Arie Achi-Ze'ev Goldbear which is; Arie is lion, which is the name he was named when was born, in Czechoslovakia. When he ran away, bravely from a work camp in Europe, with minimal chances of surviving, he arrived in Israel and changed his name from Greenberger to Goldbear. And then since his adored older brother died when the Americans freed some working camps and from a good thinking gave the starving people too much to eat and thus killed them that way, he decided that his name, forever will be, also, the brother of Wolf, his brother's name and thus in Hebrew-Achi Ze'ev.

I was brought up to be quite a proud woman and thus have kept my father's name even after being married, and hence the Goldbear in my name, and the Yehoshafat from my husband and thus, Danielle Goldbear Yehoshafat. (by the way my name, is spelled GOLDBEAR). My father is 85 years old, and retired from a very high profile position in the police and the foreign office long time ago, and is living on his good retirement money, and if anybody is supporting anybody, (never a need in financial terms) it is my father that is always there for me, at all times, like a rock. (I was never supported financially by my parents) He is very Jewish, not religious at all and the busiest person in the world, whenever I wished to meet him we would have to coordinate our schedules. He likes now days to read a lot, garden, take care of his daughter and cook for me some times. I love his Schnitzels and special meatballs. He lectures a lot for different audiences, immigrants, our age, young people, he studies at the university, involved and heads different organizations, like the congregation for Czechoslovakia, the management of the town of Haifa, second deputy to political party in Haifa. He is a well-known figure and much admired, by whoever knows him. I am blessed to have him as a father, and I always say, that in fact before I was born, I was flying up there, checking the ground, and thereafter, chose, both my parents, my mother and my father. Now days he has just published his book in English and Hebrew, telling the story of his brave escape from the working camp.

I got one mail from your office yesterday, so if there were more, why don`t you send them? Your day seems to have been full and with surprises and activities. Do you go every afternoon with the dogs walking in the woods?

It is raining so beautifully right now, with a delicate color of the twilight.

Your dog Parsley sounds nice, what do you mean that she is at a very primitive level? She wouldn't be able to read Dostoyevsky to me? Your last letter was getting better by the line like a good wine, aging nicely. I like to read about your day, your thoughts and feelings.

Winter is coming now to Israel and today was the first rain, which cleans the air and brings about a fresh smell to the air of the summer in the desert-like Israel.

I have received the art book you have sent me -thank you. It will be nice to read it per se, and also because you have thought about it and bought it for me.

Good morning, enjoy your coffee, your day, and my smile, and be good to your patients,

Yours,
Danielle

CHAPTER SIXTEEN

Jan-Paul... A Prologue

"I am over at the airport, see you soon." His voice sounded like always somewhat low and shallow, with a depressed taste to it and a mysterious, closed tone.

I was wearing my tan slacks and a white, super tight, very complimenting to my toned figure shirt. I wanted to dress simply yet very feminine and alluring. This was my chance to captivate Jan-Paul. I was so deeply in love with him. I prepared everything I was capable of thinking of ahead. My hair looked beautiful soft and blond, falling to my shoulders, freshly done at the hairdresser yesterday.

I came back home from the hairdresser stopping to see Cherie, to show off, and her assistance just caught a glimpse of me entering, she gasped for air and semi shouted" MYYYY You look FAaantastic" I smiled at her embarrassed that at my age I was like a teen ager so excited, and I did not want her to know what of, but I was glowing and it was written all over me that I am probably getting pretty and ready to meet a man. And what a man I thought. I was attracted to Jan-Paul with all my being, intellectually, physically, spiritually, I actually almost ached to the thought of meeting him, ached in my heart and my gut.

Cherie smiled, knowing all this and said "You look great Danielle", as always supporting and doing so with a graceful collected mature voice. She knew of my fears of meeting a man, The Man, after such a long time of being by myself, after Michael passed away. So many years have passed, I never found any of all the men and there were quite a few, attractive and appealing to me, and here I was going to meet a man with whom I have corresponded and talked with over the phone and got to know him for over a year and a half. I was almost exploding from the expectations. The fears.

Would I like him in person? Would he like me? "Oh Danielle he will be swept away by you. He will be smitten with you." She said re-assuring last night when we went shopping for some clothes and jewelry for a possible late dinner with Jan-Paul should all proceed as I planned and so wanted. So dreamt of. So wished. The gray body fitting shirt decorated with shiny black beads looked so nice on me, especially on top of that camisole, the lady at the shop explained to me, with its lovely delicate lace showing shyly yet fully emphasizing the feminine body it was on. Mine. I was enjoying the process although looked forward to the realization, materialization, finally, of falling in love with another man. Being a woman and feeling so. I was not a scientist now, neither a widow, but a blushing entity, so busy with discovering love again. So immersed in a new world, a world of her dreams, of her reality well mixed with her fantasies. This was an exceptional moment, reality, and event. Something that might lead to a whole new life. A whole new and exciting horizon was possibly opening now.

I was terrified not wanting to lose it. Once I tested a bit of its taste, its pleasure, its possible meaning for me for my future, I was terrified subconsciously and consciously as to how it will go.

I re-walked all over my condominium when waiting for him to make sure all was in order. The chair was at the right place, my lap top open and ready to make the right impression if needed, my women journals scattered over the leaving room table, but, but, let's not forget I AM a scientist, thus my professional journals were there as well. The right impression needed to be made and reflect me as I am, truly, A Woman, A very much of A Woman, but a scientist as well. I passed the wall mirror for the thousand times, looking briefly at myself and got my confirmation for my looks when suddenly the doorbell rang. My heart stopped beating for a second, then a very calm, collected and easy feeling overtook me and I went to the door and opened it with a smile, a very light and comfortable one. He stood there, with a light blue shirt and white pants and his head tilted to the left the minute my look descended on him. "Hello" I opened the door invitingly and he stepped in.

It was like I knew him for ages. I felt so at ease and surprisingly he seemed to feel so himself.

CHAPTER SEVENTEEN

THERE ARE CIRCLES TO LIFE

The corridor was swarming with people, as always, nurses running around, some with their faces semi closed, some with faces projecting a hurriedness mixed with some worry and softness, but most were distanced, detached and somewhat cold, but extremely efficient. I was, as always startled with the strong smell of the ward, a dominant smell projecting for me harshness and a world of a fight to survive. It is amazing how smells can translate in a person's mind to an emotional entity. Like the first rain, where ever whenever, would always baer for me with its accompanying fresh smell the memories of my childhood in Ethiopia with the soft sound of the drops on the tin roofs sending secure and protective feelings, with a soft smile to my thinking.

Now, I definitely did not have a soft smile. I stepped forward in the corridor towards Simcha's room, my steps and my figure projecting all that I felt, humbled by fate turns for Simcha, yet very strong for Josh. I entered the room and caught a glimpse of the sharp strong look of Josef's eyes, that were able at a mini second to express his so many thoughts and feelings of that exact moment, a cocktail of a welcome look for me that changed its warmth for the knife-like sharp professional gaze accompanied by a short snappy hello.

He was standing at the bed side of Simcha, busy with studying his skin color that as I saw immediately has turned a bit yellowish. Not a good sign. Part of me tried to avoid Simcha's eyes. I found it hard to look Simcha straight in the eye and encounter his soul. His sad, yet trying to look brave, knowing it all soul. But, as reality demanded, I reached down to my energy reserves and straightened my chin and met his eyes, telling him all that I felt with this encounter. All. The warm feelings I bear for him. The hope I bear for his son. For Josh. All that I can do for him and his son. All that I cannot do for him and for his son. Simcha and I did not have to talk. We knew each other so well and for such a long time, that our eyes had their own way of talking.

"Well, I will let you too have some quality time" Josef smiled at Simcha and stepped out of the room while giving me a meaningful glance conveying the urgency of which he wanted the DNA results. Josef, knew the special way of which Simcha and I were communicating. He knew that Simcha needs this quality encounter. But he also knew, as always, the bottom line priorities, thus for me to spend a few minutes with Simcha, important minutes, possibly last minutes and his whole world right now, but still there was the urgent task of locating the exact place of the mutation for colon cancer in Josh's DNA.

I bade Josef farewell with a responding quick look letting him know that we are on the same page, and shifted my whole entity, my whole being to Simcha.

He too knew it all.

Thus my big brown eyes, that were always strong and purposeful, betrayed me today and were like an open window to my heart. No, more like an open huge door, to my soul. They were soft, a little wet, and all the green in them was gone, the warm almond color took over. Totally.

Simcha reached for my hand.

He squeezed it with strength yet not strongly hurting. He squeezed it with warmth and re-assurance, and my hand responded immediately almost automatically with a "Yes" squeeze back.

The look at his eyes was starting to change from an intense one, doing his utmost to shift me back to track, transferring me his energy and strength, his last, for his child, for his future, for me, to a quiet, engulfing peaceful look, conveying his acceptance of reality.

His eyes were now shifting from the difficult task of comforting me, strengthening me, to his own world, his inner tranquil somewhat tired world.

His head moved away, as though he wanted to end our conversation. Our unique way of communicating. He wished to be by himself, with himself.

I reached for his other hand. It seems that his other hand had a will of itself, wanting, wishing, to please me, caressing gently very softly my searching hand.

Simcha's body started to relax. His stressed tensed muscles were loosening slowly, and his body became bigger and lay more comfortably more assuring in his bed.

He won. He was now fearless, laying in his bed, his empire for now, his kingdom his world, all strong and tranquil, facing what is ahead with open eyes.

Open eyes in his soul.

His eyes were closed.

His hands left mine, gently.

His breath was steady, and then stopped.

Simcha left.

My way back to the lab, this time, seemed longer than usual. My face was blank. I did not feel anything. It was like I was on "automatic drive". My senses knew the way and led me back. I did not know where I was. I hardly felt the colder air that was coming from northern Europe. They said it was going to rain today. In midsummer. Oh well. My mind could not process any thought and was just roaming around, and erasing itself, like not being. It could not even cope with the weather. I entered the elevator and as always squeezed myself in to the almost full space, hardly noticing the many lips moving on the different faces surrounding me, let alone hearing the sounds. I did not hear anything.

I knew, automatically at what floor to step out of the elevator and started heading to my lab. My pace got quicker and quicker I almost ran. I grabbed the door knob of the corridor of my lab, like it was a life saver, an anchor to the earth of life, a grip on a protecting reality.

The welcoming smell of my lab, of the bacteria grown, of the cell lines grown, awoke me abruptly. It was like I was fainting and someone had given me some strong scents to smell. Some strong perfume to revive me. My lab smells were the perfume of life for me, now. I was shaken. Terribly shaken, and now I was beginning to come back to my world.

As Simcha had wished.

Exactly as he wanted.

I passed along one of the lab's rooms and continued to my office, stopping as I usually do at the coffee corner to prepare a good strong smelling coffee for me to enter my office with. I caught a glimpse of myself at the mirror there. I could not see anything, but that the green is coming back to my big almond colored eyes. The green is back. So good. I felt the other me again. I felt in control again, heading one of the most prestigious labs in the country and one respected in the world; my own lab.

My eyes turned down, while mixing the coffee I prepared in my favorite cup, that everyone in the lab knew not to use. It was my ritual. Every morning. I opened the small refrigerator that we purchased from some money donated from a good soul caring for our day at the lab. I smiled. Shachar had remembered to buy my favorite milk. Coffee without milk, would be like an egg cooked a minute short for an Englishman. They all knew that my morning had to start with a good strong coffee, touched with some milk. I raised my eyes while closing the refrigerator, securing the milk in it, to meet Shachar's.

Her look said it all. She knew about Simcha, and she knew me well enough not to talk about it, but rather do the necessary thing now: find the exact location of the mutation.

But she also knew how to caress my emotional world with her soft look and semi sad smile, saying, that the GEL is already running comparing all DNA samples amplified in the recent hours by the PCR.

"We will be wiser in a few hours, Danielle" Her soft voice noted.

"Yes, we will" I replied, with my strong voice, uttering the latter three words that were actually symbolizing and meaning so much.

Yes, we will go through this.

Yes, we will find the location of the mutation.

Yes, we will save josh.

Yes, we will.

And that was Simcha's legacy.

I entered my office, with my coffee cup in my hand, and headed to my chair.

I sat in my big executive's chair, putting my weight back so it will tilt a bit backwards. I took a long sip out of my hot almost boiling coffee, tasting its deep strong aroma, while smelling it as well, and I suddenly felt at home. I relaxed in my chair, looking at all the different files and papers scattered around on my desk, in their own specific order.

Yes, the weather indeed changed. I was still sipping my coffee thinking that after Spring stopped by; in midsummer winter came now for a day or two, but quite elegantly and romantically. I was looking at the window of my office. There was no thunder, just a smooth, soft, continuous rain all day long accompanied with lavender-colored skies. It was nice and a time for listening to the Opera all day long when writing or thinking or sorting out these piles of papers and files on my desk.

Today, as the whole world is, as life is sometimes, it seems that the weather too, is quite confused and winter came to visit in mid-summer. But Spring will be coming soon too.

"Danielle, she is waiting on the phone" Regina's harsh voice was penetrating my quite moment in my office.

Regina could only enter like that, abruptly to my office, without knocking on the door first, if it was very important. "Who is waiting?" my voice was calm and collected. No hurry. "Yael, Prof. Tal" She answered a bit panicky. "Well on what line is she on?"

"Number two" her face reflected worry and anxiety. Yael headed the most prestigious cancer institute in Israel, in Jerusalem, and was famous worldwide.

I pressed the line on my phone, immersing totally in this new reality, my lips smiled warmly yet withholding some distance. "Danielle, hi, I have got to have some good news from you, it was a disastrous day over here." She sounded warm and inviting. I knew that kind of voice of her was used when she really needed something from me.

"I am glad you called, Yael"

She was puzzled. I could hear it through the silence over the line. She did not understand the tone of my voice, neither the words. How could I be glad to her call when she is asking so much and expecting an answer? How could I welcome her so warmly when she needs to know, now, at that minute, what kind of a mutation did the L girl bear? She was confused for a slight second. "Her sister just gave birth, Danielle, we must know if there was a mutation and if yes what was its sequence, Danielle" she said with a speedy technical voice "I know I am asking a lot, but our L-girl has a niece!?" She said when being all. Being happy thus a warm side to her voice, being an oncologist thus a technical strong demanding voice, being a colleague, a professional needing my help, thus asking for it. Questioning whether she could have it today.

"Oh, wow, that is so great" I was so relieved. I was so relieved to hear this good news.

Someone is gone. And some one is born.
Someone is gone and someone is saved.
There are circles to life.
And not all are bad.

Again she sounded confused a bit. She wondered as to why I am so relieved. "Danielle, you realize that we need an answer!?" I heard her questioning yet emphasizing. "Yes, Yael. I do. And we have."

I took a long sip of my still hot strong coffee, a deep breath and started sharing with Yael the new data we have found regarding our beloved L-girl.

CHAPTER EIGHTEEN

THE OCEAN AND CHINA,
A SAFE HARBOR

It was mid-autumn.

There was a big heat wave around the world and also here, thus I learned to sneak out very early for my morning walk on the beach, when not running on my treadmill at home. This was quite rare, since I would usually have to be the Medical center at around 8AM, for a faculty meeting, a lecture I gave or just attend to my lab, but I usually was at my office already at 7AM, before everybody got in, before the commotion, the activity started to shift to a higher gear, so I could be with myself, with my coffee, and sort out the day ahead of me, undisturbed. These were usually my most precious moments at work, when I could think and not just automatically react to reality evolving.

This morning I decided to take a walk on the beach at around 6AM. I had a very big and different day ahead of me and I had to collect myself and my thoughts, meditate somewhat and be ready for this day, this week and what it will bring for me. The sky was totally blue and the ocean was green, jade like. I liked Jade. Yes, the color was soothing and was immersed in the culture and history of traditional China for me, thus mysterious, with emperors and concubines and princes and strong beautiful women paving their way in the path of life in ancient China.

Today the Ocean and China were a safe harbor for me and my soul, and a place for my thoughts to find refuge and solace. For today was a very draining day for me. My walking pace increased while I breathed deeply the fresh ocean air, with my eyes trying to engulf, to contain, to swallow hungrily the beautiful scene and views surrounding me. Those would serve later on today as some precious food for my brain and my thoughts when facing my oophorectomy.

Yes, my own oophorectomy. Not someone else's, not a counseled patient of mine, but my own, BRCA2 gene carrying DNA-resulted oophorectomy. I wanted to go through it as smoothly, if that can ever be, as I can, and with what I truly had control of. I could not control the oophorectomy. I could not do it for myself. I had to put myself in the hands of my onco-gynecologist and I needed to stop worrying about that. I needed to shut that channel of thoughts completely so I could concentrate on what I could control and how, to best go through with my scheduled for later today oophorectomy. I could also not control the results of the biopsy samples taken from my ovaries, thus this, although being a huge burden would just have to be ignored for now. Thinking of the latter two did take away some strength from me.

Today I am stepping one more step into my reality, my personal one and I needed to equip myself with whatever and as many tools I can so I would be able to go ahead and do what is needed to be done. The sky was colored with a very grey-lavender like color and the ocean changed to a mixture of white, soft light green and gray. A nonstop drizzle of very soft, silky like rain drops, began and I was wondering how it would feel for my beach walk. I was wearing a sweatshirt, and the air was a bit cooler, and it felt like being in August on the northeast coast of the US, like at The Hamptons…. It was lovely. Now this is a good beginning. This is a good feeling and some good thoughts to be armed with for my drive to the Medical Center. For tomorrow they were expecting on the weather channel that the sun will come back, I was thinking while delaying my ride a bit longer and lingering on the beach and enjoying it.

Yes, tomorrow will be a new day! A new day for the beach, with the sun shining back, and a new day for me. The sun will shine for me as well!

Thus, I stepped to my golden CRV Honda, reassured somewhat and drove to the medical center.

"I am a good nurse, Danielle, you would love me around." Brian was pressuring me so hard, last night.

"I would make you comfortable, and I would prepare some tea for you, and it would all be easier if I would be around, in the hospital and at home with you," his voice was unusually warm and pleading. No, not warm, for Brian could not have a warm voice, but as much as his metal-like voice could have become inviting, emotional and warm. "I don't think so Brian" I answered weakly. I was torn. It would have been nice to have someone with me. A friend. It would have been nice to let go of control a bit, and have someone else take care of my well-being. Of my emotional world as well. I yearned to put my head, on Brian's shoulders and let him take care of me. It would have been nice to just close my eyes, relax my being and forget myself in peacefulness, while knowing and assured that all is taken care of and all is safe.

But I needed to feel as a woman when first meeting the man who has courted me for the last months. I did not want my first date with him to be with me in bed, probably weak and pale, dressed in a hospital gown, in a room with other patients. No. I have to be strong for a better future. For my needs. And my need to be a woman, to be perceived as a woman, as a feminine creature, just grew stronger and harder, when tackling all this BRCA business.

No, I wanted him to smell my exotic perfume, when looking into my big, endless, deep, brown eyes. I wanted him to feel a mysterious sensation when touching my hand.

I wanted him to be captivated with me physically and emotionally, as a woman. Not as a patient. Brian was an emergency room doctor. I did not want any of his professional life and experience having a bearing on our first date as a man and a woman.

So I will come a week later, he offered, slightly demanding, using a decisive color of tone in his voice, probably the one he is using with his patients.

I did not want to discourage him. I liked him. I did not want this to develop into an argument, nor an ego battle. Knowing myself, I knew I would need a few weeks, three or four to be at my best. To be as I, as I, Danielle, liked myself. But he was impatient.

"Ok, Brian, in two weeks I will meet you here in Israel," I answered with a small sweet voice, an inviting warm voice, as I was giving in to him, which I felt I was. But, it was good. It was good to look for something new scheduled after my oophorectomy. It was good to look forward to materialize my femininity after my oophorectomy.

I then remembered….

"What can I do for you?" Was Jan-Paul immediate reaction to my BRCA2 news…"Would you want me to come?"

"No," I said calmly and decisively…I had a great almost uncontrollably urge to let Jan-Paul in on what was happening to me. I have phoned him almost ten times but he would not answer…I did not know why. Was he seeing another lady? Was he ignoring me when I needed so urgently emotionally to share with him my new reality? I did not want to be with Jan-Paul any more. He has failed me and I was deeply disappointed with him. So why did I need him to know of what is happening to me? He has a right to see other women. He has a right to not answering my phone calls. Yet it was him. It was him and no one else that I so needed to share my new present with. My new future. My thoughts feelings, wants and fears. I needed to hear his voice.

But my analytical, rational, realistic part of my brain and heart protected me and I answered collected and in control, calmly and strongly, No Jan-Paul, I will go about it by myself. I actually wanted him to feel how strong I was. How strong I am. How I can be by myself. How I do not need him by me. "Where were you for the last weekend, I have been calling you for several times?" "Oh" he answered with his un-emotional distant voice "I was driving around the Keys, the Florida Keys and forgot my cell phone at the hotel."

So he is in Florida, I thought.....Came from cold Sharasesha. And enjoying himself in Florida, maybe going out with this lady friend he knew and I am here by myself. But You left him! I reminded myself. I cannot afford these paths of thoughts I reminded myself. "Can I call you, my dear?" His voice pleaded. He wanted to stay in touch.....He did not want to let go. Every minute way of staying in touch with me would mean to him a possible re uniting with me. Every possible way of letting him a glimpse to my life meant the world to him. "No, don't call and also don't e-mail to me" I added knowing when I do open that route for him I would receive at least one mail a day each day of the week of the month of the year and I will not be able to properly close the doors of my heart towards his existence. It would be a constant battle, an unneeded one.

"OK, let me know what I can do." He said. "OK" I answered. Satisfied emotionally. At least partially. Goodbye my voice managed to say and I hung up transferring myself to my surrounding and immediate reality.

I remembered by heart my letter to Pierre.
It was having the heading: *no hard feelings*

Well, I have semi-joined your club:

A week ago, my childhood best friend called me and told me that she had found that she has inherited the BRCA2 mutated gene from her mother, and thus I should consider being tested for it as well, since I had lost my mother to ovarian cancer. It is funny, because usually it is I who diagnose patients and give the genetic counseling.

So, I had my blood test a week ago, and instead of waiting a month, since they knew me, they did a fast job and I am a carrier of the mutated gene as well.

What does that mean?

1. That I have up to 54 % chance of having ovarian cancer-thus am taking action for removal of my ovaries, a simple 2 day stay in the hospital for removal of the ovaries, planning to undergo this within 3-5 weeks if possible.

*2. I am at risk of up to 85% of having breast cancer, a **possibility**, not a current reality, and in fact, because of harboring the mutated gene, am eligible to a yearly follow up with MRIs, thus if there, cancer should be detected very early. (that is again, if there, could pass a lifetime, till age 100, with nothing)*

Actually, it is rather a good result, since every 1 of 7 women now days from the age of 30-70 will have breast cancer. From ages 50-70 every 1 of 5. Anyhow, every woman nowadays, including me is undergoing mammography, for early detection, and thus it is in every woman's mind and possible future. Of the women that have breast cancer quite a high percentage will be cured. BRCA2 carriers, even have a better chance. Knowing it, and following up with MRI gives one a better chance- more than any other, non-following up, or regular woman who is not a carrier or is not aware of her being a carrier, as was I and thus following up only with mammography-a less sensitive technique- of discovering it (should it arouse) in time for treatment and total cure.

I felt that in all fairness although my situation is different than yours, and I am not sick with cancer, and did not have cancer, and it is just a possibility, that you should know.

If that information, for whatever reason, makes you feel that you would not like to continue our relationship, please feel free to write so, no hard feelings.

Danielle,

"I will accept you with no breasts, Danni, do what you need to do honey I will accept you any way shape or form. If you need to also go under a total mastectomy and take of your breasts, please consider it and do what you need to do," Pierre said in a warm protective voice.

I was puzzled. A mastectomy? Taking of my beautiful breasts? It did not occur to me. Not yet. Had I been counseling to a patient this would be a natural first step first suggestion….an oophorectomy and a double mastectomy thus reduce the risk of cancer. Reduce the existing 85% risk of breast cancer by to almost 7% or even lower as described by some published papers. "I love you Danni, save your life." His voice was even warmer and so supportive and the one he is probably so well trained to use with his patients and as a psychologist.

"Thank you Pierre," I said partially grateful for his acceptance, partially angry that this stage has risen and partially frightened. I locked these thoughts up, I was not ready to contemplate them and thus could coldly somewhat answer that it is not in my agenda and while answering gaining confidence and telling him while persuading myself that Pierre there is another alternative and it is a very tight routine screening twice to three times a year Pierre with the state of the art techniques Pierre (or was it Danielle? Was it Danielle that I was answering and so heartfuly investing in and persuading?) and a follow up with the Gyno-oncologist and a Breast Surgeon, an MRI a year and Ultrasound twice a year and even a mammography to throw in thus I would be protected and if and when the slightest "thing" (I could not yet say "tumor") would be revealed, it would be in very early stages and I would be able to" take care" of it.

"You see Pierre," I was already somewhat stronger and had summoned my professional strength, "I am actually lucky to be under such tight surveillance and should any malignant cells be discovered I would have the proper time to deal with them."

I was encouraged. Pierre seemed to be as well. In a very relaxed masculine assuring voice he add "well Danni, my love, I am here for you"

I was equipped with all those thoughts feelings and supportive men in my day. On this day. I felt the soft wind brush against my face. I felt so pure and genesis-like and strong as the rock I was looking at in the deep waters in the sea...

There was a golden ray in my horizon and hope with its strength was seeded in my soul.

Thus I wrote him,

My Darling Pierre,

It was so soothing to hear your voice after a day of tests. I was the whole day in Haifa, morning with Mammography, late afternoon with ultra sound, a core biopsy might be done tomorrow, again in Haifa, in Rashi, and I will take it from there.

I like your low, so rich voice, it comforts me.

I love the boat that you have bought me for my birthday! What a nice surprise, fantastic, I want to sail in it with you, already tomorrow, or the soonest possible.   What a nice plan to have. When and if you have the opportunity, send me pictures of it. Can you describe the boat some more, where is it now? I think I will name her "Twilight" to signify our new life together, our beautiful lavender-colored twilight phase of life together….

To have you, and the boat….I am blessed…

I am glad all your friends approve of you dating again, that is good and that is the way it should be, they all seem to be emotionally healthy, open, broad minded people.

*Yes, I am happy this minute, to have **you**, and the boat.*

I left the message on your cellular, after listening to your opening, so there is no fear of a stranger phoning, I might have talked very low, it might have not recorded.

A very good morning to you, my content-happy smile is accompanying you, this lovely sunny and blue-sky-day,

And...My Darling Pierre,

I read your morning mails with a smile, enjoying the flow of the text and the meaning of the words and what is in between the words and lines. I slept a little less well but I imagine that was natural and tonight I will already sleep dreaming sweet dreams. I have had a very nice morning; it started with your mails that have put a smile on my lips and I proceeded down stairs to prepare my coffee. This is a magical time for me, the sunrays are on the kitchen counter and the first floor looks so rich and beautiful with the Persian rugs, the wooden furniture, some Moroccan pillows and old light fixtures, with everything enveloped by the rich yet not suffocating draperies, and still there is an air of openness and a lot of light and all the greenery from the garden is entering the house through the numerous big windows. Such tranquility. Such privacy. Such musical calming silence.

Your poem about what makes a woman is so nice, accurate, and although I know it, from previous experience, is always heartwarming, even with no connection to the specific situation I am in. If the poem is specifically referred to me, from you, then it is twice as nice.

Having said that, I accept your offer from a previous letter to be examined daily by you, after all you are a doctor (does not matter what kind) and it seems that for now, you are my doctor, and since I do have to be under some kind of a follow up, why not this kind and by you, daily, some times in the mornings, sometimes at night, although personally I prefer the noon times, and for that I would have to surprise you and visit you at your office, and be examined by you, so pleasurably, on your big table, with your secretary keeping an eye on the patients, who so patiently would wait for their dear doctor, to be done with his sudden, much needed, lunch break.

Come, come do enter me and warm my heart
My heart
We are what we are, and for us, each of us, is an angel,

I am now getting dressed to go to Haifa, to the Onco-gynecologist.

I have read your deep so open and sharing letter, and enjoyed reading it again, so nicely written, so touching with no need for "defense" and thus lets me enter even deeper into your thoughts and my feelings.

That could be nice, that you would retire when I come, or at least find a lot of time to be with me, with us, with our new world.

I have received your book and started reading it, and it lets me have a small window to your soul, from which I learn a lot. I am realizing, what I already knew, how different you are from me in self-disclosure, due to your profession, your personality, your openness, your confidence, and since you know to respect other people's privacy and needs, and since I am a very open minded person, I think we might enjoy our encounter. I find your book to be very interesting from many angles, such as using a very silly cute phrase to build any situation and reality that you wish. I find this book to be very creative, and also allowing a person, with its humor, to put things in to perspective; the world does not fall down for every problem we encounter. I am still reading it. It is nice that the angels, sometimes as us, in the jar looking outside of the shop to the world, and the world is watching the angels, us in the jar. But the angels; us, are dancing and happy, not realizing, not caring that someone might be looking at them, at us, like we are something different, in a jar to look at. Because, we are what we are, and for us, each of us, is an angel, a dancing one, a unique one, a confident one.

I have to go and choose what kind of perfume, jewelry and clothes will fit my mood and get going.

It is Thursday and the weekend is approaching,

Danielle

CHAPTER NINETEEN

I Was Ripe, I Was Ready, I Needed

I laid on my lounge chair on the beach about 3 feet from the water, dozing off not really reading my book, only partially aware of the soothing sound of the soft waves coming in and out, in and out at a repeated pattern, a calming pattern, providing a certain kind of supportive consistency.

I loved being in Myrtle Beach. It was a whole new world and quite different from New York. It was a good change that I was always looking forward to, after a dynamic hectic international conference in New York where one was absorbed with the pressing reality and vacuumed to a jet pace of living, doing business, delivering and closing deals. I was always handling the latter with flying colors, participating in discussion groups, heading sessions, delivering my lecture and attending the Gala nights always beautiful and attractive as ever, a very appealing feminine figure at nights who appeared as a bright, sharp and successful scientist during the day. It took effort and energy but I have flourished doing so and my eyes were always bright and my mind was always going after and thinking of the next research to analyze, perform or participate in. I enjoyed the fast pace, the jet pace living but part of me also needed and loved anonymity and solitude.

Part of me enjoyed the long nightgowns and expensive jewelry that decorated me accompanied by the admiring glances of the male and female fellow scientist, the healthy strong laughter and chatting in the Gala nights, but definitely, definitely a huge part of me liked and yearned for walking on the deserted beach with my short torn jeans and my face bare of any make up. I belonged to both worlds no question about it. But when being in my former one I longed to my present one, just be and breath, with no need to smile to, please, be clever for and pretty in the eyes of, someone else.

Here in Myrtle Beach I could be my most inner me and be one with nature. I could inhale nature and be nourished by it, be calmed and stable and rooted to the true inner strong world of mine.

The sun warmed me and the rays caressed my body and I felt that muscle after muscle, part after part of my body was relaxing and melting and all tension was gone.

I was thinking of my recent e-mail to my friend Marian. For some reason, although we were not communicating, I felt an urge and a need to send her a Happy New Year blessing for Rosh Hashanah.

I wrote:
Although we do not like each other, Marian, we do love each other. I love you.
I am lately thinking a lot of you and thus wanted to wish you Chag Sameach and Shannah Tova.

I did not receive an answer. A small little troubling sense invaded my entity when re-hearing my father's respond to my sharing this with him.

"You are very brave, kind and generous, Deninka."

Well, brave I could understand. He meant that after all Marian and I are not in touch and it was kind of brave that I could initiate a communication with her.

Kind and generous I could also understand since she was very un kind to me and never responded to my efforts and never re-paid back with kindness or generosity to my ongoing efforts from time to time during the last 20 years, to re-establish some kind of a relationship between us, to act upon my love for her, as my friend, my childhood best friend, my shadow, something that was embedded in me, that was burned in my sub conscience although we did not like each other, apparently.

I loved her.

My soul burnt when I would hear of a wrong done to her or of a possible suffering of her.

But we needed our distance from each other. Marian harbored a lot of hostile feelings towards me that were cored and initiated in childhood and would never be there in a time of my need. She never shared with me my happy moments as my success as a scientist, or my buying a new beautiful home or marrying my beloved one my husband Michael…she always sort of tagged along with the latter not really happy for me and not really taking active part in those happy events. Neither did she take part in my sad events in life. She was not there for me in those terrible moments, hours or days of my loss, my greatest loss, the loss of my husband. She was hardly there when I, we, Michael and I fought for his life for six terrible hard months in the Emergency Unit, a battle we have lost. I was broken. I was devastated. It was incomprehendable for me to understand, to accept to absorb the notion the thought the idea that my husband, my friend, my lover and my Mentor was gone. MY EVERYTHING was gone not to be anymore.

Marian was not there for me at those hard times. On the Shivea days, when my physical body was there to meet the flowing in river of people who felt more abandoned than I when Michael left them on this earth, I had to make sure she was there too.

"Tell her to come tomorrow" I casted a sharp look at my father and almost ordered him to make her come each day of the Shivea, although I felt that she was doing so reluctantly. And her family followed her. Because Marian was one of those people that was in control of all her family and her wishes, wants and needs were taken into consideration first and foremost.

Even though, and although, I had a soft caring loving spot in my heart for Marian, I loved her, I did not like her.

So, I understood my father's reaction to my sent e-mail to her.

But still, his voice was too serious too quite containing much more then was heard. I knew my father. I knew the small nuances of his voice and behavior. We were very good friends. I thought I must ask him, I should express my doubts as to my interpretations.

I brushed it all for now under an unseen rug in my mind and smiled with my soul and my lips when getting up from my comfortable lounge chair and walking lazily towards the shy waves. The water felt good and so did I.

The next morning, on my daily phone conversation with him from Myrtle Beach to Israel I asked "Aba, what did you mean by saying I was brave, kind and generous?" I loved these talks, these chats with him. We were so open he was such a good friend and a bright wise one and it was a pleasure and a privilege to be his daughter and share his time.

"Marian is very ill now, I did not want to tell you" he said with a voice that harbored a deep pain, patience for me, a need to protect me and with all those, his voice most of all conveyed strength. "What do you mean ill?!" my voice was alarmed, frightened and fearing the worst, the waiting to be in the corner the one thing my sub conscience took a very great care not to deal with at all. The big one thing.

"She has Cancer" The line went quiet. "Breast Cancer?!" I shot out my question sharply with a demanding voice? "Yes" came the answer. "Wow" I said in a soft breaking sound. And then my natural defense mechanisms took over and I reacted a bit scientifically. "How can that be? Has not she been taking all the necessary tests all the routine screenings?" It was easier on me, addressing the technical cold matters, the scientific issues then the personal news.

The news that my childhood wonderland-mate has Breast Cancer. My so very best friend, my shadow, whom I loved so much, whom I did not like.

"Yes she has but the last one was one year ago" he pointed as a matter of fact.

He too loved Marian and was all these years in touch with her. He had his defense mechanisms on as well. He could also address it from his brain and mind portions of his soul, it was too hard to relate to it emotionally.

I have developed, with time and age a good strong friendship with him. He learned to value my closeness, to respect my achievements and to give me all the support I have ever needed in hard times and to share happily the good times. My father became an even stronger rock for me with each year passing and our relationship grew closer and better like an aging wine...My Father was, in my mind, the most important figure along with my beloved husband. They two constituted the anchor of my soul in life.

I was sitting on the high bar stool, surrounded by the beautiful art work hung on the walls, on which Jan-Paul and I have worked so pleasantly 2 years ago, over looking at the vast ocean from the glass wall to wall sliding doors at the ninth floor at my condo, but unlike the usual phone conversations from that lovely spot, I did not see anything. I was focused on my inner self and my soul was turbulent, confused, fighting its way to sanity within reality.

"But so was mine! I also had my tests a year ago?" I semi cried being torn between being so deeply worried for Marian, but also, bit by bit as the news began sinking into me, my sub conscience and conscience, I was being so overwhelmed when realizing the implications regarding my state my situation. My BREASTS. And all the feelings and thoughts came screaming their way from my sub conscience...MASTECTOMY... BREASTS...MY BEAUTIFUL BREASTS...No..I can keep my breasts, I will just tighten the screenings, the tests, I will go through them every three months instead of every six months as I do, or more accurately as I should do. Lately for some reason my tests were done once a year, it just got to be that way...may be I was too busy with work with life, maybe it turned that way because after a suspicious Mammography a doctor needed an ultrasound so there was no need to re-schedule another test so soon, and maybe I was not able to face so often each year the question DO I HAVE CANCER!

I was beginning to be personally involved not only for Marian but also as to my own situation.

"Abale` I will talk with you later. I need some time to process all this" I said smilingly to the phone so to protect my father, my 89 years old father who was my core and origin of strength yet still was my old dear father whom I wanted to sleep well tonight…it was nine PM in Israel and he needed his mind to be peaceful as could be under the circumstances… God what circumstances… his daughter is harboring a gene, a difficult Gene from which its consequences he lost his dear beloved wife and now my dear friend is about to embark the fight of her life and Me? Me? I don`t know quite well what is happening with me. Yet.

As I hung up the phone with my father's good night greetings and sweet dreams sent over, always no matter what age I am at, always his young vulnerable so talented and beautiful so strong and independent daughter, I looked around to the delicate and floating ballet dancer positioned in the center of the living room wall looking at me from her painting but I could not focus on her. She did not do it for me today. I looked at the Ocean, the lively partially angry and dynamic and to the south peaceful and turquoise and it did not do it to me as well. A certain restlessness came over me. I walked to the master bedroom, so spacious and beautifully decorated a well done job by Jan-Paul and me and paced back and forth between the bed and the lovely small bedroom balcony overlooking the deep green creek. The creek was quiet and the sun rays flickered on its water, it was tide time and the water came in streaming with strength and elegance into it, almost overflowing it. I set down on the lounge chair there and looked at it and then shifted my look towards my inner self. My most deep inner self. I started analyzing the situation calmly and analytically. As a work of science and published paper or my research results I started drawing in my mind all the facts and all the possibilities. All my options and ways of action.

My main principle in such matters rose strongly and echoed in my heart and in my mind. *EMBRACE*…embrace!! Yes, embrace it, do not fight the reality. It cannot be changed. Ever since I was found to harbor the BRCA2 Gene, I decided, as much as it was hard, to say the least, Gene the latter was, it is a Gene I have inherited from my mother whom I dearly loved and still do, it was a Gene to be found in each and every cell

I carry with in my body, thus hatred does not have a place in my vicinity. Bitterness is not a word in my vocabulary.

Neither the emotional one nor the spiritual one.

And certainly not in my mind and brain.

I felt my peace of mind returning to me. I was calm and tranquil and strangely enough full of confidence.

I walked decisively towards my laptop and wrote another E-mail to Marian:

Dear Marian:

I have just heard from my Dad what you are going through.

I am here for you should you want.
Please let me talk with you, I am at the US and there is a seven hour difference thus it should be your evening in Israel. Please let me know when it is convenient for you, for me to call you.
I very much would like to talk with you
Danielle

I pressed the send button and felt even stronger.

Jan-Paul will be phoning momentarily, shall I share this with him? Part of me needed so much. Part of me needed to have this broadcasted in the evening news. Yet part of me needed my time and my privacy and part of me knew, too well, that my strength will come from ME from within ME. It will build it self-bit by bit, hour by hour, day by day, by me and from the inner deep me.

So, I smiled when the phone rang and happily shared my beach day with Jan-Paul, remembering our conversation a month and a half ago when he discovered I am at the US.

"You are in the US??!!" his voice was surprised as insulted for not knowing and somewhat exhilaratingly happy. "Yes, I am in my condo at Myrtle Beach" I answered softly using my spoiled, longing on the verge of tearing voice. Jan-Paul knew to recognize an opportunity. It was his profession, his job. "Then, I am coming over" He said decisively, yet asking, pleading for my permission, my agreeing to his rather pushy dominating way to fact a matter.

I was surprised and felt I was caught with my guard down since this is not what I was planning for our phone call of 6 weeks ago to end with or rather to proceed and let a new beginning start. It was just a very lonely week, a very lonely night and I have decided to phone him.

I have left Jan-Paul a year ago.
After we were living together for almost two years.
I fell in love with Jan-Paul but not really with Jan-Paul
I was ripe
I was ready
I needed
After three years of mourning
I believed every written word of his
I believed the way he portrayed himself
I was too innocent
And I wanted to look the other way
I wanted to believe
Thus I fell in love with a creature of my imagination
With a creature of my wishes, wants and emotional needs
This creature unfortunately did not resemble Jan-Paul whatsoever

He may have won the battle but I won the war

Yes, he won the battle
Everything was his way
His way or the highway

He would engage in conversation only and only when he wanted or felt like it

He would smile only when he had the time for it

He would offer to dine out only when he felt he wanted

Trips to the lake or the forest were taken only when he could make some emotional space for it and for me

If he could not than we would not

We would never do something that was not really wished by him for himself

I learned to talk only when he could

I learned not to share with him my thoughts and feelings regarding a book I read, a painting I finished or remark on political events because he was really not interested

The cocktail of traits he was built of, his extreme need to control, his extreme need to be within himself, his consumed fashion with himself, then his two sons, then his business and his low, very low ability to give and his crippled emotional entity along with his extreme selfishness all resulted with me feeling deprived, with me being left out

Yes he loved me immensely, but he loved me the way he was capable of

The latter was not satisfactory

His ability to love me did not suffice

Yes he was extremely bright

He was very intelligent

He was out of the ordinary creative

And he was in beautiful breathtaking Sharasesha with his two boats

But I was getting crumbs

I was getting leftovers

Thus I won the war

He may have won the battle, everything went his way

I lost my personality there for a while

I created my own world within our mutual world

I learned to satisfy my emotional needs by myself

But then there came a moment that all the latter were not enough for me
They were not sufficient
For me, a giving, warm, embracing living creature
For me, a sharing, helping, smiling, happy person, to be around a severely, constantly depressed person
Sharasesha, the lakes, the forests were not enough anymore for me to bend so much
To accommodate so much
To cage my personality and leave my wants un tended
Thus I won the war

We headed to Seattle to board my flight to Myrtle Beach with me half almost exploding from the realization of the happiness and future that will await for me there at my home at my oceanfront condominium
He was shocked
Depressed
Could not imagine that I was and am capable of making such dramatic changes
Dramatic decisions
Without him
Bringing an un ordered path to his carefully built world
Disturbing his peace
Without his involvement and against his needs
Against his wishes
He liked me the way I learned to be
Soft
Quiet
Always waiting at home
Always having his needs come first with sometimes overlooking and disposing of my own
This is not me

This is not the world known scientist, the accomplished painter, the kind, optimistic, smiling, caring, talented, career woman

This is not me

Thus, in the past few days, Sharasesha began to be mine

Sharasesha is now mine and I could open my heart and enjoy the genesis- like view, the majestic, sugar-like sprinkled with snow mountains and the eternity- like calm, vast, assuring by their presence, beautifully all blue toned colored lakes

They were all shades of blue like a London Topaz and lighter like a Swiss Topaz

They were colored with all shades of wonderful capturing green, like pastel Chinese green and a darker tone of strong green

They were also colored with sharp yet mellow shades of Grey

But my mood was not grey

I could now enjoy, inhale, embrace and burn in my emotional world the beauty of Sharasesha

The beauty that captured me

The beauty that no longer synonyms with Jan-Paul

Sharasesha stopped representing Jan-Paul in my mind

Sharasesha stopped twining with Jan-Paul in my heart

Sharasesha was now Jan-Paulless

Sharasesha is now Jan-Paul free

And thus we drove to Seattle with me leaving in my heart the old Sharasesha and so happily and enjoyingly embracing my new Sharasesha

My new lake of a future

My new and own good memories of all seasonal colors of the trees, mountains, rivers and lakes in my own Sharasesha at my heart

The latter strengthened my decision and laced it with the much, so much looking forward to, my new life

My new world

Mine to take and mine to carve

Thus, He lost me

He lost the innocent love, the big, brown, beautiful eyes he so loved
He lost me
And I found myself again
I found an endless well of possibilities, dreams to cone true and a
Smiling Horizon
I was home. I was back
I was happy
And

Yes.

Relationships are not about battles.
Relationships are not about wars.
It is about giving and taking.
It is about giving and receiving.
Like love making.
It is about giving.
This was the way I perceived a relationship
This was who I was and what I have lived by and what I have experienced in my life.
This was me.
Thus I was at peace.
Finally, content, confident and tranquil, at my pursuit of my own future, my own bright future and back to myself and my proud entity.

CHAPTER TWENTY

India, Aqaba, Eilat and the Canary Islands

But yes, he was so overwhelmed that I could leave him.

That someone can leave him.

That I had it in me to leave him. He who was a quarterback, THE quarterback of his high school team, the handsome bright Jan-Paul Dossier could not imagine of being left by a woman. Jan-Paul was a very bright and successful investment banker and a world renowned author. His self-esteem and confidence just flourished and grew over the years. He was deeply in love with me and my image fitted well with his world and I belonged to him in his view. His male outlook on life. It was a done deal, for him, and he began to take me for granted. Yet, I was disappointed with him. I was infatuated with him, with his brightness, creativity and let's not forget his physical looks, a most masculine and attractive blue eyed large shoulders and dominating authoritively face and look. But, he did not respect my needs. As much as he loved me, as much as he adored me, as much as he was awed by my achievements and looks and was attracted to my body and character, he forgot himself, for a long period of time and thus has lost me.

He begged for us to remain in touch. I did not agree.
He begged for my permission to send me an e-mail a day. He thought, with his patience a character he mastered as a successful commodity

investor, he would win me back, step by step, starting with an e-mail slowly entering my life and then have a hold of me again, having me his again. I knew better and declined.

But, I phoned him once a month on my own time and terms and he was only too happy to always answer and be there.

Every evening he phoned from the road, the journey he has undertook on himself to reach me. He drove almost ten hours a day all the way from Washington State making his way surely and confidently through the roads the weather and through the walls to my heart.

Every evening we shared his road views and thoughts and my day at the beach, my hikes on the shore touching the teasing low waves and my writing of my papers, science papers and abstracts of my lectures to be presented in international conferences I was invited to. This time the conference will take place in *Xuzhou, Jiangsu,* a well-known historic city in China. Besides the science, when in this city, a person will enjoy the richness of historic and cultural relics of ancient dynasties (especially the Han dynasty) of China, and the beauty of its natural scenes and city appearances.

I accepted the committee invitation and was preparing my lecture and power point presentation. Of course, later on, my clothes have to be chosen carefully for my lecture day, for the day I was asked to preside as a chairperson for another session on "Cancer and Diagnostic Strategies Today", for the Gala night and the trips around and just days of meeting fellow colleagues and friends. I was enchanted by Chinese literature and ancient culture. I was looking forward to the opportunity. It would be nice to visit China again; I always enjoyed encountering traditional China, today.

"I will be at noon time tomorrow at your door" His voice was smiling and conveyed his self-satisfaction and amazement at making this long trip so quickly. I will let the guards know your name so you can enter, I answered softly yet assertively without being able to conceal some of my excitement about meeting Jan-Paul again.

"See you soon" his voice was very cheerful very happy and almost kissing me through the phone. "See you soon" I replied with his so loved saying. He always said that.

I wondered how it will be to meet him. Will it be like four years ago when I first met him and he called from the airport in Myrtle Beach that he is on his way? Then I could hardly contain myself. I was so eager so totally under his spell, a spell that was formed through months, long months of corresponding and talking on the phone.

Today part of me was closed, was fearful to open, was guarded. Part of me wanted to melt in to his body, in to his entity. But was it really His body? His entity that I wanted so much to be imprinted into, to be one with? Or the Jan-Paul that my emotional world was creating and my mind...alas was following, wanting him, That Jan-Paul, to be so, to be as I imagined as I wanted as I needed so.

I remembered how he came then.

The doorbell rang and I tried to walk slowly and contained but my heart raced.

My hand automatically turned the knob to open the door. He stood there, four years ago and I did not have time to compare his looks to the ones I saw in the picture exchange. I remembered that my eyes swallowed him, and my head was dizzy. The hunger that was built through the anticipation of so many months, the letters from Israel to Washington state, the trans-Atlantic phone conversation, his trip to Florida and my trip to Myrtle Beach, until finally, I met the man I already fell in love with 8 months ago without even seeing him.

I fell to his world as a ripe apple, three years after I have lost my mate, my husband, when looking for a totally different life experience, companion and mate. After all no one could match up to Michael, thus I looked at a different angle of life and men.

Jan-Paul was Nature to me, he was the un-inhabitant lakes combined with brilliance and creativity. He was immensely masculine and terribly attractive, with his strong blue eyes and strong face features. Not to mention his broad shoulders and strong body. My mind was attracted to his mind, as well as my body.

It was a beautiful sunny day at Myrtle Beach and the lovely ocean breeze engulfed with the mixture of salty air and a fresh smell of lily flowers came through the door with him. Everything was smiling for me.

The day the ocean, he. And I.

I was beautifully dressed with my simple white tight shirt that embraced my beautiful large breasts, contrasted with an innocent string of elegant pearl beads laying on my neckline which was generously exposed, as Michael would have said "doing justice to my lovely cleavage". I remembered how my Khaki slacks were simple yet made elegant by my high heeled brown delicate summer sandals.

My brown leather belt decorated and emphasised delicately my narrow waist.

What was there not to like?

Indeed Jan-Paul later confided that he fell in love with me there and then and for ever.

He was infatuated with me and from then on things took their own pace and dynamics, with us only tagging along embarrassedly, timidly yet so yearningly for each other.

I did not feel such a physical yearning for a very long time. For some years to be correct.

After Michael passed away I nearly died literally and physically twice in the year of mourning. I felt like I was out of my body, most of the year and just observing life from the side. With time I used every tool I could think of to get back to track, back to life, to combine my automatic fashion of day to day life with my emotional world, with me, with my entity.

I took a flight to Eilat, a Red Sea- front city in southern Israel, after the 30 days of initial mourning passed, and booked myself a room at the most expensive luxurious beachfront hotel, and tried to enjoy the beach, the weather and overcome the loneliness. But the latter was hard. I read lounging on my pool chair; I drank a cocktail while in the quiet, flat, relaxing, tranquil water of the bay, enjoying the sun set…but alone, with all these romantic couples around me. I went back lazily to my room and ordered dinner to my overlooking the bay balcony eating slowly while watching the lights of the city of Aqaba across the bay, in Jordan,…but still alone. My thoughts were still with me, my restlessness was never leaving me and my sadness was there, always as a shadow. Was it ever going to fade somewhat not to mention or hope for it to go away? Am I ever going to be happy again? I was wondering. Was I ever going to smile again? I was longing.

I had no peace of mind and then planned to travel to India to get some remedy for my sad spiritual way of life that seemed to be like my second nature now. Like a new Gene embedded in me.

Yes, I thought, I will travel to India, and stay there a month, a year and learn their philosophy, their way of meditation, so I can go on with my life and regain my, until a year ago Joy de vivre, that I was so famous for and identified with.

I will regain my peace of mind.

I will regain my inner tranquillity.

And then it dawned on me, that *I CAN BRING INDIA TO ME!*

There is no need to travel all the way to India, I COULD BRING INDIA TO ME!

Peacefulness would be found within me.

It does not matter where I am, in Alaska or India or Paris, I will not be able to run away from me and achieve tranquillity. Yes, true, I can be given the tools to achieve it maybe better and quicker in India, by professionals, as a person goes to an orthopaedic doctor when breaking a leg or to a psychologist when needing help in the latter field. But, but, *I can find my core, I can relate to and get in touch with my inner most deepest me and find my tranquillity at home at my garden with me.*

And I did.

I found peacefulness and tranquillity when learning *to accept, to embrace and to live with the world I DO have, and stop wishing, wanting, yearning, hoping for the world I could never have.*

Bit by bit when thinking and dwelling on what I do have, I stopped wanting the people, the things, the world I could not ever have again. Suddenly, I did not want them anymore. Suddenly I wanted what I have. Suddenly I wanted my own future, and a smile began to reside on my lips.

Empowered by myself, my regained peace of mind, by my smile and curious, searching, optimistic life-long self-nature, I began my life again.

This smile now was flashed at Jan-Paul. He was my new finding, my new exploration, in life, in me, a wide opened new big window that actually was a huge beautiful door with a threshold to phase number two in my life.

Would that door lead me to a pleasant place? Would that door lead me to a better place? A different place for sure. There is no better or worse I thought, there is different and for me to decide how to go on, how to navigate and what to take from that path leading from that wonderful door, wonderful opportunity.

It was mine to choose, and mine decide.

I led him in to my small beautiful condo, feeling and knowing that I am letting in a whole new world, excited, careful and yet teasingly walking to the living room, fully aware and knowing that he is right behind me, watching me, learning me, checking me out.

"Would you like something to drink?" I offered standing in the middle of the living room from where a person could see the whole, wide, ocean just lying there spread out, for the eye to enjoy. Just a glass of water, he answered quite timidly, looking a bit puzzled, letting me lead the way, the path to our getting to know each other. I moved confidently to the kitchen, my heels making a sound when reaching the tiled floor there, my motion automatically carried out, outwardly looking as if all is under control when inwardly there was a storm going on.

What do I do next? It seemed that he left everything to me. Why? Was he tired from the flight from Florida? Was he overwhelmed with me? But my instincts just carried me on and I gave him a tall glass of cold water while leading him to the laptop on the dining room table. "Would you like to see some of my presentations for the course I am preparing about "Traditional China and Medicine"?

"Yes, sure" he said very interested. Jan-Paul was always an interested party when intellectual conversation took on. He was extremely well read and knowledgeable about many subjects. He was like a walking library. It was a pleasant mind-storming and mind sharpening when talking with him. I needed to think, not very much, but still needed somewhat to think when talking with him.

I sat on the chair putting on my PowerPoint presentation on the screen, while letting him stand behind my chair, behind me, making him bend a bit in order to have a full view of my ppt, while so he will have to smell my alluring perfume, be close and aware of my blond beautiful shoulder length hair just done carefully yesterday at the hairdresser, just for him. His face was a poker face. One could never know what Jan-Paul is thinking. One could never know what Jan-Paul is feeling. I was the total contrast; so warm, showing and expressing my thoughts and feelings. I needed a mate like me in this respect. A warm one. An anticipated one. I felt that life bears its own surprises and thus I was yearning for stability in other areas. I wanted to feel comfortable and relaxed with my mate and off guard, but Jan-Paul was different. He was a very known and experienced investor in the commodity market and published many books conveying his intelligence and creativity of which people bought and paid thousands of dollars for.

But I decided to look at this latter character as a refreshing and new toy. I went along with it very flexibly and smilingly with open arms, letting him, his whole personality as is sink in to mine, amazed and awed by the complexity of his.

"This is the Emperor of the Ch'ing Dynasty" I heard my self-explaining to him while my mind was wondering at what he was looking. Was he looking at the slide or was he assessing my feminine hair? Was he impressed with the red colours I chose for this session of lecture or with my body being set there in front of him, vulnerable to his eyes and completely accessible to his searching curious look.

I turned my head towards him, further explaining about the way Chinese worshiped their gods at those ancient times, while trying to read his face. Nothing. A remote soul. But, those Blue piercing eyes, that smile of a combined timidness and respect towards me yet projecting an immense strength, strength of a man, of a male. I felt I was totally in control while being overwhelmingly attracted to him. The more time passed the more I emotionally and mentally surrendered to him. The more I gave myself to him. He did not know all that. Maybe he was in control. Maybe we both came near and nearer to each other with every minute passing.

"The view is breath-taking here" I said with my voice now even softer then before when being partly a researcher. I felt he got a glimpse of my professional personality and now it's time for a more feminine me. While rising gracefully from my chair I led the way to the balcony commanding an unprecedented view of the Atlantic Ocean from the ninth floor. A school of dolphins just passed and my eyelashes lifted slowly from him to them to watch them, amazed, as again, leaving him time and opportunity to look me over, to be impressed by me, to want me as much as I wanted him…I so yearned for that. I wanted Jan-Paul to like me, love me, want me as much as I have so longed to be his.

He smiled and came nearer to me looking at the dolphins while his hands holding the rail near mine, and after what would be considered sufficient and polite time, a few seconds, we found ourselves letting the dolphins go their way and looking into each other eyes. I waited for him, instinctively, to make a first move if at all. I was leading in other aspects, but he would have to feel that he is deciding to make a physical and thus maybe an emotional move towards me. He would have to feel that it is him that is in control. And before I knew it, I felt his lips pressing delicately at mine and his eyes, blue strong eyes, plunging deeply, strongly, confidently in to my warm, wide big brown eyes. I may have appeared soft, collected, but I was drowning in his personality. Indeed I was drowning in his hands, in his lips, in his smell, In His World.

The sun rays stroke my back warmly, the low fresh breeze played delicately with my hair and I was consumed by Him.

"Indeed, you have a marvellous view" Jan-Paul pointed out when taking a few pictures of the view, and then of me, and then of us together, hugging each other while holding the camera at arm length. "Shall we go to lunch?" he offered and I smilingly accepted, while taking my purse, my beautiful expensive leather purse, and we went towards the door with me leading the way and him leading events. Yes, him leading reality. I was his.

I locked the door and we headed to the elevators through the carpeted long corridor, both very busy admiring the lush, green view of Myrtle Beach while his hand was searching for mine, finding it giving yet holding its own. I walked erect, with pride in my personality, the later a combination of femininity and strength. A complex combination of brain, mind and womanhood. And Innocence. I was innocent and trusting to the verge of foolishness. I was raised by a rock of a father, and had the salt of the earth for a husband. I knew in my mind that not all men are as my two role models, but the draining demanding professional life and the loss of my dear one made me inclined to believe and embrace the notion that my new love would be as remarkable as my previous one.

And maybe it will. May be this was the door for me to open, experience and let another soul make its path to my heart. Maybe rocks and salt of the earth come in various ways.

Thus, I was completely and utterly open to the upcoming events, to the upcoming reality, to a different but enticing future, TO Jan-Paul.

"A chef salad, please "I gave my order to the young waitress, while smiling at her, nicely. The booth we were sitting at was secluded and gave us a lot of privacy and was chosen by him. He was concentrating on me, examining my face while I handled the waitress gracefully. I was very calm, noticing his knee nervously, strongly, trembling. Is he nervous at last? He reached for my hand on the table and held it for a minute, until our icy cold water was served. TBonze was a beautiful place for lunch and I always enjoyed, again and again, watching the boats go by on the intra-coastal waterway. A passing boat caught my eyes, and Jan-Paul turned to look what caught my attention.

"This is a very beautiful place" he said semi- smiling for Jan-Paul never smiled fully, he was too much on guard at all time with a natural trait of never fully revealing his feelings and thoughts.....so in control to an extent I have never encountered before in my life. So different from me, with my flowing warm personality, with my immediate respond at close familiar family interactions as opposed to professional interactions at which I was always collected, in control and quick only when fully knowing where it will lead. Jan-Paul was always slow responding while thinking his actions.

"How did you find it? How have you decided to pick Myrtle Beach as a place for you to live? He was genuinely willing to know. Jan-Paul rarely was genuinely willing to know. He was rarely genuinely interested at another person's thoughts, feelings and decisions.

I enjoyed his attention and his interest "well I actually have found it after a very long time of looking for an ocean front place for myself" I said smilingly and my thoughts returned a few years back at how Myrtle Beach was chosen.

It took years actually and I learned that such things are *a process…*I discovered then some years ago that I may have thought about something, may have formulated a want, a wish, a decision…but *my mind..my soul would need to process it and that might take time, all the time needed for the latter…*The decision regarding Myrtle Beach was a complex one. It started with the wonderful years I have had with Michael, my ever beloved. Michael and I were frequently travelling to the US for his and my international conferences. Michael and my relationship with him grew like an old good French wine….always bettering with time. We were like a glove and a hand for each other, like a key and a key hole, we matched so well.

"Why don't we buy a one bedroom place here in the US for the summers?" He once asked. He was so creative, so resourceful and it really was so logical, as Michael always was. To have our own place to come to every summer, since we both liked and enjoyed stability. Thus we thought together, it would be lovely to retreat each time after our work is done in the US to our own place. Yes, I loved the idea and started looking in the internet for places that were in the midst of nature, with a lake nearby, slopes for winter so the place could be rented while we work or vacation in Switzerland each winter. I looked for our new nest with so much new energy and so much affection, almost as if it was a person. It symbolized to me yet another evolvement, the great journey and evolution, our relationship was experiencing.

Always.

Life with Michael was a mixture of stability, assurance, calmness and constancy combined with creativity, imagination, hope and pleasant surprises. Life with Michael was the engine on which I could run on. The engine which provided me with the force, the power, the Jet power, to reach my high goals in my professional life. Life with Michael was what I was leaning on and what I could count on always, forever, at all times. Michael was my Gibraltar Rock!

I was looking for our new place.….

A place with a good slope and a nice snow for people to enjoy and for us to rent during the winter months in which we were not there and a place with nature and water, a lake, for us to enjoy during the summer months.

And suddenly Michael left me.
All alone in the cruel world.

I remembered again, my traumatic yet brave, desperate and decisive first trip out of my house. Out of my nest. Out of my world. Then a secure, blissful, smiling, greater than life world, that turned so harsh.

"I am going to fly to Eilat for New Year's Eve". I announced to my father. My other Gibraltar Rock. After the 30 first days of mourning, in which I somehow held up, I decided to go by myself and fly to Eilat, and spend the first holiday of New Year alone.

I travelled to the airport in Haifa, with my packed handbag containing my beautiful new bathing suits from a few months ago, and some appealing beach wear and some women journals and a book.

I needed to be out of the house after 5 long months of battling for my husband life and after a month of mourning in which I actually did not comprehend, and could not and did not accept my huge, tremendous loss. My decisions were made through my intuition. I was not alive and aware and could not make informed decisions since my whole entity was not with me. My body just went through the motions every day but my soul did not reside in it.

The sun greeted me in Eilat and the beautiful Red Sea waves smiled at me with the flickering sun rays playing on them and with them. After arriving to my large luxurious suite with a balcony overlooking at the capturing view of Aqaba, Jordan, Eilat and the Red Sea, I changed quickly to my new bathing suit and looked at the mirror to catch the appealing site of the feminine body appearing there, with my big large beautiful breasts and my so thin waist…I have lost a lot of weight, I was not aware of that until this minute.

But I was numb. It did not do anything for me. I heard Michael's voice in my mind, as always, inquiring, what do I see in the mirror. Did I have a chance to look at the mirror and what did I see? He always asked wanting me to always know feel and appreciate, how beautiful and attractive I was.

The figure in the mirror, this time, did not register in my eyes and my heart.

I found a nice place down on the beach under a big blue umbrella and my body stretched like a cat's body on the spacious, luxurious lounge chair. The sun was caressing me. The sun, but no one else was. Yes, I could detect the eyes of both men and women sizing me up, looking at me with appreciation, paying their respects or envy feelings to the way I looked, like from a Vogue magazine....the right colours of my bathing suit which hugged tightly my feminine figure boasting my beautiful breasts standing proud and in contrast to my thin curved waistline.

But still, it was only the sun that caressed me, and each and every direction that I looked to, I saw them. I saw them, him and her, her and him, and I was with the sun and the Red Sea. My eyes shifted up as I heard the waiter offering me another drink. "Yes, please" I smiled warmly, and when he turned away I was still with him and her and her with him.

A certain uneasy feeling crept through me. A certain restlessness was catching me. My most ever soothing entities, the sun and the ocean, were not able to deliver. They were not doing their job. An enormous abyss of sadness suddenly took over me and I no longer enjoyed my escape.

I realized then, partially, that I cannot escape. I have to face reality, look forward, and be creative and change my strategy for life, for enjoyment, for life by myself, not alone but with me, and to learn to smile again, to myself, to me, from the bottom of my heart.

I went up to my lovely suite to change for dinner. I chose my jewellery carefully, in a way that it will match my mood and my clothes and the event: Dinner at the hotel luxurious patio. My eyes searched for my perfume bottles and my mind deliberated which one should I use, should I spray the light summer evening fresh flowers cologne or should I use the tempting alluring slightly heavy rich and somewhat sweet other one? I chose the former.

Striding to the dining room, the maître d` stood there all smiles and warmly so eager to host and show me to one of his best places, I smiled a small aloof smile and let him lead the way to my chosen seat. Definitely one of the best. It pays to look gorgeous. It might pay to be alone. I sat satisfied with my table, commanding the view of Aqaba, Jordan and the Sea, and relaxed for a minute. My eyes browsed slowly from one coast, of Jordan to the other of Israel, and rested on the Red Sea in between, now calm and steady as evening approached. I lifted my lashes to take a look at the big wide room, filled with tables and murmurs and chatters, in which expensive cologne and perfume smells were intoxicating along with the capturing horizon.

I saw him and her, and also her and him.

Him and her and her and him.....

This does not work for me, I thought.

I got up decisively and walked briskly towards the exit with the maître d' running after me, his face worried and his eyes questioning, and his hands apart all conveying his disappointment from my leaving along with his fear as to why.

I ordered some dinner sent to my room and ate it looking at the flickering lights of the harbours of both pretty cities in Israel and Jordan. Aqaba and Eilat. *And the seed for changing my strategy for enjoyments, for trips abroad, for living my new life, was placed in my emotional world, and in my mind.*

The question was, how, what tools do I use, how do I make my eyes see, me and me, not him with her and her with him. But rather, me and me, with a satisfied, calm sense of living and enjoyment?

I did not know yet how, but I knew that with time I will find the way. With time. But I was always in such a hurry, I always needed things done yesterday, matters solved two days ago. Right Now!

I need to let this new motion be processed in my emotional world and my mind and my subconscious will find the solution.

It will float one day as a finding in my head.

"So did you find it right away? Did you look long for this kind of oceanfront property?" Jan-Paul's voice penetrated through my mind, on its way passing through many fogy layers of years, feelings, thoughts and contemplations.

"I am here" I said with an energetic cheerful voice "Wow, great, fantastic" he said, so happy I was independent and taking my fate in my hands and travelling by myself, to exotic places as I loved.

"Did you meet the Prince yet?" The prince of Spain was getting married and I laid comfortably on the lounge chair on the beach of Lanzarote in the Canary Islands.

Evyatar was as usual joking with me and so happy that I called him from the beach of the Canary Islands all the way to Israel, to Jerusalem. The flight was long but bearable, especially with my decisive resolution to go about and see the world as others do. I did not want to miss anything, or to be left out. Time is passing and I too wanted to travel as all my friends and colleagues were. Thus, the oceanfront luxurious hotel in the exotic Canary Islands came to mind. It would be the perfect adventure, the best way to re-start travelling by myself to my chosen destinies, as there was an ocean, nature, quiet and luxury to enjoy. I was sure this will be the first, no actually second step after Eilat, to my new life with me, but a more successful one as the destination was so alluring and offered privacy, secludedness and a possibility not to be judged by society for being alone. Not to mostly feel her and him, and him and her, but me and me. I and I.

The way was very beautiful, with trees lining the road and here and there a red tiled roof with white washed walls was standing, overlooking the farm.

I was determined to succeed this time. Thus all was wonderful!

"Welcome Dr. Goldbear" The front desk person smiled at me warmly. "Is my suite ready?" I answered with my mind already dreaming about the oceanfront suite that I have booked from Israel, and how lovely it had looked at the internet and my eyes shifting quickly but elegantly to the badge he was wearing. He was the manager of front desk. "Yes, absolutely, Dr. Goldbear" His voice was assuring, and his eyes were appreciating my long blonde hair, falling down beneath my shoulders. He was busy assessing me, and I let him. I might need his assistance. I was busy assessing the lobby. It was extremely luxurious, built in a Spanish style, with the floors tiled with bright pricy marble   and the front desk with deep mahogany, wine- burgundy coloured thick wood. All surrounded with arcs leading to corridors and beautifully greened patio that caught my eyes as well as my ears with the calm and tranquil sound of a waterfall, the water flowing down from stoned shelves overlaid with terracotta coloured pots, hosting rich, vibrant array of coloured geraniums, a sight that captured me and made my heart bit faster anticipating the beautiful suite and vacation awaiting me, on this almost deserted Canary Island. The latter with its untamed beaches and rocky beautiful shores, hiding golden, small, sandy beaches on which one of them My hotel was built.

My expectations from my suite were fully met and more. The arched balcony tiled with Terracotta coloured tiles was overlooking the beautiful golden, sandy beach that was awaiting me. As I anticipated, royal blue large umbrellas were scattered along the shore, under each were two beach lounge chairs covered with thick, yellow gold coloured mattresses. My eyes noted two. Two under each umbrella. My smiling face turned to examine the rest of the beach and my eyes were caressing the north side showing an un-obstructed view of the horizon, boasting the crystal clear blue water of the ocean surrounding the Island. To the south direction I was glad to detect some toys. I would love to rent a water motorcycle and enjoy the spacious water, open horizon and be in the middle of nowhere, with myself and nature.

I could not get to the beach fast enough.

My new beach lavender bag in my right hand, and a sarong thrown nonchalantly low over my thighs tied elegantly yet sportful, and brown-golden beach high heeled sandals hugging my narrow feminine ankles, I went down the stony stairs leading to the beach with my eyes already busy searching for the most convenient place to enjoy the water, yet have some privacy. "Madam would like an umbrella? "The beach boy was inquiring politely. "Yes, Madam would" I said pointing to the chosen place to which he gladly led the way and moved the lounge chairs to a comfortable position so the umbrella would be in between them providing some shade.....In between the TWO lounge chairs.

I decided to make the best out of it and spread my beach wear all around and made myself comfortable and at home, for the moment.

My sarong was left deserted on the other chair, along with the upper part of my bathing suit, the bra.

It was the Canary Island, considered Europe, and "when in Rome", I enjoyed bathing in half a nude, as other women were, in the surrounded vicinity.

The sun was exactly the right temperature, with its rays caressing me, my body and my spirit. I was beginning to unwind and relax, feeling my muscles one by one responding to the warmth of the fresh calm breeze coming from the quietly humming waves of the ocean.

It was soothing. A proud, white seagull caught my eyes and I got up from my chair to follow it to the water. I stopped for a moment to appreciate the view, the serenity, the calm world I was in and my eyes brushed all along the shore. As my gaze was resting at the north side, I detected a young couple walking hand by hand right on the edge of the water. I noticed they were looking at me. They were looking at me for quite a long while and my mind was processing this reality wondering what are they so attracted to and that they are TWO. Yes, two of them, her and him, him and her, hand in hand. "But what are they looking at" I was wondering, when standing there looking at the shore, the waves and them. "Could it be that they are looking at my breasts? No, most women are bare at their upper body."

"They are noticing my Scars "I realized and for a minute felt embarrassed. I lifted my shoulders proudly, with my large, big, beautiful breasts showing even more, bearing my two pink delicate Scars, each on a different breast, from lumpectomies done during my PhD years. "Michael loved my breasts! With my Scars! "I thought. He always said how carved and adorned they were…the nicest in the middle east….in the world….he would add while smiling, with his eyes flickering with a bright shade of green when telling me.

And so, I disposed these TWO, these him and her, and walked proudly to bath in the tempting lake-like calm water.

"It is indeed a beautiful place to live" Jan-Paul voice interrupted my line of thoughts, again. "Yes, the water culture is very developed around here" my tone was soft and my eyes were hugging a boat that navigated quietly on the intra-coastal-waterway from New-York, to Florida.

We both followed it sliding delicately along the water.

And then, for the first time, after many years, it dawned at me! "They could not have detected my Scars! They were at least 50 meters away from me. My Scars are very thin, delicate pink, beautifully carved on my breasts. All these years I was thinking and feeling in the bottom of my soul, the bottom of my entity that they were looking at my Scars, My Scared Breasts, but No, they were just looking. Just looking at me. Probably appreciating my narrow waisted, fully breasted appealing figure.

They were not seeing *my Jewelled Breasts!*

CHAPTER TWENTY ONE

THE OCEAN WAVES, THE VIOLIN AND THE BREEZE

"Here you are" the professional artificial voice of the waitress called my attention to her, the big nice salad she has just placed in front of me and to Jan-Paul who was studying satisfied his big Rueben sandwich splashed with melted cheese. His blue eyes shifted to me waiting for my respond to the nicely decorated plates of food and the enjoyable relaxed atmosphere. His strong gaze, amplified by the strong deep blue colour of his eyes, brought me to the present with my gut all filled with anticipation, wonder and want. Will I enjoy meeting him? I so wanted to. I wanted to be done with my quest for a mate. I needed to be done. I needed to give myself to someone. I needed to be loved again. And most importantly I needed to love! I needed to give.

He squeezed my hand over the table, again, with his knee shaking so vigorously, but his face calm as a quiet lake…maybe a silence that is sometimes manifested before a big huge storm…

TBonze was full with people enjoying their lunch and the chatter was almost not noticed or heard by us. We both were so captured now with each other. We both were so deeply studying…feeling….wanting to please each other. We were suddenly in a hurry to finish lunch and be on our way. What way would that be? Where will we go? What will we do? On our way to the parking lot, there was electricity between us. A building chemical tension was felt between us and the quiet was full of sound. The sound of our hidden craving for each other. Our eyes scanned the parking lot for his grand rented car, and once we located it Jan-Paul gallantly opened the door for me to enter, while looking at my slim feminine ankle engulfed in a high heeled summer sandal and smelling my fresh perfume. I felt he is mine. But I also felt, with some fear, with some excitement, with some wonder and pleasure that it might very well be that I am his as well.

He backed up from the parking space and looked at me and there and then our mouths just had their own wish will and personality and my lips were pressed by his, and my tongue searched hungrily in his mouth. I sucked his tongue like there is no better nectar. Like I have not drunk for days. I was so thirsty.

He pulled back, and started driving away. To where? "Your mouth is all smeared with my lipstick "I said smilingly and softly. He took a hand-kerchief out of his pocket, and looked at the mirror to wipe his lips while I had re-freshened my lipstick on my warm full lips while still full of the emotions, feelings and tantalizing warmth that were spreading in my soul and my body. My body was awakening from a very long sleep. It has been over three years since I have been kissed by a man.

We drove in a silent. A silent that soothed us. No words were needed. A mixture of comfortable, relaxed, unwound feelings were playing with an electrical, magnetic, unbearable, attraction for Jan-Paul in me. For a minute the latter took over and then the former. And then the latter was overwhelming me again. Jan-Paul cruised through the roads silently, navigating his car, his ship, our yacht for this day to somewhere. Myrtle Beach was always a nice place to drive through. A pleasant laid back place to enjoy.

My eyes caught suddenly the Marriot hotel sign. "Oh, this is the hotel I wrote you about as a possibility for your stay here, did you book it?" I asked stepping to reality. "No, I booked the Holiday Inn" I was a bit dis-appointed. I was not planning in staying with him, but the Marriot was much more luxurious in Myrtle Beach and on the water, on the ocean. Of course it is also pricey. And, Michael and I have stayed in the Marriot, always, when in San Diego. I liked the Marriot. I wanted the Marriot.

It represented for me the Ocean which I loved, nature, away from the city, luxuriousness and a feeling of being at home.

Jan-Paul seemed to catch it all at once. He was like an animal, intuitively assessing the reality, the moment, processing and responding immediately as needed towards the right direction of His want and need and desire, his prey; Me. Jan-Paul was a very bright and successful commodity trader and did excellent when playing in the commodity market. His radar the top of the art and worked quickly and efficiently. When he wanted.

"Would you like me to book a room in the Marriot?" His voice was so comforting and suggesting and obeying, aiming to please all at once. "Yes" I responded, simply. The car tires squeaked and a u turn was taken on the spot, and we were heading to the Marriot Lobby when the bell boy took the car keys from Jan-Paul. I was not really aware of anything, just going through the motion, just flowing with events, here and now, with here and there, a small touch to steer, navigate reality the way I wanted. Of the latter I was not fully aware. In my mind. But apparently I was aiming there, with Jan-Paul.

"A room with an ocean view?" The front desk man asked looking at Jan-Paul. Why do they always refer to the men? I wondered in my mind. "Yes, please" Jan-Paul responded politely.

"Oh, we have some beautiful ones"

It was early November with the tourist season over and I was sure that they had quite a few rooms, with reasonable prices.

"How about an oceanfront room" I interjected softly but decisively

"Oh it would actually cost only slightly more and we have room number 413 available" He answered sweetly and accommodating, this time looking at the both of us, smiling at me and re-assuring Jan-Paul. "We would like to take a look at it" Jan-Paul suggested agreeing. Wow, my heart leaped when we entered the room and the whole front wall was a glass door to the balcony commanding the most beautiful view of the ocean with a proximity that made you feel like you can actually touch it. You can actually immerse in it. You can wet your hand in the softly autumn grey waves approaching you again and again and again…I was holding the rail of the balcony all captured with this overwhelming soft grey laced with the white foam when I heard Jan-Paul talking to the bellboy "we will take it" I smiled. "Why don't you wait here Danielle and I will check in and bring my suitcase"

"OK" I smiled, pleased and conveying my pleasure to him.

I stood there, not aware of the time, with my back to the room, facing the Beauty of nature, when I heard the door slam and Jan-Paul's steps approaching me from behind. He placed himself adjacent to me with his hands wide spread on the rail looking at the view. His hand moved slightly and touched mine. I did not move. He came closer to me from behind and as I expected, as I longed for, as I demanded with all my senses, his hands cuffed my beautiful large breasts that were felt so easily through my tight white shirt. I did not move. I cherished the moment being all consumed with his hands. With my breasts. With his clasping moving massaging hands on my breasts. Oh what a feeling. He leaned back and sat on the chair behind us while pulling me over with him. We both sat there, I cradled in his arms, his body and his hands still caressing my chest. I was spellbound. The breeze, the soft sound of the ocean, his hands caressing me, his murmurs in my ear, I did not care, although for a slight second it entered my mind…we are on the balcony. Luckily, Jan-Paul was still in control and rose us up and led us to the bedroom.

He took me again and again and again like the waves on the shore never ceasing to come never tired of coming from the ocean to the shore again and again and again…He came to me strong and soft, slowly and quickly, I was like clay in his potter's hands.

In his hands, his body His desires, and Mine.

The see-through, soft white pale banana colored curtains, moved slowly and rhythmically with the wind accompanying Jan-Paul's movements inside me. With the autumn wind getting slightly stronger so did he. With the autumn wind letting go for a minute leaving the magical curtain standing still, so did He, and I was crazed, almost could not contain the waves of warmth, the waves of elevated pleasure, the waves of spiritual conquest that came through me, washed me and left me yearning for more…

I could not wait for dinner to end. We were sitting across the elegant table in one of the most pricy and known restaurants in Myrtle Beach, conversing civilly like the afternoon did not occur. The afternoon with it's soft, full of emotions of love, accompanied with a flare of basic animal mating… as in nature, but loving animals. It was clear, now, that I was deeply in love with Jan-Paul, and he was infatuated with me.

I could not wait for us to be body to body, breath to breath, in bed or on the floor, the place did not matter to me, time stopped and all that I felt was the enchanting sensation, the magical world, everything disappeared, only my physical and emotional elevations were storming in me, defining me, consuming me.

On the way back we discussed politics. When on the elevator we discussed Eastern Asia philosophy. When coming out of the bathroom with just a towel engulfing my body, Jan-Paul was sitting on the sofa and with his hand waving me to come closer. I did. "Take the towel off" I dropped the towel to the floor. His eyes cruised my body, his face a poker face, but his mouth blurred out with no control "wonderful" His voice was husky and his eyes still flowing all over my body, stopping here and there, focusing on my beautiful jewelled breasts, and repeating "wonderful" I stood there as a Venus, giving my self to him, to his eyes, to his soul, to his yearn and lust.

He did not have enough of me. He could not take his eyes off me. He was numb. He was overwhelmed. With my femininity, with my beauty, with my strength and my softness, all there for him to view, to take, to enjoy.

And thus he took me again, on the floor, on the carpet, with me yielding, giving.

And he took. He took for himself, semi forgetting me.

But I gave.

He was like the vast ocean down below the balcony, lazily caressing the golden curvy yearning shore

"Oh….I need to foreplay a bit more," He mumbled and I wondered… but have let the physical pleasure and the spiritual elevation take course.

"Take, Danielle, do like me…take" He said in a strong somewhat hoarse voice. Take? I thought? I do not take in love, I do not enjoy taking when lovemaking, when mating…*I give!! The utmost highest level of pleasure is to GIVE when lovemaking…thus two cords are played with so much harmony in a delicate artful shining and meticulously made VIO-LIN*…No, I do not take when love making I receive and give…I am like a flower being watered, like a stream being filled by the ocean…I receive and I am being filled…and I give….more and more….I give….these latter two intertwine together, once the former is on high a mountain and the latter in a valley and then they turn places and pleasures, like a concert well conducted. Like an Opera well written and composed. After which, all descend from the seventh heaven, satisfied and embracing each other.

I was like a small pussycat that has just finished liking her delicious bowel of vanilla milk.

I placed these thoughts in the bottom of my mind and continued to love Jan-Paul.
He loved me back. Strongly, muscularly, intelligently and creatively. He and the Sharasesha Nature, the breath-taking lakes and the deer.
He loved me back.

CHAPTER TWENTY TWO

THE TIME HAS COME!

"Would you feel less feminine?" Evyatar's question was standing there in the air, in my heart, in my emotional world. My feet enjoyed the rough yet soft touch of the sand while walking barefoot on the dunes, half listening to the waves. I was getting emotionally ready for my oophorectomy. Scheduled this morning.

"No, it does not affect me that way at all. I do not perceive it as a feminine organ, or better yet as an organ that represents my femininity.." I told Evyatar. And that is exactly how I felt. I wanted it done. Done quickly. To be over and done with it and with the danger it carries. My mother died of Ovarian cancer. My beloved mother probably transferred the BRCA-2 Gene to me. Along with some beautiful much loved other Genes. I loved my mother with all my heart and have never connected in any way form or fashion any ill thoughts or feeling regarding this latter gene. It is one of my genes that needed extra care and attention in a unique, medical and scientific way, and that is what it was all about. For me. I longed to be with my mother again. To share with her my accomplishments, my life. She was always so proud of me. So loving and supporting me. She was my shelter when I needed…and for a long time….always. I was extremely lucky to have been born to such parents as I have.

Life is a package deal. I thought. I might have this "attention demanding" Gene, but as I said at my Father's 75th birthday gathering, I have chosen both my parents when being in the endless light-floating cloudy sky when embraced by the Stork, before I was born. I was lucky with my family. I was lucky with the man I loved. It was a miracle to have had such a childhood, such a family, such a husband, such a career…thus strengthened I walked full of energy to my jeep, heading to the medical centre.

On the way while driving, I switched of my entire emotional world, and became very remote and analytical.

I was glad I wrote Brian a month ago not to come to Israel to meet me. I needed to be by myself and with myself.

From now on, my way of handling my operation was to flow with the events, not to be emotionally involved and to be in control to a certain point, observe and be aware to a certain extent, and the rest is up to fate, to the doctors, to the people whose hands I have put my life in.

"Hi Dr. Goldbear" The receptionist in the ward knew of my coming and welcomed me with a full warm smile.

"Hello" I responded being very remote, and sat down to just wait for the process to start and procedures take place.

My vitals were taken…I was passed from room to room….from doctor to doctor….then to a nurse…and another nurse and finally given my hospital PJs feeling very stripped from my identity, now, merging with the view at hand….the hospital, the patients, the staff, and me just a number, with my wrist plastic bracelet.

It was strange to be a "nobody" a "no one" Just another number, just another "Thing" that "decorates" the room, the ward, the hospital, this world I was in right now, like one of the pieces of furniture or vases scattered around the corridors here.

The next morning I was walking up and down the corridor, with my left hand towing the IV on wheels with me. My right hand religiously holding my "kidney" for I might throw up again, like all night long after the operation. I was miserable, but smiling, somewhat happy that the worst is behind me.

"Oh, I did not know you were throwing up" Gal was apologizing from the other side of the corridor quite loud, all trying to appease me, his face conveying warmth and care.

I did not fall for it.

He was truthfully and genuinely caring for me, after all he operated on me just the day before. But in order to stay strong I had to remain detached. Emotionally detached.

I smiled back and looked at the nurses that were lined up near the reception counter all looking at me. "I must be quite a ridicules spectacle, with my hospital PJ and my IV in one hand and my "kidney" in the other…shlapping along the corridor"

"No, Danielle…you look more beautiful than any of us on a good day with your long beautiful blond hair and your fragile figure conveying such determination" She cried out admiringly.

"You should have seen my Mother….what a beautiful woman she was" I answered. And thought….Why?

My mother has died in that exact ward after eight months of a long, brave, battle. I was there every step of the way, all day long, taking care of her in all possible aspects. Medically, emotionally, looking after my father as she had requested. I was there 100%.

I had to remind myself and the whole world of how beautiful and strong she was.

It was good to have my ovaries out. Time has come. And as Kohelet says there is a time and place for everything and the time has come to have my ovaries out.

Now it is time to start a new phase, a new kind of life, letting into the latter, my gene, given to me from my mother and just having it as a part of my world. Strict surveillance and follow up needed like twice a year having an Ultra Sound, and a breast surgeon check-up, and a yearly mammogram, and MRI along with an onco- gynecologist check-up would just become part of my yearly routine and that is it.

I will just learn to live with it.

And I did.

I learned to live with it.

And with the sad knowledge that my Darling Pierre was killed in a car accident on his way to the airport. On his way to me. On his way to be with me after my oophorectomy.

I was grief stricken and was in the process of learning to live with my routine, the MRI, the Ultrasound, the mammography and the yearly breast surgeon check-up.

But without Pierre.....

I lived with it in Israel.
I lived with it in Myrtle Beach.

Until....

The table was orderly loaded with files and memos and things to do now, and matters to take care of later.....The room was my "Operation Room," The Pit....all was scattered, but in a fashion that I could under-stand and carry out further instructions of, the Chief of this Operation Room: Me. The Ocean looked beautiful as always, and the breeze was softly moving the curtains, but I was focused on other matters. My mind, my entity, all of my self was captured and pre-occupied with what the near future held for me and how I can possibly navigate and control it toward my favour.

I was multi-tasking, talking on the phone with my doctor in Israel, sending e-mails to Israel and thinking how best I can find a good breast surgeon and a good medical centre, and have a double mastectomy after having an Ultrasound and MRI to make sure I am still healthy.

I understood two things.

One, I may have a window of opportunity to reduce dramatically the chances of having Breast Cancer, as Marian is already experiencing it.

Two, *IT IS TIME FOR MY BEAUTIFUL JEWELED BREASTS TO GO!!*

Yes, the time has come for them to go.

I have had them for many years. Many years. They were loved and adored and cherished. They were fondled, caressed, and cradled. They were always getting attention and were an "object" of desire. Of lust. They were formed as if by an artist; large and big, yet still holding themselves proudly, and were a source of physical and emotional enjoyment.

Yes, I liked being eyed due to their beauty. I liked being lusted due to their voluptuousness. I liked being appealing and attractive and thought of tremendously feminine due to my two beautiful jewelled breasts.

But I am a woman in the core. I am a woman inside me. Inside my heart, my mind, my personality. I am a woman due to my feelings, my thoughts, my perception of who I am.

Not because of my fingers, or my lips, or my breasts.

This is how I feel.

And this is the most important matter. With, or without my two Jewelled breasts, I will feel the same 100% woman.

Men will still fall in love with me. Men will still look at me. Men will still seek my presence. For, a woman can possess the most desired build, of her body, but her kiss, her look, her voice her moves could all be offending and un-appealing if that latter "womanhood" is only a shell.

Only an outside, very, thin, cover.

If she does not possess the inner "womanhood confidence" then after a few dates, a few entangles, a few "intimate meetings" the magic will be gone for a man, for the kind of a man that I am attracted to.

Yes, Men will still love me, but most importantly, I will continue to love myself. My breasts do not define me. No, not at all. My heart defines me. My mind. My personality. My dreams my wants, my talent and yes My Genes....All of them.

Yes, I will be very feminine, still and more. Because I feel that femininity is in a core, in the inner-most, deepest, place of a woman. It is the way she kisses her man, it is how she caresses him with her eye lashes, with her thoughts, it is how she responds to his touch, to his eyes. It is something that a woman is either born with or not. It is not an acquired capability. I feel femininity engulfs so many characters of a woman, of me, the way I think, the way I smile, the way I walk and the way I look upon this world. It is all then combined and conveys itself to my man.

And he feels it. And he wants it, needs it and yearns for it.

For me, my femininity is not defined by the pair of my thumbs, or my nails or my arm, butt or the pair of my breasts. The latter being appealing to someone, is an added bonus, but cannot stand by itself and can absolutely be absent.

Now, I know that some women are different. Some women feel that they like, and need and want their breasts. That their breasts mean the world to them, and thus they would do all that they can to preserve them.

That is very good, I thought. What is good for a person and makes them happy is the most important matter.

And what is good for me and makes me happy is the most important for me.

Neither my feelings, nor another different woman's feelings are the right ones or the wrong ones.

They are all the right ones, each for every kind of a woman. We are all different genetically and thus we wish and want differently.

And, so are men.

They differ in their wants, needs and wishes. And so long as no one hurts or offends another, then that's ok too. Each man will look for the woman that captures him.

And each woman will look for the man that captures her.

This has been since Noah's Ark and this will go on to the end of ages.

So, I concluded to myself, my man will be enchanted, captured and attracted to me. He will be spellbound by me, by Danny, the way she is.

The way I am.

The way I will be ...soon.

Thus it is time, if I am still healthy, to undergo a double mastectomy.

And start a new phase in my life. A phase of less stress. A phase of less worry. A phase of less threat.

A more calm and restful phase.

I started smiling.

It can be a good change. A welcomed change.

I felt a warm re-assuring feeling. A comforting one. But I knew better. I have to put a boarder, a limit to the involvement of my emotional world. I have to be all mind now and concentrate on the task ahead. On my goal ahead.

I have to find the best breast surgeon for myself, and undergo a double mastectomy.

I have to reduce my very high risk of having cancer. Breast cancer. Marian is now battling with breast cancer. She had undergone the same tight surveillance, the same tight follow up of the recommended tests for the last year, as did I.

And she is now having the battle of her life.

I was 56. Only 2 years to go until the age of my mother's ovarian cancer and death. Only 3 years to go until the age of Marian's breast cancer and such a tremendously difficult battle.

Part of me wanted to be there for her. To protect her. To shield her.

But no, this was not my reality. She did not want it, she did not want my support and my closeness. She chose not to answer my second warm,

worried e-mail. She wanted to leave the doors of our relationship closed. I respected her wishes and summoned all my will power, all my energy and mind, to go through this path, quite by myself, quite alone, and successfully.

I can do it.

Others have and so can I.

The phone rang. "Danielle, I have scheduled your MRI for the day after you land." My family doctor was there, calling from Israel, so nicely cooperating with me. His voice was matter of fact, like I liked it to be, help-ing me and being there for me all professional. No emotions.

This is how I could handle it and go through it, like a General execut-ing his well thought strategy, no emotions involved.

"Thank you Ranan, I will see you then within a few weeks" I have answered my voice well collected, projecting calm and decisiveness. Exactly how I was and what I felt.

Ming.....the sound of an incoming E-mail called my attention.

My eyes examined the mail with a sharp look and mind when reading the message from my friend in Israel. All my friends and colleagues were now recruited to the mission of finding me a good breast surgeon, a good medical centre, and a nurse to help me for the days I would need after my mastectomy. While reading, and assessing the information I started typing my letter to my close friends:

My dear friends.

The time has come for me to undergo a double mastectomy.

I talked with my father and he shared with me that my childhood best friend, my so close and loved friend, Marian, has been diagnosed with breast cancer.

Since we both bear the same BRCA2 cancer causing gene, and since both our ovaries have been removed four years ago, it is time for me to shift from the strategy of a very strict follow up of my breasts, to remove them, and thus to reduce my risk of breast cancer dramatically.

The time has come to say goodbye to my breasts and depart from them.
Danielle

I finished typing...and my mind was already contemplating, quite joy-fully, what kind of breasts do I want...cup D as I had? Maybe cup B? Maybe have just a flat chest, no reconstitution?

Whenever I had the opportunity I took my bra off. All my life.... when swimming nude, when being at home....it always gave me a sense of freedom....a sense of relief....a sense of nature....

All my life I was a D. This might be a chance to enjoy another possibility. Yes. Re-fresh myself. I was heading towards 60, nature was taking its course, I did not feel I want a D any more.

No!

I was suddenly, so relieved. I knew what I wanted. I knew it immediately. I want a new me. I want a young look refreshed by a boyish flat chest accompanied with my thin feminine waist, and carved body. The contrast between a flat, boyish, young chest and such a womanly body would be amazing. I liked it. I loved it. I was beginning to be impatient to have it.

I toyed in my mind with the latter thought, saw myself in my imagination, dressed in tight flattering sleeveless shirts and small little vests and shirts that I was never able to wear with a D, how cute would that be. Oh I smiled so happily. I already was in love with my new figure, my new form, my new self.

And bathing suits....I could now go with the tiny almost non-existent bras, and tiny little almost nonexistent evening camisoles and upper wear, those lacy see through, delicate, thin bras, those so feminine ones and small little jackets engulfing me tightly, Wow I will be so attractive. I will feel so attractive.

I feel already now, so attractive and feminine.

And thus.....while sprinkling islands of hope on my future, I felt I gained an ocean of smiles....

"Let's go shopping!" I cried enthusiastically to the phone, to my best friend Cherie. "I want to go shopping for some tight little beautiful sweaters for AFTER, for some nice little almost non-existence shirts and camisoles... And, imagine, I would be able to wear colourful materials and fabrics"

The latter were not dominating my current wardrobe. My wardrobe was quite classy and filled with solid colors, more appropriate for my full nice breast.

Now I can play with more colors. Yes! The painter in me was over joyed. The artist in me was already assessing the limitless world of colors and shapes that would be introduced to my world.

We went shopping!

And when I returned home I wrote:

I am breaking for once my wish and writing to you, because it is very important to me that you understand, that I was in touch with the other men I told you about, because you led me to understand that we; in fact, in reality, not in romance dream-wish, cannot be together, and you cannot make this transformation from living alone to being in a long committed and exclusive relationship, sharing, and having my needs come first for you, as if they were your own, and thus harbor in yourself a need to make me happy.

I want to share with you how it all evolved so you will understand.

I met these 2 last men who were writing to me; for the first time when I landed in Israel from the US- after crying even at the last minute, in New-ark airport, in my conversation with you. Even then trying to find a way to be with you, only later well understanding when landing in Israel, that I cannot think for you, and I cannot understand for you, how precious and rare, what we both have together, is. Time is a precious commodity as well (and I have re-learned it and re-experienced it very intensely for the last 2 months) - and thus they started to correspond with me. At this time, you and I were not in touch, with me being in a very deep, depression, longing for you - something that was denied from me, and trying to get some energy from nowhere, since I was too drained and broken, to enjoy myself at home in Israel. My father was very sad to see me like that.

And then I was shocked with the discovery of my Gene, and I needed all support that I could have from wherever I could receive it, since unlike Marian, there is no husband, no children no colleagues from work, for a support system so much needed in such occasions, and as most women usually have.

I was so devastated, that I had to call you from time to time, even though I felt there is no future for us, I just needed to hear your voice and share with YOU, somewhat of what is happening with me.

Meanwhile these 2 men fell in love with me, which was no surprise, and I NEVER got THE MAIL from you, the one and only one I told you that you CAN send to me, on our conversation in Myrtle Beach, the one telling me what I wanted to hear from you.

I was ill, and I was feeling terrible. You were not mistaken, and were not misled. I was not "busy" with these 2 men (I was a bit offended when you said that, I was confronted with a possibility of having to face cancer which was very frightening, and I was aching tremendously physically, and was alone, and you were in Florida, fishing and enjoying yourself, a reality that you chose, because if you had wanted, we could have been together), it was an added comfort, needed at a very stressing time, I did pass 2 general anesthesia operations within a very short period of time, and was very frightened, and suffering physically and emotionally, and more so, knowing you will not be there for me.

I do not feel I have to feel guilty or apologize for dating when in MB, since I have been so depressed and so very heavily hurt by you. It was tried as a remedy and a way to go on with my life. I feel I have done way much more than any woman in my position would have done regarding putting in effort and trying to save our relationship. But I did not succeed.

You have hurt me several times Jan-Paul, when after E-mailing in March 2006 to August 2006, you led me to believe that all that is bothering you was the physical distance between us. When I came finally to

Myrtle Beach I was sure we will meet and then after some long, back and forth, hurtful letters, I found out that in fact you were on your way to see another woman in Florida.

And then when you finally proposed to me in San Diego, and I returned proud and radiant to Israel, and was so happy and you retracted after a few weeks. I was very hurt.

And then in Sharasesha, the happenings of which you know.

My heart thus needs some mending, a lot of love and as you said in the phone, some "confidence installing."

You wanted to hear me say, well I will: "I love you Jan-Paul, I love you so very much."

I am a very strong woman, as you know, but with this strength, lives another character and in peace; I am like a little, small puppy, craving for your touch, your love, your attention and affection, your care.

Since you are very intelligent, you will read in between the lines and, you will realize that this is a cry-out from a woman to her loved one.

I am not a person who plays ego-games. You are much stronger physically and emotionally then I. I have cried so miserably before leaving Sharasesha and it did not touch you at all. You could not realize what we will lose, and with you busy with concern about your money, and marriage issues, you could not realize what you will lose. I could not make you see, and cannot make you see. These 2 men saw it and knew it as every normal person would, and they were working on me with all their power and trying to get me at all cost. They realized what I am about, what life is about, and what is important and what is not.

As I finish this letter I realize, that telling you all the above was a minor need for me, the major one is telling you what was bottled in me for many months, and is that: I love you, Jan-Paul, so much, and wish I could whisper that in your ear, while feeling you near my body.

I love you, Jan-Paul,

I love you from the bottom of my heart.

Let me know that you have received my mail.

I landed in Israel on the 1.11.11 and my MRI was scheduled for the 2.11.11.

My Taxi driver was waiting for me and I was quite tired from the long transatlantic flight, some 5000 miles. Although first class, still, I had to stay in my "mind mode" to face what is waiting for me in the upcoming weeks, months, future;

My double mastectomy.

I had to focus and concentrate on my tasks, of finding the best breast surgeon for me, the best medical center for me, the best support of family, friends, and colleagues.

And I have to go through the operation, the hospital and bid goodbye to my nice, big, jeweled breasts.

Yes, I had to smilingly let them go. No, I am not letting them go, I am welcoming something new. I am welcoming and embracing and lovingly waiting for my new body;

My new flat young looking chest.

As time passes, and life goes on, a person has to know how to face changes and new realities. I have to know, and understand and emotionally accept all that fate and life presents me with.

Thus, I embarked for Israel and my new phase in life with determination, energy, and focus on the "to do" list. Yes, from time to time a worried thought crept to my mind. To my emotional world. Will the operation pass ok? Will I be found still healthy and cancer free, thus be able to go straight through a double mastectomy and have my new breasts? Oh, how I wanted to be past that time already. I promised myself some "strawberries" as I call them, some presents, some self-indulgent, good things for "after".

I will enjoy the summer and the beach with a new smiling face lips and figure. I will stop worrying about the un-controllable. I will plan my life so every day will count and every moment is enjoyable. I will pay attention to THE IMPORTANT matters. I don't care anymore if another small wrinkle will appear. If another tiny cute pound is residing on my behind or feminine tummy. If I have this ring, or that jewellery, or if the floor is re-done with beautiful black hard-wood.

I will turn, even more intuitively than I ever knew to do, to my inner self and indulge my inner wants, wishes and needs.

Like the need to create. The need to express myself, the need to smile, be calm and give!

Yes, these simple and small needs are the important needs I should want, and would so like to attend to.

I would love to attend to them.

I can't wait to attend to the latter.

I was beginning to transform. To change. From within. It is a process. It was a process that was already going on inside me. A process that was ripping. A process that was maturing. A transformation that was continuing to take place, inside me, since I suffered my first loss:

My mother's death. I was young, 30 years old, and realized for the first time that we, all of us, I more truly, are not strong forever and not all is good forever, and hard and harsh and devastating things happen.

It took me many years to understand that. To accept that. And learn to live with that.

Michael's death, sharpened that understanding strongly. I hardly made it back to life after losing him. I almost gave up on life, but decided with my mind and brain to hold-off the "giving up on life" until I am more rational. More aware and informed of my options in life.

I waited a year, and my basically inner positive, smiling, strong self, prevailed, and life seemed, again, appealing, attractive, and full of challenges worth taking, while enjoying the path.

Thus, every adversity seemed to add to *THE PROCESS*.

The process that I was going through in understanding how to better face life.

This process equipped me and gave me the tools to look forward with open eyes and confront and deal with adversities coming;

Leaving Jan-Paul, whom I so loved,

Embracing My Gene when it has been detected a few years ago, and having my ovaries removed.

My life was like a nice little boat in my beautiful lake. My lake that harboured my success and fame in the science world, my unique relationship with my "hard to find such" a husband, my beloved Michael, for over 20 years, my warm, interesting childhood surrounded with a supporting loving and nurturing family…and much more…My life, I felt with tremendous satisfaction was a beautiful lake…sometimes a bit rocky, sometimes with turbulences, but the laced, foamy waves were always brought to a calmed, mirror-like, beautiful blue-lavender coloured lake. With the water crystal clear and cool and fresh!!

And now, it is time for me, for yet, to calm another wave, a high one a mighty one, but still only one in a vast spacious big alluring lake…….....................

"Hello, Dr. Goldbear, I have not seen you for quite a while" Tamir said when opening the door of the taxi for me.

"Yes" I smiled warmly. I was focused internally. I was not channelling any energy for anything other than the long road of events awaiting me. He was now in a world very remote from mine, and I was going through the motions, even without realizing it. Without realizing him. All my attention was to the important matters at hand now, and thus, I sat in the taxi on the way to the hospital on the 2.11.11, heading to my MRI, a bit tired from the long flight of the day before, and the jet leg that did not let me get much sleep.

I was very calm looking out the window watching the Mediterranean Sea with its wavy nature of today, an autumn day. It seemed a bit grey, here and there some strikes of blue, and glittering small little dots appearing and disappearing, playing with me, my eyes, and with the ocean.

It matched my mood, somewhat.

"Are you comfortable?" Her voice has penetrated my armour, my wall bordering the world from me, the nurse asked. I lay there under the MRI, heavy, threatening, machinery. "Yes, all is fine" I answered automatically and thought, how will I pass those 40 minutes now, of invading repetitious noise of the MRI, and time? How will I pass the operation? Will I be able to go through with my plan and undergo a double mastectomy or, god forbid, will I be found having cancer now with the MRI and the Ultra-sound? And should I be lucky and be found healthy, would all my other tests; heart, lungs` functioning and blood be ok, satisfactory and enable me to go forward? To go through my now so craved for, double mastectomy?

And how will I do it all alone? All alone at home after such a major operation.

Yes! I would think of what would be my next painting…my next hero-ine…and I found it. I was beginning slowly and calmly, with my muscles beginning to unwind and relax, planning and seeing in my mind and imagination, the next subject of my next new painting!

It would be Miriam!

Yes, and the colors surrounding her would be of the grey, blue, laven-der, and white-laced waves, of the ocean that I saw today, on the drive to the hospital.

"I would like the table to be over there" I motioned to Jan-Paul. We were all, Jan-Paul, Wilson and me cleaning and moving around the fur-niture in the room that was designated to be my Studio. *MY STUDIO!*

It took several months of asking, nagging, reminding and protesting until that day finally came, I am going to have a piece of space, in the big huge building down town Sharasesha that Jan-Paul has owned, and it is to be my own space, my Studio.

It was an important matter to me, and I needed something of my own, in His House, His Town, HIS FRIENDS, His family, His State, His life.

CHAPTER TWENTY THREE

NATURE, JAN-PAUL AND HER WITH LONG EXOTIC NARROW EYES

I did not know exactly what and how I will paint. What materials I would use, what kind of colors, canvases, and truthfully, how to hold a brush! Any brush. What kind of brush.

"Do you want your easel over here?" Jan-Paul inquired. The room was quite clean and very big. My heart and my lips were starting to relax and to smile. I was beginning to fall in like with the place. It was large and spacious with huge big windows over looking the street, the main street of small Sharasesha, WA. a city of 2000 people. A passer by there and a passer by here, they walked and looked inside at what was going on. It is a big commotion to take place for small Sharasesha. I looked back smiling half feeling I own the place, my chest straight and up proudly, "this is my Studio"

We were driving a lot, for the past two years around Sharasesha. The most popular place in Sharasesha was Wal-Mart. Wal-Mart was where people went to entertain themselves. We have exhausted the different restaurants; may be 10 or twenty, to eat breakfast in or lunch or dinner, thus the travelling, the driving trips, one to two hours each way were becoming a habit and a way of life, a way to get out of the house, out of Sharasesha, and re-fresh our selves and our spirits.

Luckily, the view and nature caught me, and I was in love with Jan-Paul. But, I was tremendously and utterly in love with Sharasesha. There was no cure for it. I was tantalized, enchanted and enslaved by the nature, the raw nature, inhabited by almost no people, which Sharasesha commanded.

Either genesis-like, bare, majestic mountains, when in summer, engulfed with sage, or when driving higher, covered with endless tone of green colored trees, or numerous lakes that resided majestically wherever a person would bother to look. Each differs from the other, by the blue green shade of the water, by the hills or mountains surrounding them and the way the sun caressed them and their wavy or sometimes still, mirror-like, water.

Nature was at its best in Sharasesha and it always caught me breathless. My eyes could never have enough of it. My soul was always thirsty for more. And my mind and inner world needed it to sooth the rocky days, to calm my spirit, to be in touch with me. With myself.

I was so at awe with Sharasesha and its beautiful magnetic bewitching nature, that I needed to find a way of affirming it. A way of recognizing and confirming its grandeur. A way to re-live it with my own personal fashion.

I started to take pictures of the beautiful vastly open wheat fields that were glittering with golden rays all the way to the horizon with nothing, but nothing to intrude on their being. I took fantastic pictures of the snow covered mountains, the ice shining lakes, and the endless, green, blue, brown and yellow shades softly brushing the canvases of Sharasesha.

I took hundreds of pictures. And then a few more hundred pictures. And more.....And more. But my hunger, my inner hunger was not satisfied.

I took them when the sun rose. I took them at twilight time. I took them in the evening, at noon time...but nothing seemed to quiet my hunger for some elusive feeling, for some vague, undefined yet search in my soul.

Thus I began to start thinking about painting all those godly created worlds of limitless, endless colors.

I was very unsure with my decision. "How would I paint?" I thought. "What would I paint" I contemplated. "How would I mix the colors, what brushes should I use, what kind of colors should I use, do I want to paint with water colors?"

All these questions and more were circulating through my mind, for days, for weeks, for months. From time to time I looked at my calendar and read and re-read, in my "to do" list, to take some painting lessons.

I already phoned and found a teacher.

I already talked with her on the phone and enquired the details of the lessons she gave, the times, the schedule, the cost.

I already looked up and found exactly where she lives and how to get there.

And then one day, *the Process* reached an answer, a solution, a decision - I felt so confident! Yes! I want to paint. I want to paint, by myself, with no lessons, no influence none what so ever, that I can control knowingly.

I do not want to take any painting lessons.

I want to do it by my own. By myself. With myself. And only with myself.

Yes! I want to paint with oil colors on canvases.

And there and then we went, Jan-Paul and I to Wal-Mart to buy some kits, for oil painting, including small 10" by 10" canvases and an easel.

I was in the seventh heaven, Jan-Paul was sceptical and went along with my desire, on a small scale, so the investment would not be too bad financially.

He was very sceptical.

I was not even aware of any consequences, negative or positive. The only thing I felt was that I wanted to paint. No. That I needed to paint.

I was a very established and known scientist, and I did not pay any thought or attention to how my paintings, if any, would turn out. That was not a thought or a consideration. My need, my feelings, my resolution led the way.

I was at my Studio, my clean nicely furnished New Studio, with my new small little set of oil paintings, some brushes, some turpentine and a few canvases.

I sat on the sofa chair that we brought over and looked at the nice, red, rug that we spread on the floor, and was happy and content with my new toy, My Studio, a place that satisfied so many of my needs, here in Sharasesha.

I wore the apron we have bought and placed the smallest canvas on the easel, comfortable, like a fish in a pond. I took a brush and looked at the different oil colors that I have spread neatly on a table beside me and chose the red. I dipped the brush I chose, not a too wide one, not a too small one, and started applying the color on to the canvas.

I did not think.

I did not hesitate.

I was all alone in the Studio. My Studio, with My colors, My easel, My brushes and My imagination.

At those days I was re-reading Pearl Buck's books.

I was addicted to her. I admired her way of writing and was always sorry to finish a book.

I especially was impressed and touched with her books about women.... I identified with some of her heroines. I was feeling so, because, I realized there and then, that I, as a woman, a career woman, a woman who navigated her life through good and challenging times both, felt as a strong woman. .A woman with strength.

After about an hour, Jan-Paul came from the adjacent office, his office to look at my work. He wanted to see how things proceeded.

He passed the easel and stood looking at my painting. My new painting. My first art work. My art work.

I could not know what he was thinking. Jan-Paul had a poker face. One could not guess what went in his mind. His eyes were the usual ice cold blue. No expression whatsoever. But, But, he did not leave immediately. Jan-Paul was a person that analysed matters immediately. He was bright and brilliant. He had no patience and if what was in hand did not interest him, he would immediately leave.

But he stayed. He was examining, assessing the painting. His eyes went up and down. Left and right. His eyelashes moved and his dark blue pupils went here and there.

He sat down on a chair, taking all what he saw in the painting, in.

I could feel he was intrigued!!

That was good.

I could feel he was impressed. I was puzzled, surprised happy and questioning…is my painting good enough to capture his attention? I just painted for my pleasure, for my mood, for my need, for consummating my Studio and feeling that it is mine. Mine.

Jan-Paul said nothing, got up and left to his office and I was left with my thoughts and questions, with my doubts and my satisfaction, a cocktail that very quickly disappeared as I felt the need to play some more with the different colors.

At that time I was re-reading "Imperial Woman" by Pearl Buck and was captured with the strength, beauty femininity and intelligence portraying the concubine who rose to be an Empress. I was totally captured and impressed, and calmly yet excitingly dipped the brush to the prepared royal colors of green, yellow and purple.

I was not aware of the time passing or passers by that were glimpsing curiously inside my Studio and some times watching me paint. I was in another world, a timeless world of colors and concubines and queens and empresses.

I was consumed with the figure in my mind, admiring her for her inner strength, for her know how and the capabilities to navigate her way in a cruel world of harsh difficult surroundings and adversities. This was as how I perceived her…the woman of my adoration…and what she represented for me personally.

I inhaled the smell of the oil colors, so pleased and relaxed, remembering the times I was always inhaling the smells of my lab, enjoying it, being greeted in the mornings by it, feeling at home with it, drawing confidence and assurance from it…like a wonder of a perfume, a pricy luxurious cologne.

Now, I felt the same with the smell of the canvases, the smell of the oil colors, the smell of the turpentine. The smell of MY Studio, the smell of the immerging painting, My Painting. *My own new painting, my own new creation!*

I was in wonderland. My hand seemed to have a will of its own, controlled by my imagination, my dreams and possibly, probably my inner world.

The small little canvas was beginning to harbour nicely the three colors that I have chosen, appearing quite appealing and pleasing to the eye. My eye.

I then changed to a finer brush and decided to paint HER. To paint her as a concubine…to paint her as a princess, to paint her as a queen, as an empress!

And thus for the next days, and weeks, My Profiles of Her, emerged from the different canvases, with Her long exotic narrow eyes, harbouring intelligent pupils, looking femininely to the upper side, with her eyelashes lifted in such a capturing feminine way, almost enslaving all that would look at Her.

She appeared soft, she appeared strong, she appeared reigning, and if necessary to the outsider watcher, subdued, with some feature always accompanying *HER*, Her long, elegant, fragile, but strong neck, Her exotic narrow enchanting and bewitching eyes, shooting a glance convey-ing a mixture of temptations, extreme femininity and strength, Her curved shoulders, screaming to you of her womanhood mixed with royalty and her lips, as voluptuous and full and luscious, colored red, alluring yet with decisiveness.

Every morning I hurried to the Studio to see the previous day creation, to see her in another version of my dream of my perception of a woman, a strong feminine princess of a woman.

Every lunch time Jan-Paul would stop by, assess, examine, and sit for a few seconds absorbing my creations, my art. He would bring my lunch with him, my salad, and I would eat, all consumed in my magical world of colors and empresses. Not necessarily the Empress of China. Not necessar-ily an empress of a country a land or a continent.

My empresses were reigning over their lives, their fate.

My empresses were the queens of their world, facing it straight on and decisively navigating their way through adversities.

One morning, when I came to my Studio, the door was blocked. I could not get in as the whole entrance was filled and taken by huge big boxes containing huge big canvases. And new oil colors. Not a kit from Wal-Mart, but fifty different oil colors of all variety of tones, all ordered from a catalogue of one of the best art enterprises in the US.

Jan-Paul has thought and concluded to himself that I was immensely and uniquely talented, and thus I should paint using the best of colors, and on an array of sizes of canvases.

I was surprised. I was overwhelmed. I was flattered and was threatened. I was a bit intimidated.

How would I, a scientist, and a very successful, and world-renowned, paint on such huge canvases, with real good quality oil colors.

Jan-Paul thought that I could and would and will enjoy it and will produce excellent art.

I was so happy emotionally that Jan-Paul felt so. I needed his long with-held, affirmation. I needed his marvel, his admiration. I needed him to be impressed and yielding his encouragement. And finally I got it.

"Will I succeed in filling his expectations?" I wondered.

Will I be able to arise to his anticipations?" I feared.

"No! I am not painting for any person's expectations or anticipations, I am painting for my own need, pleasure and desire" I sternly answered my doubts and fears.

I raised an imaginary wall sealing me and protecting me from all out-side influences and pressures and decided to continue and paint according to my whims, wishes, likes and desires.

It was an emancipating decision and feeling. A freeing one. Now I could continue and paint on the big huge canvases, with the new wonder-ful shades of every color I could think of, and enjoy the process, emotion-ally, physically, and creatively.

CHAPTER TWENTY FOUR

My Atelier, Smoky Topaz, Summer Turquoise and Ruby

"Are you ok? It passed quickly didn't it?" the inquiring voice of the nurse in the MRI room entered a fraction of my world. I was surprised to find myself there for a second and then resumed reality "I am done with my MRI! Finally" I thought satisfied as this has taken so much effort and transatlantic phones and e-mails to coordinate.

Although I just landed yesterday, I was all energy and purposeful" Yes, thank you" I responded her, not letting her voice enter my entity even through the smallest narrowest cracks that were still open to the world. I was walled-in by my own wall. But I was not completely sealed in.

I got dressed and went through the motions to get out of there as soon as possible, like I was hunted. I needed to be home. I needed to paint.

Tamir dropped me at home, after a few futile trials of making conversation during the drive home when my attention was totally focused and my entity was fully absorbed with the color of the sea, the Mediterranean Sea. Its waves, its strength, its calmness. The confidence it projected towards me. The assurance I withdrew from its rhythmic, never letting down, always being there, wavy character.

And gradually she began to take a form. Her neck, long, thin, curvy yet delicate, showing the pride side of her character along with her strength.

Jan-Paul used to say that they are all Royal, Aristocratic....my women. I was all consumed with my painting, after the MRI, almost did not feel myself arriving home, rushing to my Studio in the Atelier, on the second floor in my home at Zichron. "Is that the right grey?" I contemplated when my brush strokes caressed the canvas lightly, while I deeply breathed in the comforting smell of the oil paints. I looked at the lapis lazuli blue I loved and mixed it with some Chinese green and a touch of white and light cream to create a background that will match her long, lush, feminine hair. It went down to her buttocks in a wide and wavy fashion. Hair, and long aristocratic necks were becoming like my trade mark in my paintings. They were becoming an integral part, a dominant part of my women. The women I have been painting for the last two years. They were becoming a part of my style. I was developing, without realizing, without knowing, A Style. A style of my own. I was becoming an Artist!

And it was good. I loved it.

Along with the latter "trademarks" of mine, my hand as with its own will, independent of my thoughts or control, started painting Her eyes. Yes, they were shaping themselves to The Exotic eyes, my women usually bear, along with a deep, wise, semi smiling, aware, gaze. Sometimes the gaze was also sad. This time, as I looked at Miriam, her gaze was strong, deifying, conquering, in control! I liked her. I felt stronger. I felt calmer. I felt more at ease in the world. In my world. In my Current world.

Without thinking I felt the urge to decorate her. I changed to a thinner brush a lighter one and with one curvy, enjoyable stroke, I painted her long Princess-like dress. All of a sudden, it was colored and decorated, in an embroidery like fashion. She looked like a princess....No, like a queen. She had her emerald jewels around her neck, her rubies on her dress, her turquoise on her sleeve, and yes, she had her one and only long, very long and curvy earring, going down from her ear, almost touching her shoulder. Like most of my Jewelled women. One and only one, long, mysterious, curving, jewelled, earring.

I stepped back to asses her and my breath was taken away. She was beautiful. She was majestic. She was in control.

She was, also as I had noticed, my first woman to be one with a flat chest. And her décolleté was marvellous.

She was so feminine, alluring and appealing.

And I was ready for my double mastectomy.

....

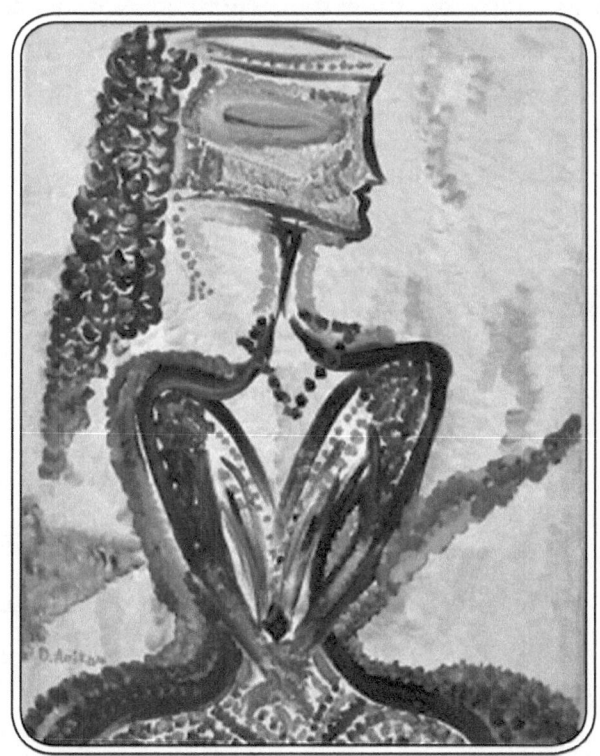

"Is it over?" this is all I could manage to say. I was not feeling clear and the room was full with murmurs and instructions and answers and questions.

"Yes, it is all behind you" Some one answered, warmly.

I was rolled to my room.

I opened my eyes, to see my surgeon, the head nurse, my friend Eden and a few other unfamiliar faces all looking at me with warmth, admiration and anticipation, all waiting for me as I was some one of importance. Their looks conveyed the utmost respect and honor a look can possibly convey.

They all thought I was extraordinarily brave.

I looked back amazed, happy, absorbing and relieved, I have my new flat chest. I am out of danger.

And...Jan-Paul was standing there, puzzled, serious, feeling out of place, yet totally there for me.

Eden had contacted him and he decided to come.

He was there day after day after day.

We hardly talked; he was just there, reading, following me, being there.

For the next days I focused on one minute at a time.

I slept very calmly and comfortably, as I felt safe.

And step by step I learned to focus on one day at a time, and then one week at a time, and very quickly I found my women were calling me, and my Studio was lonely and thus I colored my days, with the oil paints, the canvases, and the sun rays that entered my window at the studio and also my window at my soul, my life.

Pergolesi was playing loud and I was immersed in the music, and my hands were immersed in my new painting. I was in another world, with colored tones of Pergolesi's harmony taking me far away, and my soul concentrating deeply on my new developed style of painting with my hands cooperating lightly and easily.

I was drawn now, along with the use of different colors that matched my mood and needs at the time of painting, to release my spirit, in several ways, the large, long elegant, curvy brushstrokes along with dotting, small and big, creating backgrounds or decorating my women, with their breathtaking beautiful jewelry. Yes, their Jewellery seemed to expand

Her, in Smoky Topaz, Summer Turquoise and Ruby Jeweled Scar

from the one and simple long alluring earring, through the novel idea of my colleague "Transform The Scar on A Woman's Breast in to A Jewel" by Dr. Dorit Amikam, thus, adorning their breasts. And so when I was lecturing in Conferences about my research I was also showing my art work accompanied with the latter new evolving philosophy of Dr. Amikam: *Transforming the Scar into A Jewel*". There was an evolution in my way of painting and my recent images of women. They were jewelled and adorned on their body, their dresses, and recently I have come to realize, that on their lush, wavy, long beautiful hair, they carry a wonderful Tiara.

I liked it.

Yes, my painting had evolved, in many levels and phases. I began with the inspiration of her imperial woman, the Chinese Empress, in my Studio in Sharasesha, and then, one day when boating with Jan-Paul, on the beautiful Bonaparte Lake, I came to it!

"What are you so happy about?" He asked. "Did you catch one"" He looked towards my rod with interest, all ready with the net to help me unhook the fish and release it back to the lake.

I liked fishing with him, but always wanted to release the poor things. "No, I just thought of something" I replied, murmuring, mostly to myself.

The water was dressed with a kind of green that I could never paint, it was so quiet and relaxing, the motor off, and the oars lazily hanging to the sides, and there were only Jan-Paul, I, the lake, and God. I did not know where to look first, to the tall towering genesis-like mountains, to the bewitching green vast of soft water, to Jan-Paul, or to the fish that from time to time leaped out of the water to breathe some air. I was also looking inside me, apparently, because I came with this intriguing idea, as a woman, as a scientist, a molecular oncologist, that the Scar, on a woman's Breast, should be looked upon as A Jewel!

Yes! Many women would have liked that. It can and might give an additional support to women harbouring a scar on their breasts. It might give a whole new outlook as to the scar, to their body, as to their relationship with their husbands, their significant other, their workplaces, their families and friends, when they feel differently regarding their Scar. Thus, most importantly, it might provide them with a totally new fresh and beautiful outlook as to *their relationship with Themselves!*

"We want hundreds of those, Danielle" Annabelle was telling me when we finished creating the new desk calendar harbouring twelve photos of my "Jewelled Breasts Women" one for every month. She was going to send them to Knesset members in Israel, to head of Cancer institutes and clinicians, all over the world and to people, men and women. She was so excited with this project and celebrated my idea of "Jewelled Breasts" manifested by my beautiful, strong, feminine women, harboured in my paintings.

At a Gala Night with Her Lovely Scar....

She was not the only one. Requests, invitations, admiring comments and embracement regarding my novel idea and the paintings came storming and streaming in all the time.

"I have to tell you how deeply you and your art and your novel idea have touched me" She said. And they kept coming after lectures accompanied with my art, after and during exhibitions of my art that included that part of it as well as all my art and paintings of women and Life. There were e-mails to my website thanking me and appreciating my novel approach and my "women". It seemed that many women and men all around the world were moved, very much, and touched, and could identify, with my "Women and Jewelled Breasts".

"I would like to purchase that one" He said, pointing admiringly to one of my painting exhibited in my single person exhibition. "May I introduce my wife?" he asked, with a voice bearing volumes of respect and admiration. I remembered him from my lecture a few minutes ago.

I remembered when ending with my closing sentence *"Every little drop of hope and strength in an ocean of genes, realities and decisions, is a drop that may allow all to view our ocean in light, blue, calm colors with some decorating white waves, strongly but surely pave their way through. May my paintings add some droplets of strength...and bring a smile to the lives of women..."*

He was magnetized to me, to my lips, to my entity.

He was following every single word, and his eyes were following every single movement of mine. He was hypnotised to me, my art and what I represented for him. It was hope! His wife was battling cancer. He wanted to let my art, my strength, my vision enter their castle, their home...in hope.

I gave him the painting.

And thus, as Cherie my friend from South Carolina, was saying, I kept touching people's life. And my own. I moved from the latter so important and fulfilling theme, to my new them....just Women and Life. Not just.... But Women and Life.

And as Pergolesi kept playing, my hands kept painting, putting onto the canvas, my smiles, my wants and *the color of my soul.*

The dramatic concert of Pergolesi was suddenly accompanied with an irritating sound. It took a few seconds for me to realize that. And then a few more to interpret it to the sound of the phone. Who is calling now? I wondered. They will stop. I liked my protected wonderland right now. But it kept ringing and ringing, and the more it rang the more reluctant I was to leave my canvas.

It then stopped, I smiled relaxingly. But alas it came back.

"Yes!" I barked to the phone impatiently.

"Hi Danielle, I was looking for you, how are you?" Her voice sounded so hopeful and pleading.

In an instant, I became all professional, all of me a scientist and a colleague "Yael, boy am I glad you called, I was looking for you for some time now!"

"Yes, I have landed this morning and saw all these messages that you have left me"

She answered all still conveying hope.

"Did you find anything, Danielle?" She asked

"Yael, you probably remember as I told you that germ line mutations in the tumor suppressor gene p53 are associated with the Li-Fraumeni syndrome."

"Yes, I remember, Danielle"

"With the latter characterized by a wide range of neoplasm occurring in young adults and children namely early-onset of breast cancer, variety of sarcomas, brain tumors and leukemia, right?"

"Yes, Danielle and you have said that molecular testing of her blood DNA, our L-girl blood DNA, did not show mutations in either *BRCA1* or *BRCA2* genes. You have found no BRCA mutations in her DNA sample." Yael sighed heavily. We were both on this project and wanted so much to solve it. There were children and family members to consider, and it was also important for the L-girl's sake, to find what caused her aggressive cancer. It was also important for Yael.

It was important for me.

"She was a very young woman of 25 years old exhibiting an early-onset of bilateral breast cancer, and she was from a family with an otherwise negative history of cancer." Yael wanted to remind me delicately, as though I did not know, with a somewhat worrying voice.

I knew it all too well.

"Yes, Yael, this is why I have thought of checking another angle, another gene, this P53 gene, as I have suggested earlier on our conference meeting"

"Yes!?" Her voice conveyed hope, questions, dynamic, life, strength.

"We have detected in our lab a novel P53 mutation in the L-girl DNA. The latter novel p53 germ line mutation discovered in her, as a daughter, was not found in both of her parents, and we repeated this for several times. Thus, this latter mutation is a *de novo* alteration."

"What are you saying Danielle? You have found a new mutation in her DNA, a one which was never seen before in the world, and on top of that, are you telling me that this mutation does not exist in her parents DNA? "She sounded surprise, extremely interested, and I could hear from far away how her mind starts working, assessing, thinking and wanting to solve the world problems for the children of our L-girl.

I was too.

"This *de novo* transition of A>G, never before detected in the world, which was revealed by us at exon seven, converts aspartate with asparagine". I added

"I see" she murmured.

"Since this tumor suppressor gene, *P53, which* is located on the short arm of chromosome 17 encodes a 53Kda phosphoprotein implicated in an array of cellular processes including   cellular regulation of DNA repair and programmed cell death, this transition that we have detected, of the latter amino acids, compromises dramatically the ability of the protein to function normally, Yael"

"Yes, yes, and hence the aggressive cancer she battled." Yael commented.

"We cannot exclude the option of parental mosaicism Yael, parental mosaicism does apparently account for some sporadic or new mutations in genetic disorders, Yael."

"So what are you telling me Danielle?" I had more of her full attention. She was preparing herself for some more news.

"Taking into consideration the latter possibility, Yael, means that there is a plausible risk of the latter novel mutation being harbored by other offspring of our L-girl, Yael, and her extended family. "

"I see, you are saying we might have a way of knowing whether her children and brothers and sisters carry this terrible mutation."

She sighed confirming and somewhat in fear of what the future and the results of such testing might hold for these dear family members. Hope and freedom for some, and maybe challenges for others.

"Exactly, Yael! Send me the other DNA samples, of the rest of the family"

She hung up, as usual, no goodbyes, all consumed in her work. I understood, accepted and as always was there and ready for her next phone call, with her next families and women.

Yael did not know that I had just undergone a double mastectomy.

Nor did I want her to know.

It was a non-issue for me.

I was done being a molecular oncologist for today.

Pergolesi continued to play, and I returned to my painting.

CHAPTER TWENTY FIVE

MY LAKES, PINK TOPAZ, AMETHYST AND SCIENCE

Jan-Paul was back in Sharasesha and his e-mails kept coming....

And I answered:

But What I chose to remember....

But what I chose to remember is the gift I have been given. The gift of a whole month. No, six weeks of being in heaven. Six weeks of living in a dream world. During the day, most of my entity was thinking when will the night come. During the day, floating through reality, partially not being there, and waiting for the night to come. For in the night I could be in your arms. I could feel, sense, smell and melt in to your strength, masculinity, and beautiful strong blue gaze.

Every morning, I nibbled on the delicious apple strudel that we so happily and childishly went to buy, and sipped my strong, hot, smelling and freshly brewed coffee that you have made for us, looking lazily at the ocean, feeling content and relaxed and smilingly planning the day ahead with you.

Watching the whales` show, or people watching in a sun drenched corner cafe, or driving to Rancho Santa Fe. San Diego did not lack places to go to and enjoy one`s self. And we did. We so enjoyed ourselves, helping ourselves to the best the city could offer. The weather was playing along with us, like everything else did.

People smiled at us, the dolphins came every morning to bid us good day and the sun shone every day, with new colorful rays. Every day.

The world was smiling to us.

At the Zoo, as you explained to me about the different fish and animals, I was listening to your voice, taking in and absorbing your body-build, smiling at your laugh and waiting to be embraced by you, at night.

The meals were memorable, the Opera was touching and elevating and the surf in the ocean was always playing for our eyes.

As we returned to our rented oceanfront villa, the light, see-through curtains would be delicately moved by and play with the ocean breeze, as our bodies did, together as one.

I loved you then. You loved me then.

And I thank you for that.

This is what I am going to remember, all my life.

This is what will always bring a smile to my lips, for I have been loved and made love to in a maddening fashion, and lived in a seventh heaven of my own, for these six beautiful, innocent, and lustful weeks.

Thank you, Jan-Paul.

I returned from San Diego to Israel another person. Harboring new and tantalizing feelings, harboring an embedded experience in my entity, for life.

For such memories is what the world of a person carved from.

For such tastes of life and sensual experiences are what the stones and bricks of personalities built from.

And I was so lucky to have another memory added to my beautiful, luxurious pearl-like string of memories, which made a precious necklace, every woman would be indulgingly enjoying and proud to wear on her delicate, long, feminine and elegant neck.

Yes, The Marriot in Myrtle Beach SC was the Prologue, The ocean front Villa in San Diego was the beginning and Sharasesha in Washington state was the end, of a rocky, beautiful and hard at the same time, special seven years spanning relationship, with Israel spicing it up.

Thus I thank you.

I was preoccupied with my various activities, very much involved with my new world.

I enjoyed my exhibitions, breathing the air of art, oil paint, canvases and bohemian encounters.

I loved spending my late mornings drinking coffee at the galleries where my art was shown, lazily inhaling the air of the latter world and letting it capture me, my sense and my being.

And then one late morning my cell phone sang, announcing a close friend is calling. I wondered who it could be, phoning now, in this beautiful day, already approaching mid noon time, while I was in Bat Shlomo, visiting my art exhibition. Bat Shlomo was such a small, little, precious stone-like village of only some few hundred families, at which a famous art gallery was located. I chose that gallery, for my art show, partially for the prestigious name the gallery had and partially because of my inner connection with nature as the gallery resided among the mountains and valleys of the Carmel Mountains and was planted in the midst of the lush greenery and trees and beautiful flowers scattered all around, with the sounds of horses and cows and chickens making their way through the day. I liked that. And also it was ten minutes from Zichron.

I looked at the caller id number and my heart leaped.

It was Marian.

How come? What does she want from me? What is happening with her? How has she been since battling her breast cancer? I have not heard from her in years…so many years…too many years….

All those thoughts and more raced through my mind, with the sound of the song from my cell phone, Ava Maria, my favorite and designated only to close friends, mixing, with the so lovely cows mooing and horses trotting sounds.

"Hello?" My voice sounded anticipating, welcoming, wanting and yearning at the same time.
"Daniel, I want to see you!" Her voice sounded as harboring all those feelings of mine, yet more decisive in making her wish.
"Daniel, I need to see you!" She did not ask, she stated.
"I am at the art Gallery in Bat Shlomo, where they show my oil paintings, would you like to drive up and have a cup of coffee at their small country like restaurant?" I offered, asking, pleading, wishing.

I too wanted to see Marian.

I missed her.
Let bygones be bygones.
I want her in my life.
I want to love her. I want to hug her.
I want to smile to her.
I also wanted, needed, to let her know that she has saved my life.

Yes. She has saved my life. When phoning a few years ago and making me schedule my BRCA-DNA test.

"Yes, yes, I am right nearby, see you in a few" her voice sounded relieved.

My eyes caressed her fragile body. My eyes feasted on her delicate porcelain skin, that was still so smooth, no wrinkles, so beautiful. My eyes drank her light, blond hair, flowing softly with the wind and her so light colored pastel blue eyes, that I realized, were caressing me.

We were sitting, with our cups of coffee getting cold, because we could not have enough of each other. We laughed and smiled and cut to each other sentences...all like when we were young, two innocent girls, one the shadow of the other.

I did not care about anything. I just was so happy to have Marian back in my life.

It was good to share my happy moment of my art show with my long-time friend, my close heart mate, my shadow from my childhood, as we were both now more relaxed, sitting there, two classy, flat chested women, sipping their coffee and finally, closing circles and opening their hearts to each other.

Now, I felt, I am stronger, with Marian back in my life and at my side.

Now I felt more whole, more secure, hugged by her acceptance as I loved her back.

Marian.

And I was standing there, with the microphone clipped to my lacy brown tight see-through jacket, that showed my red edge-laced camisole, and did justice to my open feminine décolleté and my impressive wine-burgundy-colored necklace, glittering with garnets and rubies, one hand holding the power point slide changer and the other busy with the laser pointer, my voice full of dynamics, and rich with texture explaining the next slide, which was showing one of my paintings. I walked to the left end of the podium, and all eyes were flowing me, like when I lectured the 101 basic genetics in the university when all 200 pair of eyes were magnetized to me following every and each gesture, every and each change of tone, every and each explanation of mine. They, in 101 Basic genetics were mine to carve, mine to shape, as those now in the "Artist lecture", who came to the opening of my Single Person Exhibition of 56 of my paintings. They smiled when a smile was due, their eyes reflected surprise, when I surprised them and their hands rose up to present a question when presented with an interesting intriguing and challenging subject.

They were mine.

Like clay in the potter's hands.

They were mine because I was so fully immersed in my painting experience, like a fish in the water, like a mermaid playfully teasing the waves, and I was able to convey my feelings, my thoughts, my philosophies and insights, through my lecture, using the different tones and sub tones of my voice, and letting my body movements and dynamics add to my reach to them. To all of them. To each and every one of them. Making eye contact with her, smiling at him, and asking them all.

And in the while having them smell the tantalizing, exuberating, enticing smell of my studio, my oil paints, my canvases, and hear the music of my colors, waltzing around with my choices for the day, dancing with their hands and hearts on my canvases with me as their coach.

"Yes, this one took quite a long time to paint" I was answering a woman who appeared extremely taken and absorbed in my lecture.

"And how did you choose the colors?" She kept on

"What is your name?" I questioned with a smiling interest

"Bar" She answered with some shyness mixed with pride and her green beautiful eyes shown with excitement

"Well, Bar, I was thinking about this painting for a long time, during the days and the nights. My subconscious was thinking about it too. No, not about it, but about Her, The Woman that I wanted to paint. No, not the woman I wanted to paint, but the woman I wanted to create, to give birth to, to spot-light and rise above all, at that time and phases in my life."

I paused for a second to let that sink, to let her and all of them process, and maybe participate in a minute way, in the birth of an art creation….. The birth of a painting.

Her eyes seemed expecting more. The gentlemen sitting near her was all in suspense. The silence in the lecture room was loaded with anticipation.

I moved my laser pointer to the painting, and then with my clear soft yet confident voice continued" I wanted to show her mourning devastated feelings of losing her husband, yet carrying his child, thus a new life, in, within her."

The room was still very silence and they were all consumed with the painting shown in the slide on the screen.

"I wanted to manifest her infinite grief, thus her eyes are somewhat sad, yet she is strong and looking forward, thus they are big, wonderful and colored as the color of sand, and gold, which is to have the cocktail of the desert she was walking in, and gold, as a jewel. They were also harboring some turquoise, which is again the color of a beautiful sky in a nice day, maybe somewhat hot and hard day in the desert, but also the color of a refreshing, young full of power semi-precious stone, the Turquoise" I added.

I could feel they wanted more. They needed more. That woman, that painting caught their imagination, swept their hearts, touched their souls.

"Why did you use the color of deep Burgundy and pink?"

A warm, strong voice, full of curiosity came from the left far corner.

My eyes shifted to locate this inquiring voice, as all heads of the audience were looking back to see who's voice it was. It was obvious he was touched by the moment, the experience and the depth of the painting and what some strokes and colors could mean.

"I wanted and needed to make her feminine and delicate, thus I jeweled her with garnets, and rubies, with pink topaz and amethyst, and I decorated her with lush, long, wavy beautiful hair, she is very soft and feminine, inside and out" my voice carried on so softly, navigating them all through the different features with my laser pointer moving on the slide display of the painting.

"Was she suffering? Was it very hard for her?" Another soft voice, so participating in the current scene, was asking delicately. They were in the desert with her. They were taking part in her journey and in my journey, my painting. They were needing a closure. They needed to know what has happened to her. They cared!

"Would she survive the desert? Would she survive the harsh dramatic events that challenged her life?" A voice full of strength and confidence, so optimistic, rose from the center of the lecture hall.

My eyes met a strong brown gaze, accompanied with strong confident features of a beautifully dressed woman at her prime, maybe at her 60ties. She wanted her to survive. To succeed.

I could feel it. They all could. And they all wanted.

"Yes, she would survive the desert. This is why her dress is so dynamic and moving. She is moving with confidence and assurance along her journey facing her challenges with the full brush strokes of her so determinately moving dress, the latter playing with the wind, but not carried with the wind. The latter is moving while taking charge, while controlling, and the brush strokes move her powerfully forward. Yes! Forward! Like her profile was painted, looking forward, and colored with a strong ruby-brown-earthy color, thus she is majestic, yet her legs are rooted to the ground and her world is here and now. But she is majestic, and this is why her neck is brush stroked with a long elegant stroke, yet is still feminine, thus it is long but curvy, very curvy."

A sound of Awe was heard. An Awe that conveyed amazement, relief, admiration and warmth for Her.

"Yes, feminine yet strong, a queen! This is why I also accessorized her with a decorating Tiara, resting so peacefully and in place over her lush, long beautiful, yet possessing their own mind and will conveyed by the carrot-golden-red-colored hair." I passed my laser pointer, softly, caressing her hair on the screen.

"This is when, why and how the novel saying of my colleague Dr. Dorit Amikam "Her eyes as Jade...Her Lips as A White Pure Lily...and Her Spirit will Quarry The Rock..." was emerging and created. This is a sentence that also describes my Women, my paintings, all of them"

A wow was heard throughout the hall. Murmurs, soft, floating in a hush manner, were passing around.

"I painted her future with hope." I added.

They were all looking at the name of the painting:

"Mourning the loss of a loved one but staying strong and embracing New Life: looking forward to the birth of her child...the fruit of her love..."

"Does that represent all kinds of women?" He asked from the front row.

It was a question shared by many. I could tell from their affirming eyes, and questioning faces.

"Women, in all shapes, kinds and forms, harbor their own specific unique personal strength. They may be enchanting and mysterious like beautiful jeweled mermaids, they can be vulnerable at a sad path in life, crying big beautiful pear shaped lovely tears, they are jeweled and harbor big mesmerizing, luring yet intelligent strong eyes....They are WOMEN.... and they are all strong."

I went to the next slide and the next, with my laser pointer, showing that painting, this woman, and my voice accompanying the presentation, decisively assuring that all of my feelings and more are captured and conveyed to the canvas by my brush strokes and presented in the various paintings, my paintings, via the colors, sometimes strong, dark and tantalizing sometimes fragile with their pastel tone and light, soft touch, featuring a woman, in various paths in life. Yet always, always, strong in Her way, Her own Personal way, varying ways from woman to woman, as we are all different, but the same....we are strong.

And he e-mailed again and again.

There was not a morning that my mail box was lacking a mail from him. He soothed and comforted me, pleaded with me and offered the seventh heaven. "Anything, Anything," just so I will return to him.

"Anything…anything, just share your life with me. I cannot see the rest of my life without you…please….we will work it out….I will change….I will….our love will win."

He pleaded.

He showered me with gifts and flowers all the way to Israel….

Thus I answered:

My Love,

My Jan-Paul,

I just answered the door bell, and a man brought a huge package sent to me. I was a bit reluctant to accept it, since I did not know the sender, a Mr. Ran Toren. The man said not to be worried, it has been thoroughly checked and it is not a bomb. Maybe it is from my accountant, the tax returns that I am expecting I thought, but no, it is way too big of a package, and the box was filled with Hebrew written words.

He said shall I open it with you? I said yes. We opened it, and WOW, a beautiful basket filled with all sweet things and chocolates and such. You see, someone loves you, he said. I was puzzled, the box was sent from Israel, and had Hebrew written all over, Yes, but who??, I opened the nice paper accompanied, and there I saw, I saw the name of my beloved, My Jan-Paul. My heart missed a beat and as the man walked back to his car, I cried after him, it is from my lover, my Jan-Paul, from the US, He was all smiling and said you see, there you are.

I entered back to the kitchen all smiles, so Jan-Paul has sent me a package, how nice, how much I would have liked to kiss him now softly, again and again.

Thank you my love,

That was such a nice beautiful surprise, coming in the right time the right day and the right moment.

I am so happy with our love.
I am coming.

And I flew back to him.

He met me at Sea Tac, the airport in Seattle. He was excited as a school boy. His strong blue eyes, hugged me, swallowed me, caressed me along with his arms and his whole body.

He changed.

He treated me like the most valuable, beautiful, irreplaceable porcelain doll.

We stayed for a week in Seattle WA. where I was invited to lecture about my colleague and friend Dr. Dorit Amikam's and my, two break-throughs in Science.

The first being the novel nucleotide C-Di-GMP affecting cell cycle. My research showed that C-di-GMP causes blockage of the cell cycle at the S-phase, thus S-phase arrest. It was characterized by increased cellular thymidine uptake, reduction in G2/M-phase cells and an increase in the number of S-phase cells, all the latter accompanied with decreased cell division, when cancerous cell lines were treated with C-Di-GMP.

And thus the novel nucleotide C-Di-GMP was being presented as an anti-cancer agent in this international conference.

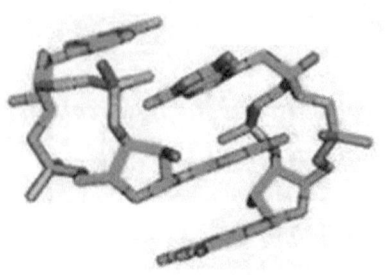

The Novel Nucleotide C-Di-GMP

The second breakthrough was the effect of the novel, naturally occurring latter nucleotide on the lymphoblastoid CD4+ Jurkat cell line. When exposed to c-di-GMP, Jurkat cells exhibited a markedly elevated expression of the CD4 receptor. The latter receptor plays an important role in the mechanism of which HIV enters the cells of the immune system.

Interestingly and of additional importance were the other observed effects of the nucleotide on immune system cells like the finding that c-di-GMP naturally enters these cells and binds irreversibly to the onco-protein P21ras. Again it caused Cell-cycle arrest also with the immune system cells. All the effects described appeared to be unique for c-di-GMP.

I was very proud of my research work and findings.

Not every scientist can enjoy having a breakthrough and establishing a totally new research field that did not exist before, not to mention 2 such novel research fields, as I enjoyed.

I received from my fellow scientists all the recognition and respect for that and enjoyed it.

I was busy the whole week with discussion groups in some of which scientists from pharmaceutical companies were very interested in my presented science work, and many lectures, and I also met a few people from Spokane and promised to come to lecture there as well.

I loved going to Spokane, because we always visited the art galleries in Coeur D'Alene in Idaho, in which at one of them I presided over the board of directors, as they have asked me to, and where I showed and presented my much admired oil paintings. It also presented a very tempting chance to consummate my renewed relationship with Jan-Paul in our favorite Hotel, in Coeur D'Alene, overlooking the lake there, and having our dinner at our favorite spot, in our favorite restaurant at the top floor of the hotel, celebrating with a huge, humongous, beautiful, barrel - like half a glass of ice-cream…and in other ways as well..

And I shared My Lakes with him …We went bicycling around Sun Lakes, becoming one with the genesis view, look, and atmosphere.

We fished in the Sharasesha River and boated to A No Man, secret, hidden islands there and named them as we wished, making them our own and bathed in the nude, with the crystal clear sprinkling water caressing my flawless arched back, along with Jan-Paul's eyes. There was no one but only the blue sky, looking at us.

We fished in the beautiful Conconully lakes.

We returned home at around 9 PM, and I was peaceful and content, blissfully tired from a long day at the lakes, my entity tranquil and my ears listening to the roar of the pick-up when Jan-Paul was trying to back it up with the boat, to the drive way.

I loved that roar.

It symbolized for me a cocktail of nature, rugged life, barefoot -no heels, no power-suit and most of all, moments to be cherished with my loves...him and they...

Almost each day we went to our afternoon dip in Green Lake, absorbing the pure nature surrounding us while eating our dinner and looking at the sun set with him, I, and the lake the only witnesses to our bliss....

I shared with him my most beautiful lakes, Bonaparte and Beaver, where we bathed in the jade-toned, green, water and forgot all reality.... forgot the world....and our entity existed only in the purest way, in the purest moment, in the God-like kissed surrounding, so quiet, so beautiful, so deserted, only for us to enjoy, only for us to become one with...

I shared my lakes with him....they became Our lakes.

Yes, our lakes.

And I thought of my friend and colleague's idea and feeling, nicely put in her sentence "Empowered By The Past...Capture Your Present...And Carve Your Future...." by Dr. Dorit Amikam.

The sun is smiling, and hope is always there, and Sharasesha now shares us both, my science, my art, and since my darling Ginger passed away, our two new dogs Cleo and Cinnamon....and the lakes.

Yes, I am A Woman with A Lake…a lake of hope, a lake of dreams, and my beautiful, big, brown eyes are looking forward with contentment and confidence………

THE END

www.ingramcontent.com/pod-product-compliance
Lightning Source LLC
Chambersburg PA
CBHW031613240626
47153CB00002B/737